Livin' Large in Fat Chance, Texas

Books by Celia Bonaduce

Fat Chance, Texas Series

Welcome to Fat Chance, Texas

Slim Pickins' in Fat Chance, Texas

Livin' Large in Fat Chance, Texas

Venice Beach Romances

The Merchant of Venice Beach

A Comedy of Erinn

Much Ado About Mother

Livin' Large in Fat Chance, Texas

Celia Bonaduce

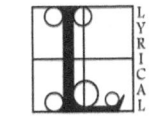

LYRICAL PRESS
Kensington Publishing Corp.
www.kensingtonbooks.com

LYRICAL PRESS BOOKS are published by

Kensington Publishing Corp.
119 West 40th Street
New York, NY 10018

All Kensington titles, imprints, and distributed lines are available at special quantity discounts for bulk purchases for sales promotion, premiums, fund-raising, educational, or institutional use.

Special book excerpts or customized printings can also be created to fit specific needs. For details, write or phone the office of the Kensington Sales Manager: Kensington Publishing Corp., 119 West 40th Street, New York, NY 10018. Attn. Sales Department. Phone: 1-800-221-2647.

Lyrical Press and Lyrical Press logo Reg. U.S. Pat. & TM Off.

First Electronic Edition: July 2016
eISBN-13: 978-1-60183-433-1
eISBN-10: 1-60183-433-0

First Print Edition: July 2016
ISBN-13: 978-1-60183-434-8
ISBN-10: 1-60183-434-9

Printed in the United States of America

This book is dedicated to

Almiyi,

a tough old bird.

ACKNOWLEDGMENTS

Writing a book series—let alone two—can test a person. Storylines to plot, deadlines to meet, style guides to follow. But that's nothing compared to the strain it puts on your family and friends. "Please read this," "please proof this," and "please laugh at this" was only the beginning. My family and friends have bought my books, attended launch parties, come to readings, and taken copies of The Venice Beach Romances and *Welcome to Fat Chance, Texas* to Little Free Libraries around the country to spread the word. In creating the world of Fat Chance, Texas, I've tried to convey the sacredness of friendship. I've learned from the best.

PART ONE

Chapter 1

The *clang clang clang* of the dinner triangle zapped the morning air. Dymphna looked down the hill to see Fernando, the café's proprietor, standing, hands on hips, staring up at her and Professor Johnson as they made their way from the farm into town. "Breakfast is served, Your Majesties," Fernando yelled, then stomped back into the café.

"Why ring the bell when we're in shouting distance?" Professor Johnson asked. "Why does everything have to be some sort of drama?"

"Where would Fat Chance be without drama?" Dymphna asked.

"Probably a lot further along than we are now," Professor Johnson said.

Dymphna took in a deep breath. She wondered if the country's Founding Fathers were this exhausting.

At first glance, the town looked much as it did when Dymphna first saw it three years ago. The buildings still leaned to the left. Tumbleweeds still convened on Main Street. The creek that ran behind Main Street, around to the front of the Creekside Inn and through the lower portion of Dymphna's farm, continued to glint in the sunshine. The town still sat in the confluence of several hills.

She looked up at those hills, rising like fingers above the town. She remembered how they looked when she first saw them . . . wild like the rest of this territory. Unfriendly. Forbidding. Nothing like the lush green acres now covered in grapevines that marched in perfect rows as far as her eyes could follow. She felt sure she could detect the faint aroma of the wine that was expected to follow soon.

Her eyes shifted to the newly paved road that ran from the county highway down into Fat Chance. That, she thought, might be the biggest change of all. She remembered her own first encounter with the crevice-riddled ravine that was the gateway to her future when she and her little group arrived.

She thought back to the feeling of dismay when they reached the turnout on the highway that ran above town. Dismay turned to anguish as they carefully made their way down the ravine and into Fat Chance. She remembered thinking: How was anyone supposed to live in a place like Fat Chance when you couldn't even get there from here?

But get there they did.

The townspeople always called the ravine "the trail," a subtle signal that no matter how awful things were, they were going to look on the bright side. Now, in place of the ravine there was an honest to goodness road with shining asphalt glowing in the morning sun. It looked to Dymphna like a lava flow, pouring into the town before stopping abruptly at the bottom of the hill.

She never said it, and neither did any of the others, but she really believed that the road signified to all the survivors of the original group that they'd gone the distance. They'd made something of themselves.

There was no denying that Fat Chance, Texas, had come a long way since the small band of strangers made their way down the battered trail, hoping to muscle through six months in the ghost town in compliance with the will—and the Will—of dead billionaire Cutthroat Clarence, who decided he needed to make amends to some of the people he'd wronged in his life. While he never felt he'd actually stolen money from any of them, when push came to shove, he didn't want to die without righting a few of the many wrongs he'd committed on his way to building a financial empire. His goal was to return the *opportunity* to make something of themselves. And so he gave them Fat Chance, Texas. The inhabitants had been through their baptism by fire, and now were reaping the rewards of their own American Dream.

As Dymphna and her boyfriend, Professor Johnson, made their way down the hill they held hands and stared at the new road in the distance.

"It's a thing of beauty," Professor Johnson said, giving Dymphna's hand a gentle squeeze.

"I don't want to be rude," Dymphna said. "But if I hear one more word about asphalt, I'm going to scream."

"I thought you were happy about the new road."

"I was," Dymphna said. "I *am*. But I think paving the trail is enough. You know I think paving Main Street will ruin the esthetic of the town."

"Fat Chance has an esthetic?" Professor Johnson asked.

Dymphna said nothing. This was very old, very familiar territory. She and her boyfriend were on opposite shores of this murky issue.

In the year and a half since she and Professor Johnson had declared themselves a couple, she had never been so harsh with him. Professor Johnson didn't let go of her hand, but they continued their walk in silence. Dymphna watched Thud, Professor Johnson's bloodhound, zigzagging through the banks of the little creek. She tried to think of a way to smooth things over without apologizing for her throw-down about the road. She was sorry they'd had a disgruntled moment, but it would be wrong to act contrite. She *was* sick of talking about asphalt.

Thud resembled an energetic ghost in the cloud of dust he kicked up on his way down Main Street. At the sound of the triangle, the zigzagging had come to an end. Thud made a beeline to the café, where breakfast was waiting.

"You know," Professor Johnson said, as they watched the dog climb the stairs through the haze. "If we extended the asphalt all the way down Main Street, we wouldn't have all this dust."

"I know," Dymphna said, trying to keep her tone even. "You've mentioned that."

A thousand times!

Professor Johnson held the door to the café open for Dymphna. When they were first figuring out how to be a couple, it took a while for Dymphna to get used to Professor Johnson's manners. He held doors, pulled chairs from tables, and walked curbside. The first time he leapt around her to get to the edge of Main Street's boardwalk, she'd bumped into him, almost falling into the street.

"What are you doing?" she had asked.

"Walking on the outside," he said.

"Why?"

"To protect you."

"From what?"

"Your petticoat getting splashed by a runaway buggy?" Professor Johnson finally said.

Dymphna had looked down at her jeans and cowboy boots as if expecting them to have morphed into ruffles and high-buttoned shoes. Dymphna smiled at the memory. Professor Johnson could be exasperating, but he was certainly one of a kind. She touched his arm in what she hoped was a conciliatory gesture before heading inside.

She squinted inside the doorway, adjusting to the dim light.

"Get on in here," Pappy said irritably. "You know Fernando won't serve breakfast until we're all accounted for."

Dymphna shot a quick look at Professor Johnson. Pappy and Professor Johnson had been butting heads since the group first straggled into Fat Chance. Pappy was, inexplicably, the one to greet them and show them the ropes. He was a huge man with wild white hair and beard, and a cranky disposition, giving the impression of a polar bear perpetually emerging from hibernation.

Thud had already settled at Titan's feet when Dymphna and Professor Johnson took their seats between Titan and Powderkeg. Powderkeg roared a greeting and fell into immediate conversation with Professor Johnson about the fledgling vineyard that now sprouted on the hills. The two men were full of plans for "growing the town," an expression Dymphna couldn't stand. Dymphna felt herself relax as she sat next to Titan.

Like Dymphna, Titan tried to steer clear of town politics, even when the town consisted of only eight people. Professor Johnson and Pappy had enough views for all of them. And Powderkeg was loud enough for all of them.

"Glad you finally decided to waltz down the hill before the food got cold," Old Bertha said.

When the group had arrived in Fat Chance, Pappy said he'd "set his cap" for Old Bertha. As Dymphna reached for a buttermilk biscuit in the center of the table, she wondered if Pappy would ever give up. He'd gone so far as to buy Old Bertha a miniature mule, but Old Bertha continued to play hard to get.

"You have to keep the mystery alive," Old Bertha, the queen of unsolicited advice, once told Dymphna.

Dymphna wasn't one to express these things, but she did question the soundness of Old Bertha's philosophy. Dymphna guessed Pappy and Old Bertha had to both be upwards of eighty. Dymphna wondered which would go first—the mystery or one of them. But Dymphna had to admit, Pappy's pursuit never seemed to lose steam.

Dymphna looked around. Less than a year ago, the original band of Cutthroat Clarence's beneficiaries were the only people in the café at any hour of the day, let alone seven thirty in the morning. Now the place was buzzing with cowboys from the neighboring Rolling Fork Ranch. Once Fernando Cruz set foot in Fat Chance, bringing with him his culinary wizardry, the town started to come to life. At first, it was a slow trickle of cowboys and ranch hands stopping by for a quick meal. Dymphna remembered the first time she walked into the café and saw a stranger sitting at one of the tables. She stopped dead in her tracks and stared. Polly, the town's hat maker and part-time waitress at the café, had snapped Dymphna out of her trance.

"What are you staring at?" Polly hissed.

"Who is that?" Dymphna asked, pointing a finger at the ranch hand's back. It was incomprehensible that there was a new, breathing human being in Fat Chance.

"It's a *man*," Polly said, cheeks reddening as she went to refill the cowboy's coffee mug.

Dymphna had forgotten that Polly worked at the café solely to meet guys. There were *very* few men in Fat Chance. One was old enough to be Polly's father, one old enough to be her grandfather, one was taken, and two were gay. Slim pickins indeed. When Polly talked Fernando into giving her the job, Dymphna thought it was a very kind gesture on Fernando's part. But now, Dymphna viewed Fernando as a visionary. With Polly in the picture, there were men at every table.

The sight of a cowboy was now commonplace. The new challenge was trying to get Polly's attention. Dymphna looked over at Polly, coffeepot perched sassily on her hip as she flirted with a tableful of long-legged men in jeans and cowboy boots.

"We'll never get more coffee now," Old Bertha groused, following Dymphna's gaze.

"Oh, let Polly have her fun," Titan chided. "I can put on another pot."

Titan half rose from his chair before sitting back down. Dymphna smiled at him sympathetically. When it was just the handful of locals who ate at the Cowboy Food Café, meals were a little more relaxed. If you needed butter, you went into the kitchen and got it. If you needed coffee, you put on a fresh pot. But Fernando put a stop to the casual approach once the place started attracting customers from out of town.

"I have a reputation to keep," Fernando had announced.

"Oh?" Powderkeg said, coaxing the ancient coffeemaker into producing one more pot. "Since when do you have a reputation?"

"Since now," Fernando growled, his voice bouncing around a nearly empty room. "Stay out of my kitchen."

Within weeks, Fernando had his reputation and a full restaurant. Word spread that Fernando's food was the best for miles around.

Until the new road was put in, anyone driving to Fat Chance had to park at the turnout at the top of the hill and walk down. After a meal at the Cowboy Food Café, few diners wanted to immediately climb the steep, gouged trail. As the café gathered a following, the reputations of the other Fat Chancers grew. Powderkeg's leather shop now had a backlog of saddle orders. Titan's forge was busy night and day making shoes for horses and mules. Old Bertha's B & B took in guests of the ranchers. Cowboys consulted Polly for gifts for their girlfriends, mothers, and wives, and Dymphna's knitwear and fruit jellies sold briskly at the grocery store. Although Professor Johnson's museum wasn't a hot ticket, visitors to town often stopped in to see the professor and to discuss the vineyard's progress. The promise of a new winery in a year or so had captured the imagination of the whole area.

The only downside to this new prosperity had been the lack of a decent road into town. As more and more cars and trucks clogged the turnout, the county, which had conveniently ignored Fat Chance's existence for centuries, miraculously and suddenly decided to put in a road from the turnout to the bottom of the hill. The locals were divided on whether they should take up the challenge of extending the asphalt all the way through town. Pappy, Powderkeg, Fernando, and Professor Johnson were in favor of extending the road while Dymphna, Polly, Titan, and Old Bertha wanted to retain the charm of the town with its sun-bleached boardwalk and dirt road. It was certainly not the biggest calamity to face the people of Fat Chance, but it was dividing them.

"I say we pave Main Street and just be done with it," Pappy said to Professor Johnson.

There appeared to be no getting away from the topic.

"I agree," Professor Johnson said, although this was no surprise to anyone.

Although she was tired of the topic, Dymphna was happy that

Pappy and Professor Johnson had finally met on common ground. Bolstered by Professor Johnson's vote of confidence, Pappy continued, raising his voice so the rest of the table could be included, whether they wanted to be or not.

"I think I'm more qualified than the rest of you to make this decision," Pappy said. "We're putting in the road."

Dymphna sighed. So much for common ground.

"What exactly qualifies you?" Professor Johnson asked.

"I'm the mayor, aren't I?"

"No, you're not," Professor Johnson said. "How many times do I have to remind you that no one elected you mayor?"

"Remind me all you want," Pappy said. "I came with the place."

"He did come with the place, Professor Johnson," Titan added. "You can't deny that."

"I'm not denying he was here when we arrived," Professor Johnson said. "I'm just pointing out that he's not the mayor."

"So you're saying we shouldn't put in the road?" Pappy asked.

"No," Professor Johnson said. "I'm just saying you're not the mayor."

"If it helps to get the road put in," Powderkeg said, "I have no problem calling Pappy 'Mayor.'"

"You can call Pappy whatever you want; nobody can put in a road unless we vote," Professor Johnson said.

"Whose side are you on?" Powderkeg asked Professor Johnson.

"Here they go again," Titan said to Dymphna.

Dymphna looked around the table just as Polly arrived with more coffee. Of all the changes Dymphna had observed in the years they'd been in Fat Chance, the 180-degree shift in Polly's personality was probably the most marked. Polly had been little more than a teenager when she set her black-and-lace tie-up boots on Texas soil, her kohl-rimmed eyes observing everything and everybody with suspicion. In New York City, where she had been raised, Polly fought hard against rules. In Fat Chance, there were no rules. Polly, like all of them, was free to decide who and what she wanted to be as the mood struck. The big difference between Polly and the rest of them was her age. She could shrug off convention more easily than the rest because she hadn't adhered to it as long.

"Hey guys, anybody need a fill-up?" Polly's eyes shown from the exertion of flirting with the ranchers.

"Warm-up," Old Bertha corrected. "Does anybody need a *warm-up*? This is not a gas station."

It drove Old Bertha crazy that Polly couldn't get her automotive and waitressing terms straight.

Dymphna felt tears fill her eyes.

She would sure miss her band of misfits now that she was leaving Fat Chance.

Chapter 2

Cleo could afford good lighting.

In the last decade, she'd had several lighting specialists customize her bathroom, her walk-in closet, and bedroom. Now, catching a glimpse of her determinedly preserved face in an upstairs hall mirror, she made a mental note to soften the hallway lights as well.

Cleo knew Wesley was down in the library, but she made no attempt to rush. She was rich and he was her attorney. He had arrived without an appointment. Therefore he had to wait. It was the unspoken rule.

Well, it was one of the unspoken rules.

As she made her way down the curved double staircase—she always walked down the left one as it featured her good side—she saw her butler, Jeffries, standing outside the library door. He looked up at her impassively. When Cleo was a girl, her mother taught her to navigate stairs without ever looking down. Now that Jeffries had caught her gaze, she couldn't break eye contact by looking down at the marble steps.

It was another damn unspoken rule.

Cleo's life was riddled with them.

As she reached the bottom step, Jeffries gave a brief nod and opened the door to the library. Cleo stood ramrod straight as she walked through the door. She was always on her guard around Wesley, and being on guard required good posture.

"There you are!" Wesley said, standing up to greet her.

"Yes," Cleo said, accepting a light kiss on the cheek. "Here I am."

He smelled like expensive bourbon—her expensive bourbon—which he made a habit of drinking whenever he waited for her. Cleo went to the Waterford decanter and poured a small amount of bourbon into a glass for herself. She raised it in a toast. Wesley had settled back on the couch. He raised his glass silently and checked his Rolex.

"Early for you to be joining me in a cocktail," he said.

"It's five o'clock somewhere, as they say."

"Actually"—Wesley checked his watch again—"it's five o'clock *here*."

Cleo was grateful for her latest shot of Botox. She knew her surprise didn't show. She'd kept Wesley waiting a whole hour. She actually felt a little guilty, but Wesley showed no signs of annoyance. He appeared as unflappable as ever.

She took a seat in a wing-backed chair opposite the couch.

"With the money I pay you, I know you can afford your own bottle of Elijah Craig," she said, taking a healthy sip of the amber liquid. "So I assume we have some business to discuss? Something that couldn't be handled at the office?"

"Not exactly," Wesley said.

Cleo knew Wesley well enough to know that no subtle body language or facial expression was going to give her any clue as to why he'd come to see her. She studied him. He was a handsome man, around her age. In his fifties, he was effortlessly fit and could claim a full head of hair that was just beginning to gray at the temples. It occurred to Cleo that he'd had the same amount of gray for the last five years. Maybe Wesley had his own beauty secrets. She found the idea intriguing, probably more intriguing than whatever brought him here unannounced.

"What exactly do you mean by 'not exactly'?" she countered.

"We need to talk about Fat Chance," Wesley said. "I thought you might be more comfortable discussing it in private."

Cleo downed the rest of her drink and stood to refill her glass.

Cleo couldn't deny that Wesley seemed to appreciate the motley crew of Fat Chance. He had met them all once three years ago when the lot of them gathered in this very room to hear the terms of her father's will. Her father was known to the media as "Cutthroat Clarence" and his word was law—apparently even after he was dead. He had fashioned a bequest for a bunch of strangers, who were invited to Cleo's house. In the DVD that served as his will, Cutthroat confessed that he'd stolen something from each of them—either directly or indirectly—and he wanted a chance to make it up to them.

They were each going to receive a bequest from Clarence, but there was one condition: They must live together in a ghost town for six months. At the end of those six months, Cleo was the only member of the original band to leave. Technically, her nephew left with her, but it was only to finish out his contracted year at the university. He was always going back.

She was never going back.

She took a deep breath as she sat down.

"All right," she said. "Let's discuss it. Although I would hardly say I have an interest in that awful little town."

Wesley raised one eyebrow. There hadn't been an arched eyebrow of that caliber since Mr. Spock. Cleo suspected he had watched *Star Trek* as a kid and practiced in front of a mirror. She knew a studied gesture when she saw one.

"In that case, I guess I'll leave," Wesley said, rising slowly from the chair.

"You might as well tell me," Cleo said hurriedly. "After all, I'm already in for your ghastly hourly plus my best booze."

"You know I'm worth every penny," Wesley said, sitting down and swirling the cut-glass tumbler in his hand. "And every sip."

"I don't know why you're interested in Fat Chance in the first place," Cleo continued, annoyed that Wesley was toying with her.

"I am pledged to look after all your holdings, no matter how humble," Wesley said, saluting her with his glass.

"Oh, please," Cleo said. "Don't tell me that claptrap works with your other clients."

"Actually, it does. And don't change the subject. You would have to be made of stone not to want to know what's going on there. And you only pretend to be made of stone."

"You're too kind."

"Besides, your nephew keeps me posted," Wesley said. "I'm just passing along family business."

"Elwood keeps me posted, too," Cleo said defensively.

"Well then . . . ," Wesley said, rising once more.

"Oh, all right," Cleo said. "The high-and-mighty Professor Elwood Johnson doesn't check in as often as he might. But as we all know, cell phone reception is spotty out there."

Cleo knew this last statement didn't make any sense; if Elwood could reach out to Wesley, he could certainly reach out to her. She looked at Wesley. From the tight smile on his face, she could see that he saw the faulty logic as well. She would never admit to her lawyer that her nephew kept her at arm's length.

Did she detect a glint of *pity* in his eyes?

I'd better not, or he's fired right now!

"Well?" she asked crisply. "What's going on in Fat Chance, Texas?"

"Everyone is very happy that the county suddenly took an interest in the place and paved the trail," he said.

"And you were a good soldier and did not mention that I made that happen—correct?"

"Correct," Wesley said. "Although I can't for the life of me figure out why you wouldn't want credit. You've never been the anonymous-donor type."

"That just proves you know nothing about me."

"Really? Name one other instance when you didn't want credit for . . . anything."

"The people of Fat Chance, who need help, like to think they don't," Cleo said. "The people of Beverly Hills, who don't need any-thing, thrive on their conjured neediness."

"I don't get it."

"Basically, you get points for helping here in Beverly Hills, but condemned if you even offer a hand in Fat Chance."

"That should be a T-shirt," Wesley said.

"It's too long to be a T-shirt," Cleo said. "Not to mention you'd never sell any in Beverly Hills, so why bother?"

Wesley laughed his $1000-an-hour laugh.

"I'm not paying you to come up with T-shirt ideas," Cleo said. "What's happening with Titan?"

"The forge is still hot, pardon the pun. And he still has the bull he bought, apparently," Wesley said. "Seems he's getting some hefty stud fees. Sound business decision."

Cleo smiled. Only she and Titan knew that Cleo had given him the money for the bull—actually her four-karat engagement ring from her decades-defunct marriage to Powderkeg bought the bull. No need to bother Wesley with those details. Clearly, he wasn't im-pressed by her quiet, grand gestures.

Cleo was jealous that her nephew seemed to be much more forth-coming with Wesley than he was with her about the happenings in Fat Chance, but she pushed the feelings aside. She was much more interested in hearing about the rest of the townspeople she'd left behind in Fat Chance two years ago. She shivered at the memory of her humiliating and futile attempt to rekindle her romance with her ex-husband. She'd failed rather publicly. "Publicly" in Fat Chance was a relative term—did eight people even qualify as "public"?—but the memory still stung.

Wesley quickly completed his update. Fernando had worked his magic opening the Cowboy Food Café, a fact Wesley might have pointed out with a little less enthusiasm had he realized Cleo ran the café before Fernando set one boot in town and had not had anywhere near the success of Fernando's Cowboy Food Café. Her nephew had united everyone when he discovered grapes growing in Fat Chance. The entire town was now banded together, planting vines on all their property. They'd created a vineyard and now all of them were working toward building a winery within a year—just in time to start producing their very own wine.

"And it's all going smoothly?" Cleo asked, somewhat surprised.

"Who said anything about things running smoothly?" Wesley replied.

"Are you withholding gossip?"

"No, Your Honor. But with this group, when does anything go smoothly?"

Cleo tried not to think about Fat Chance very often. She had put in her six months and hightailed it back to Beverly Hills, but her life was never the same. She'd eventually worked up her nerve to return to Fat Chance, hoping for another chance with her ex-husband, Marshall Primb, now going by the moniker of "Powderkeg." But she had been too late. He was in love with a woman from the sprawling neighboring ranch, where she worked as a pilot.

Wesley's voice intruded on her thoughts. "Am I boring you?"

"No!" Cleo said, realizing she'd gotten up and was staring out the window. "I was just . . ." She turned to face him, trying to keep her expression neutral. "Anything else?" she asked.

"Not much." Wesley yawned. "Oh, apparently Powderkeg and that pilot broke up."

Chapter 3

Dymphna had to admit, now that Fat Chance had a road, the fact that they could get Professor Johnson's Outback up to the farm was pure luxury. It would have been hard to sneak off if she needed him to carry her bag up the trail.

The sun was rising over the farm as Dymphna tucked one small bag into the back of Professor Johnson's SUV. She felt guilty taking his car, but not guilty enough to stay. The farm was still in shadows, but she was able to make out Thud's form shooting through the open back and climbing into the passenger seat. He was extremely agile for a large dog. Or at least, extremely determined.

"Thud!" Dymphna called in a hoarse whisper. "Get out of the car."

Dymphna tiptoed over to the passenger side and opened the door. Thud thumped his tail. She grabbed his collar. As soon as she was in range, Thud dealt her a slobbery kiss. Dymphna wiped the drool on her sleeve, grabbed his collar, and pulled. The dog didn't budge.

"Come on, Thud," she said. "Get out!"

She was not usually this stern with the bloodhound, but there was no time to lose. Dymphna had hoped to be gone by the time Wobble, her crabby rooster, crowed. Even though it was still mostly dark, she could hear Wobble flapping around the yard. The rooster was putting his all into it this morning, looking like a vintage Kellogg's Corn Flakes ad, perched on the fence and flapping his wings in the hazy morning light.

"I'm going to miss you." Professor Johnson's voice pierced the fog.

Dymphna started.

"I was hoping I wouldn't wake you," she said.

"You didn't," Professor Johnson said. "Thud did."

Dymphna knew a scowl from her would not matter in the least to Thud, so she didn't bother.

"I . . ." She paused, then started again. "I just think it's easier this way. We said goodbye last night . . . and . . . I mean, I'll be back. Soon."

"Will you?"

"I have your car," she said, trying for a confident smile.

"And I guess I have your farm," he said.

He had a point. While she was gone, Professor Johnson would be here, taking care of her goats and chickens, as well as packing the orders that came in for her jams and jellies. He would also have to keep an eye on Dymphna's friend Crash the duck, who remained a wild bird but would show up at the farm every now and then to let her know he was fine.

Both of them had agreed that it was time for Dymphna to return to Los Angeles and collect her Angora rabbits. Professor Johnson and Powderkeg had made a climate-controlled environment here on the Fat Farm that was just waiting for the rabbits. When she and Professor Johnson had first started discussing the details of retrieving the rabbits, their relationship was not as strained as it was now. She couldn't put her finger on it, but it seemed as if when times were tough, the entire town pulled together. When they first got word that the trail was to be paved, it seemed like the answer to their prayers. The asphalt wasn't even dry before the bickering began. While the town prospered, both sides claimed victory: Professor Johnson's side thought the uptick in the town's prosperity was due to the new access to town and would only get better if they continued paving Main Street. Dymphna's side felt that as long as people were making their way into town, why ruin the historic nature of the place? Folks in the area were well aware of the squabbling among the Fat Chancers and snickered about Team Professor and Team Dymphna. It was idle gossip for those not involved, but tensions were running high at the farm. Neither Dymphna nor Professor Johnson took things lightly.

As the time approached for her to leave for Los Angeles, Dymphna felt she was escaping. Her thoughts turned more and more to her life in Santa Monica, the days before Fat Chance, the years before Professor Johnson. She'd had a good life there, living in the guesthouse of her best friend, Erinn. Erinn was a Broadway playwright who had reinvented herself as a TV producer and documentarian. Erinn's family had become Dymphna's family. Fat Chance had completely overwhelmed Dymphna and she'd somehow never made it back to Southern California. Now she was homesick, day-dreaming about long walks along the coast, drinking tea at Erinn's sister's tea shop in Venice, catching up with how her rabbits were doing from Erinn's mother, Virginia, who had been watching over the three rabbits that remained in her care. Virginia had moved into Erinn's guesthouse when Dymphna made the bold move to Texas, but Erinn had said Dymphna would always have a room in the large Victorian on Ocean Avenue that Erinn somehow managed to hang on to, even with her feast-or-famine career.

Although unspoken, neither Dymphna nor Professor Johnson was sure she was going to come back immediately. Dymphna kept pushing away the thought that she might not come back at all. Tears pricked her eyes. This farm was as close to "home" as any place in her life.

Of course I'll come back, she scolded herself.

"The rabbits will love it here," Professor Johnson said.

The sun had made its way over the hills. She could see him clearly now, his T-shirt and sweatpants wrinkled from sleep, his hair wild from last night's passionate goodbye. Dymphna's heart lurched when she saw that he was barefoot—he had obviously run out of the house as soon as he understood what the empty side of the bed meant.

Of course I'll come back.

"Were you going to say goodbye?" he asked.

She knew if she looked at him, she would see the little boy who no one got to see but her. The little boy who trusted her not to hurt him.

So she didn't look. Instead, she tugged again at the dog.

"Thud, seriously," she said. "Out."

"Do you want to take him with you?"

This is why she had wanted to leave while he was still asleep. He could be such a dear man—when he wasn't infuriating her.

No," Dymphna said. "He's been at the farm for years now. I don't think he'd want to go back to Los Angeles."

"But you do?"

"For a little while," she said softly.

"Get out of the car, Thud," he said evenly.

The dog jumped out of the passenger side and Professor Johnson closed the door with a solid *thwack*.

"It's a long drive," she said. "I really better be going."

He nodded.

"I washed the car," he said.

"Oh?" Dymphna looked at the Outback. Now that the sun was up, she could see it was sparkling clean.

"Thank you," she said.

She started to put her arms around him. She wanted to hold him and say all the things that she never said. She loved him. He was the best thing that ever happened to her. She would be back. She took a deep breath, but he was the first to speak.

"If Main Street were paved, the car wouldn't be completely trashed by the time you got through town," he said.

Dymphna kissed him on the cheek, gave Thud a squeeze, and got in the car.

As she drove quietly through town, she passed the Creakside Inn, where Polly still kept a room in Old Bertha's place. At one point, Fernando and Powderkeg had both been boarders, but over the last year or so, they'd built living quarters behind their businesses. Dymphna smiled as she thought about Pappy, who was often an overnight guest at Old Bertha's, but nobody was supposed to know that. As she made her way down Main Street, all the storefronts were still dark. She knew it would be awhile until she saw these buildings again, and it unsettled her. She'd been seeing these buildings every day for almost three years—the longest she'd ever stayed in one place. She wanted to memorize every little detail in case . . .

There was no *in case*. She would be back!

Polly's shop, called Polly's Tops, Hats and Tails gave way to Professor Johnson's establishment, once a saloon called the Booze-hound, and now a museum dedicated to the history of Fat Chance. The museum was a labor of love that Professor Johnson was sure was going to pay off one day. Every now and then, his enthusiasm for the town did manage to engage the interest of a random cowboy who had come to town to buy a saddle or boots, but Professor Johnson's overkill approach usually had the man making excuses and escaping the museum within minutes. Next was the Cowboy Food Café, which Fernando had made the shining star of Main Street.

When they'd first been challenged to spend six months in Texas, Professor Johnson's aunt Cleo had run the place. She was the one who instigated the custom of all of them meeting for breakfast. Cleo was long gone, but the rest of them still met for breakfast five days a week.

That counts for something, doesn't it?

Dymphna was not a fan of confrontation, and the morning town meetings often left her with no appetite. She gripped the steering wheel firmly.

Who cares if Pappy was elected mayor or not? As far as she could tell, only Professor Johnson.

Next to the café, Dymphna saw the darkened windows of the bank and jail—both Pappy's domain long before the rest of them arrived. After that, Powderkeg's carpentry shop. Powderkeg's skill with leather went back into the older man's past; he was actually a belt-maker who went from craft fair to craft fair when he'd first been discharged from the army in the early seventies. It was at one of those fairs that he first met the very young heiress Cleo Johnson. Although that marriage didn't last long, thanks in part to Cutthroat Clarence's intervention, Dymphna's romantic nature hoped that Cleo and Powderkeg's brief renewal of passion when they first arrived in Fat Chance might have stuck. Dymphna had only heard about Cleo's life as one of the richest women in the world when Professor Johnson made his weekly call to his aunt's mansion in Beverly Hills. Of course, the news was always a little hazy by the time Professor Johnson recapped their conversations to Dymphna. Cell phone reception was still only accessible in one spot on Main Street and temperamental at best. And Professor Johnson never had much interest in the interpersonal side of things. Cleo could be a challenge, but Dymphna had really been pulling for her, both at the beginning of her rekindled romance with Powderkeg and when she came back six months later to try again, only to find Powderkeg was already in love with someone else—a gorgeous pilot from the Rolling Fork Ranch.

Dymphna shook her head. She was full of romantic ideas back then. She was feeling much more practical these days. It was probably Professor Johnson's pragmatic side rubbing off on her. Because he was nothing if not pragmatic. Granted, he was the one who discovered grapes—not only grapes, but grapes of *historic significance*—

growing in Pappy's backyard. And now everything revolved around the grapes. The whole group had decided they could parlay the grapes into a solid future. According to Professor Johnson, everything was on track to start producing wine within another year.

Fernando very vocally disagreed with Professor Johnson. Fernando spent his high school years helping his father work the vineyards in Napa Valley, and could out-wine-snob Professor Johnson any day. Fernando thought the grapes needed at least another two years on the vine before anything drinkable could be produced. It seemed to Dymphna only time could settle this argument, but Fernando and Professor Johnson discussed it heatedly almost every day.

Dymphna was now rolling past the last store on Main Street, Wally's Groceries. Old Bertha ran the store, but even newcomers to town knew about Wally. Wallace Watanabe, a recently released petty criminal who went by the name Wally Wasabi when Dymphna first met him, was one of the original band of Cutthroat's beneficiaries. When they'd first arrived in town, Dymphna suspected Wally had a crush on Polly. Then, Dymphna suspected Polly had a crush on Wally. Wally turned out to be a romance writer who had a following even he didn't know anything about. A lucrative deal with a prestigious New York City publishing house put an end to any possible romance in Fat Chance. So many romances took wrong turns here.

Was her romance next?

Dymphna looked on the bright side. In the course of just under three years, Fat Chance now claimed a literary star. Although not the same caliber as Cynthiana, Kentucky, which could point to Robert Kirkman of *Walking Dead* fame as one of its own, Wally Wasabi's career was just beginning.

On the other side of Main Street, Dymphna saw a light shining through the rickety walls of the forge. Titan must be awake. She applied the brakes. Should she go say goodbye? Her breath caught. Titan had been her best friend since she'd met him at Cleo's house just before they'd all heard the news that they'd be going to Fat Chance. She remembered the two of them walking up the longest, best-manicured driveway Dymphna had ever seen and her telling Titan how nervous she was. He promised her he'd be her wingman—and he had lived up to it.

Dymphna sat staring at the forge. She and Titan had cooked up a plot to distract the pro-asphalt people, who were so gung-ho on "improving the town." But neither of them was a match for Professor Johnson or Pappy, so they stayed silent.

Dymphna wondered if Titan would ever mention their plan now that she was gone. Should she go ask him?

She let her foot off the brake and gently pressed the accelerator. She wasn't very good at goodbyes.

Chapter 4

As he and Thud made their way into town, Professor Johnson could see the tire tracks the Outback left on Main Street earlier that morning. There was no missing Dymphna's frown as she drove away. He wondered if perhaps he shouldn't have mentioned the road.

"Let the dust settle" had never seemed so apt.

He knew he tended to obsess about things. This character trait had ended more than one relationship, but he was surprised to find it annoyed Dymphna. She was always so easygoing. Thud ran ahead as soon as he saw Pappy and Old Bertha and waited at the front door of the café for them to open the door. The trio entered the café together, Thud oblivious to the fact that Old Bertha harbored a not-so-secret desire to have the dog banned from the restaurant.

She certainly can go on and on about that, Professor Johnson thought, shaking his head. *Some people are just relentless.*

By the time Professor Johnson had gotten down the hill, Titan was making his way up the boardwalk. Two cowboys stopped him. Professor Johnson could see by their gestures that they wanted to order horseshoes, but Titan was shaking his head. The cowboys shrugged and went into the café. Titan stayed on the boardwalk, looking around. Professor Johnson thought he looked worried.

"She's still missing, Titan?" Professor Johnson asked, walking over to him.

He saw the huge, brown biceps and forearms clenching with tension. Titan had been a bodybuilder before his life in Fat Chance, and his job at the forge kept him in perfect form.

"I'm afraid I'm never going to see Fancy again," Titan said, without taking his eyes off the street. "She's been gone almost two months. I'm starting to give up hope."

"Don't feel that way," Professor Johnson said. "Sometimes we don't see Crash for months, and he always comes back."

Titan gave Professor Johnson a watery smile.

Fancy was a one-eyed buzzard with a broken wing, who had taken to Titan when the group first moved to town. She limped along beside him to the café every morning. She waited patiently for him to appear after breakfast, at which point she would limp back to the forge, Titan taking tiny steps so she could keep pace. They were quite a sight, the giant man and the tattered bird. As more and more people came to town, the sight of Fancy frightened some people. Titan was afraid he would have to keep Fancy locked in the forge in the morning, but Powderkeg built her a special hitching post around the side of Main Street. He also fashioned a leather glove for Titan. Their latest morning ritual was that they would leave the forge, which was across Main Street, and Fancy would hobble over to the hitching post. Titan would lower his arm, Fancy would climb up on the leather glove, and Titan would deposit her on the hitching post for an hour or so.

Professor Johnson once asked Titan if it wouldn't be faster to just carry the bird over to the hitching post, but Titan looked at him scornfully.

"I don't want her to feel handicapped," he said. "I always tell her, 'You're handi-cap-able!' I don't want to ruin whatever self-esteem she has left."

Professor Johnson remembered turning to Dymphna once when Titan was out of earshot, to ask if she thought buzzards had self-esteem. She did. He kept his opinion to himself. Dymphna and Titan were crazy· about animals. Any discussion about anthropomorphizing would only cause hard feelings—and who was he to say what was right or wrong?

I do have a PhD from Harvard in natural sciences, and that should count for something, he thought.

But in Fat Chance, it actually didn't.

"I'm wondering if I did something to offend her," Titan said. "Maybe she really didn't like being stuck on the hitching post every morning. Maybe she found it degrading."

Professor Johnson thought a crippled buzzard who feasted on carrion feeling degraded by *anything* was a little farfetched, but he kept his thoughts to himself.

"Or maybe I've been too focused on the forge," Titan continued.

"I've started to work on a life-sized sculpture of Cinderella's carriage."

Dymphna always said that horseshoes were Titan's bread and butter, but he had the soul of an artist. He made jewelry, housewares, and sculptures that looked like they had been fashioned from lace instead of metal.

Professor Johnson knew better than to say what he was thinking, which was:

We're in the Texas Hill Country and she's a lame buzzard with only one eye. She's lucky she's gotten this far.

But he could feel Dymphna's gentle disapproval at the very thought of these words coming out of his mouth. Instead he said, "Let's go in to breakfast. She knows your routine. She'll come looking for you one of these days."

"Do you think so?" Titan asked hopefully.

No.

"Of course," Professor Johnson said, steering Titan toward the café.

Dymphna might not be here, but there must be somebody in that café who will have a comforting thought.

"Any sign of your damn bird?" Old Bertha called out.

Okay, maybe not.

Titan took a seat at the far end of the table, shaking his head dolefully. Professor Johnson sat next to him. Under normal conditions, this was Dymphna's seat—but these were not normal conditions.

She'll be back, Titan," Pappy said gruffly. "She's a tough old girl."

That's not what you said ten minutes ago," Old Bertha said under her breath.

Professor Johnson looked up quickly. Titan didn't seem to hear it, or care.

"We'll get up a search party," Powderkeg offered. "Remember when Thud got bitten by that rattler and we looked for him until we were dead on our feet? We could do that again."

"But we didn't find Thud," Titan said, listlessly stirring his coffee. "Dodge did."

Dodge Durham was Public Enemy #1 in Fat Chance, having tried to steal the town out from under them in the early days. He ran the store in Spoonerville, which was the only place to buy supplies for miles, so there was no getting away from him. But nobody in Fat Chance had anything to do with him if they could help it. The fact that he had saved Thud from dying from a snakebite drove them all crazy. He was also the man who begrudgingly sold Rocket, his prize bull, to Titan when the bull refused to stay on the ranch. Dodge always acted as if he'd done Titan a favor selling the bull to him, but everyone from Dripping Springs to Fat Chance to the Rolling Fork Ranch knew the bull had a mind of his own. From time to time, there was speculation as to where Titan got the money to pay Dodge, but Titan and Rocket weren't telling.

"We know a lot more people now," Polly said, as she put a plate of pancakes in the center of the table. "I'm sure we can get the boys to help."

Polly called all the new cowboys and ranch hands "the boys."

"How old is Fancy?" Fernando asked, appearing suddenly from the kitchen.

"I have no idea," Titan said. "I mean, she's been with me three years and seemed like an old soul already."

"I'm not asking how old her soul is," Fernando said. "How old is she in years, Pappy?"

"Beats me," Pappy said. "One day she wasn't here, the next day she was."

"You must be able to narrow it down more than that," Professor Johnson said.

"Let me think," Pappy said, leaning back in his chair and closing his eyes. Everyone stared at him intently. He looked up. "Nope. Nothing comes to mind."

"Why do you want to know?" Professor Johnson asked Fernando.

"Well, maybe she's rebelling. She might be looking for more of her own kind," Fernando said. He looked meaningfully at Titan. "If you know what I mean."

"I think she was happy with Rocket and me, don't you?" Titan asked Polly, a tremor in his voice.

"Oh yes," Polly said, putting down the coffeepot and hugging his massive shoulders. "There is no doubt whatsoever that Fancy loved . . . loves you. Maybe she just needed a break?"

"Why would she need a break?"

"Why does anyone need a break?" Professor Johnson asked.

No one in Fat Chance had an answer.

Chapter 5

Dymphna didn't waste any time sightseeing. She'd made it to Los Angeles in three days. The SUV hadn't given her even a hint of trouble, but started to buck like an unbroken horse coming up the California Incline, about a mile from Erinn's beautiful Victorian home. Dymphna looked down at the gas gauge, although she knew it was full. She arrived at Erinn's as the car let out a *bang-bang-bang.*

This can't be good.

Erinn and Virginia must have been watching from the window, because they were in the front yard before Dymphna was even out of the car. She was overwhelmed by hugs, kisses, and tears as Virginia enveloped her. Erinn hung back, grinning but avoiding the emotional tsunami that always seemed to accompany Virginia.

"You look so healthy!" Virginia said. "So tan! You're wearing sunscreen, aren't you?"

"When I can get it," Dymphna said. At Virginia's look, she added, "But if I run out, I always wear a hat and gloves."

"Nice save," Erinn said under her breath.

"I heard that," Virginia said mildly. "I know you're waiting for me to be old and deaf, but we're not there yet."

It was good to be back.

"Let's get your bags," Erinn said, pulling Dymphna's backpack onto her shoulder. "Looks like you'll be staying awhile."

Virginia and Dymphna looked at Erinn with matching quizzical eyebrows. Erinn nodded to the Outback.

"That car isn't going anywhere," Erinn said, heading into the house. "You threw a rod."

"How does she know that?" Dymphna asked Virginia as they followed Erinn into the house.

"How does Erinn know half the things she knows?" Virginia said. "She just does."

Dymphna looked around as they entered the dark hallway. Nothing had changed since she'd walked out the door three years before. She heard a tinny barking coming from the kitchen and the clattering of tiny toenails on tile.

"Is that Piquant?" Dymphna asked.

"Yes," Virginia said in reference to her Chihuahua. "I have to keep him corralled now when people are coming over. Age has not improved his disposition."

"Does he bite?" Dymphna asked in surprise. Piquant was never a charmer, but he wasn't violent.

"He tries, poor dear," Virginia said, steering Dymphna toward the noise. "But he only has four teeth."

"I'll take this upstairs to the guest room," Erinn called after them. "Mother will take you out to see the rabbits."

Virginia opened the door into the kitchen, where Piquant was barking so forcefully he had backed himself into a corner.

"Piquant," Dymphna said in a soothing voice. "Don't you remember me?"

The dog suddenly quieted. Dymphna sat on the floor about three feet away from him and opened her hands, palms up. The tiny dog looked at her, then walked over slowly. Dymphna didn't move. Piquant climbed into her lap, put his front paws on her shoulders and licked her face.

"Did you miss me?" Dymphna said, finally picking the dog up and holding him to her. "I missed you, too."

"I see you haven't lost your touch," Virginia said. "Nobody relates to animals like you."

"You should meet my friend Titan," Dymphna said, breaking a rule she'd made for herself to not relate everything to Fat Chance. "He adopted a lame buzzard, and a bull who wouldn't stay with his owner. He puts me to shame."

"I doubt that," Virginia said as Dymphna rose to her feet.

Dymphna carried Piquant as they made their way to the back door. Virginia turned to Dymphna. "I know I've told you that only Blanche, Earrings, and Spot are still with us. I cremated the other darlings and scattered their ashes in the roses. Kind of freaked Caro out, but it passed." Caro was Erinn's large Himalayan cat, who became friend and protector of the rabbits, even before Dymphna departed.

Dymphna, still cradling Piquant, looked at the floor. "I'm sorry you had to go through that," she said, her face flushing. "I didn't think I would be gone so long."

"That's all right," Virginia said, but her voice shook. "You loved the little guys, I loved the little guys. I'm just sorry they aren't here for their next adventure in Fat Chance!"

Dymphna was about to say she wasn't sure when they'd all be on their way, but she held her tongue. As she walked out the back door, her breath caught as her old life came flooding back to her. The guesthouse she'd called home sat nestled between two trees at the far end of the yard. It was a perfect replica of the main house, except for the guesthouse door, which Dymphna was glad to see was still red. The rabbits were housed in yet another Victorian—their hutch designed by Erinn's last boyfriend, Christopher, a local artist and craftsman. Dymphna was sorry to hear that the two of them had broken up last year; she always thought Christopher would love Fat Chance. But early in her friendship with Erinn, she had learned not to pry.

When Erinn, a TV director and producer, was working on a show that involved investigation, there was no stopping her, but that door did not swing both ways. It used to hurt Dymphna's feelings that Erinn never wanted to share what was going on in her life. But now she understood a little better that perhaps Erinn herself didn't always know what was going on. Dymphna certainly couldn't articulate what was going on in her own life right now.

Piquant's squirming in her arms brought Dymphna back to the present. Virginia was staring at her as Dymphna put Piquant on the porch.

"Is everything all right?" Virginia asked.

"Yes, fine," Dymphna said. "It just feels strange to be back. I . . . didn't think I'd be gone so long."

"Ready to say hello?" Virginia asked, gesturing toward the Victorian hutch. Dymphna laughed as she spotted Caro lying in the sun on the roof of the hutch. It was as if he'd stayed in one place since Dymphna left. But of course, he hadn't stayed in one place. None of them had.

She was surprised to find herself nervous. Virginia reached in and pulled Spot out of the hutch. He was enormous! Dymphna took him in her arms and breathed in his sweet smell. He settled immediately into her arms.

"I think he remembers me," Dymphna said softly.

"Of course he remembers you," Virginia said. "You're hard to forget, you know."

Dymphna gave Virginia a grateful smile.

Was she hard to forget?

And was that a good thing or a bad thing?

She picked each rabbit up in turn, telling them about Fat Chance, and how they would all be going for a long car ride, though Dymphna wasn't sure exactly when that would be. She warned the rabbits that life in Texas would be very different. For one thing, they would no longer be sharing their space with an old dog that was smaller than they were, and a house cat that was equally furry. Instead, they were going to be part of a real farm, with chickens, a rooster, and four Angora goats.

"Once I get you settled, I might bring in some more brothers and sisters for you. But we're going to take it slow," Dymphna said, although running her fingers through the rabbit mohair, she was itching to start making yarn with it as soon as possible. The Angora goats produced lovely fiber, but to Dymphna's mind there was nothing quite like yarn spun from rabbit hair. She had a roster of loyal customers and she couldn't wait to present them with new shawls, scarves, hats, and gloves.

After reacquainting herself with her brood, Dymphna gave Caro a quick pat and she and Virginia walked back up the porch to the main house. Dymphna could hear voices coming from the kitchen. She couldn't identify all of them. Then she heard a laugh, which she could identify immediately. It was Erinn's younger sister and Virginia's youngest daughter, Suzanna.

The other voices must belong to Suzanna's husband, Eric, and their children, Lizzy and London. Dymphna remembered talking to Erinn on the phone the day London was born. The connection from Fat Chance was, of course, deplorable, so Dymphna hadn't been sure she had heard correctly.

"*London*, did you say?" Dymphna had said into the phone, circling the spot in the street for the best reception. "The baby's name is London?"

"Yes, his name is London," Erinn said. Did Dymphna detect a

note of annoyance? With the dead space and popping sounds that accompanied every call, it was hard to tell. "What's wrong with that?"

"Nothing," Dymphna backtracked. "It's just . . . unusual."

"Really, *Dymphna?*"

Dymphna stopped in her tracks. She knew her name was uncommon, but she wasn't to blame for that. It had been her parents' idea; she didn't choose it! But she let the moment pass. It was easy to let irritants from California fall by the wayside. She wondered if the reverse would be true. Would Professor Johnson's annoying habits seem less offensive from a thousand miles away? She would be interested to find out.

As she opened the screen door, Dymphna saw that Virginia was glowing with happiness at the sound of her two daughters chatting away in the kitchen. Dymphna never spent much time thinking about family. Her own upbringing had been complicated and she didn't like to dwell on it. But now that she was in her early thirties, the idea of having more than animals to care for seemed vaguely appealing.

"There's our girl!" Eric said when he caught sight of her.

Dymphna was instantly enveloped in Eric's bear hug, which lifted her off the ground. As soon as she was back on her feet, it was Suzanna's turn to zero in on Dymphna's personal space. Dymphna looked over Suzanna's shoulder to see Erinn leaning against a counter, hands wrapped around a cup of coffee. Dymphna smiled weakly at her. Erinn smiled back and shrugged. It wasn't that they weren't happy to see each other; it was just that they were two kindred spirits. They both knew what the other was thinking.

I know you love me without your squeezing me to death.

Suzanna let go and scooped a toddler off the floor. The boy had a riot of red hair and freckles.

"This is London," Suzanna said. "London, this is your long lost auntie Dymphna."

London, who had been looking at her with laser intensity, suddenly snapped his head around, showing Dymphna his cowlick instead of his face. He made a little "humph" noise. Suzanna looked stricken.

"He's really happy to meet you," Suzanna said. "He's just shy."

"I get it," Dymphna said. *I really do!*

"And I know you remember Lizzy," Virginia said, pulling a

taller, slimmer version of the toddler Dymphna remembered, into view. "Lizzy, do you remember your auntie Dymphna?"

What's all this? I don't remember Lizzy ever calling me Auntie. Dymphna smiled at Lizzy. If these women, who were her adopted family, wanted the kids to call her Auntie, that was fine with her. *No one else will probably ever call me Auntie.*

"Hello, Lizzy," Dymphna said. Before she could stop herself, she added, "You sure have grown."

Dymphna sighed. She had hoped to come up with something more original, something less cliché. On the other hand, Lizzy probably hadn't heard enough clichés to be tired of them yet. Lizzy was a little more sociable than her brother and smiled shyly. She still had a head of ringlets. A pair of pink glasses perched on her upturned nose. There was no denying Eric and Suzanna Cooper had very cute kids!

Details flew fast and furious. The Rollicking Bun, Suzanna and Eric's tea shop and bookstore, was doing well. They still lived in the huge apartment over it, but were thinking of buying a house on one of the neighboring streets now that they were a family of four. Suzanna and Erinn were raised in Napa Valley, although given their age difference, they grew up a decade apart. Suzanna, Eric, and Fernando were the same age, spent their high school years together, and collaborated at the Rollicking Bun until one fateful summer eight years ago. Eric and Suzanna declared their love for each other after a massive earthquake sent a bookcase crashing down on Eric, and Fernando decided he wanted to spread his wings by opening a bed-and-breakfast on Vashon Island. The fact that Fernando was now spreading his wings in Fat Chance was thrilling to them all. It was almost as if life had come full circle for them.

Suzanna said she was so happy Fernando had opened his café and was successful. She tried to send him recipes, but all her emails bounced back.

"It's almost like you guys went to the moon," Suzanna said.

"Cell phone reception is horrible out there," Dymphna said, trying not to sound defensive. "Communication with the outside world is tough."

"Fernando mentioned that," Suzanna said. "He'd call me from a town on a ranch . . ."

"Yes, Spoonerville," Dymphna said. "The Rolling Fork Ranch is so big it needs its own town. We get our supplies there, too. It's our link to the outside world."

"When you live here," Erinn said, "where communication is instant, it really is hard to believe there are still places like Fat Chance. What do you do about weather reports?"

"We're surrounded by cowboys," Dymphna said. "They can read the signs."

London started to get restless, and within an hour the Coopers piled back in their minivan and headed back down the coast to Venice Beach. Virginia and Dymphna took the rabbits out to the rabbit run that Christopher had built for them before he and Erinn broke up, then Virginia retired to the guesthouse.

Erinn was sitting at her computer in the front room when Dymphna came looking for her. Dymphna knocked softly on the gleaming wood archway, in case Erinn was busy and didn't want to talk. Erinn looked over her half-moon glasses and waved Dymphna in. Caro, who had been sprawled across the large desk when Dymphna entered, leapt up and curled up on Dymphna's lap before she'd even fully sat down on the sofa.

"Have you missed me?" Dymphna cooed, stopping herself from saying, "Have you missed your auntie Dymphna?"

"He has," Erinn said, before adding matter-of-factly, "We all have."

Erinn shut down the computer and laid her glasses on the desk before joining Dymphna. Dymphna felt guilty. She'd been on such a wild adventure in Texas that she probably didn't stay in touch as well as she should. She could only blame the lousy cell phone reception so much.

"I want to hear about everything you're doing," Dymphna said, a little too eagerly.

"I can't complain," Erinn said. "Well, I suppose I can, but as Immanuel Kant so brilliantly put it, 'One who makes himself a worm cannot complain afterwards if people step on him.'"

Dymphna recalled Erinn's penchant for quoting philosophers and writers. Dymphna had no idea who Immanuel Kant was, nor was she sure if Erinn was feeling like a worm. If she was feeling like a worm, that would be worth complaining about. Wouldn't it? Dymphna decided to eat a piece of chocolate from the side table instead of addressing the comment.

"I've finally clawed my way to the middle of this ghastly profession," Erinn said, joining Dymphna in a piece of chocolate.

The "ghastly profession" was being a director/producer/camera operator for various History Network shows. She'd dabbled in food and design shows and had been fired from several reality shows, but she'd found a home at History. Anyone but Erinn would be thrilled with this career. But anything less than making a comeback as the toast of Broadway (which she was in her twenties) would always remain a letdown for her.

"Are you working on anything interesting?" Dymphna asked.

"I have a first-look deal right now," Erinn said. "That means the network wants to hear my ideas before I take them anywhere else."

"That's good, isn't it?"

"Very good," Erinn said. "I just haven't come up with anything I want to pitch."

"You'll think of something," Dymphna said. "Don't worry."

"Why would I worry?"

"I know you kind of have permanent writer's block when it comes to writing Broadway plays, and I just thought you might be afraid you were freezing up again."

"I wasn't," Erinn said. "Until now."

Chapter 6

Dymphna had been gone a week and Professor Johnson sat alone in his museum, the weight of Fat Chance on his shoulders.

He had no one to blame for his current circumstances but himself. He'd had a fine life in California, with tenure at a prestigious university, a place where people had respect for knowledge and advanced degrees. He had returned to Fat Chance as soon as he could ethically leave the university. It was hard to believe his grandfather's crazy experiment had worked in the first place, but that they continued to flourish in this tiny sun-blasted town was a miracle.

Of course, "flourish" might be an overstatement.

Professor Johnson sighed. Dymphna had surprised him with a call. He'd hoped she was calling to say their "break" was over, but she only called to tell him the Outback was not going to make it back to Fat Chance. He wasn't sure what to do. He really had no money to fix the car. He'd put what was left of his capital into the Great Grape Gamble, as had everyone else in town. Professor Johnson was sure that in a year's time, maybe two, with the proper care, Fat Chance would produce wines with *Historic Importance*.

At first, everyone in town was behind the plan. But as the venture required more and more capital, tempers were fraying. The support on which Professor Johnson counted for the delicate "road situation" was split on "the grape situation." Powderkeg still stood with him, but Fernando and Pappy had jumped ship. Professor Johnson felt thwarted at every turn. He had researched the wine business thoroughly and could not understand why everyone didn't just fall into line. He had to admit that Fernando, having grown up and worked in the vineyards of Napa Valley, had some interesting insights. But why was he so emotional about everything?

This was, after all, strictly business.

Professor Johnson had spent most of his own inheritance getting a liquor license for the museum. During the eighteen hundreds the place had been a bar, and Professor Johnson had high hopes of returning it to its former glory, but with a twist. The Boozehound would become a tasting room, with an interactive museum helping people understand not only how their wine was made but also the history of Thomas Volney Munson, the Texan who saved the French wine industry during the late 1880s when he grafted mustang grape rootstock onto sickly French vines. The fact that the grafting was still in operation was the exciting hook Professor Johnson was looking for. People would flock to the Boozehound! Perhaps the liquor license was a bit premature, but he was always prudent in his choices. If only he could sell his fellow investors on this. He had to admit, he was safe *and* sorry.

The Boozehound was attached to the Cowboy Food Café by an adjoining archway. Professor Johnson could hear Polly talking to Fernando about her latest crush. Professor Johnson tried not to listen. He was busy deciding if he should ask the people of Fat Chance if they should buy a centrifugal de-stemmer with must pump for $4,000, and Polly's chatter was distracting. He already knew that Fernando would be opposed. Fernando considered himself the wine expert in Fat Chance and seemed to buck Professor Johnson at every turn.

"Wine is art," Fernando had said. "You don't force it. You wait for it and see what unfolds."

"Wine is science," Professor Johnson replied. "You control it and invest in the outcome."

"We're talking about mustang grapes," Fernando said. "Yes, most vintners bottle the wine quickly, and that's a shame. But we have an opportunity to make a really great wine—if we cellar the wine for three, four, or five years."

"Why do that if you can get a wine people will drink right away?" Professor Johnson asked. "The 'drink it now' wines are perfectly respectable. Why wait for the profit when we can have it now?"

Grapes were apparently like politics. You could talk about it for eternity, but you weren't likely to change anyone's mind.

Professor Johnson looked down at Thud, who was sprawled on the floor in a patch of late-afternoon sunlight.

"Ready to head back to the farm?" Professor Johnson asked,

frowning through the archway as Polly's voice bounced off the walls. "I don't think I'm going to get anything done today."

Thud thumped his tail but didn't move.

"Is that a yes or a no?" Professor Johnson asked as the bloodhound's tail hit the floor again.

Thud and Professor Johnson both looked up as Titan came in.

"I hope I'm not bothering you," Titan said.

"No, not at all." Professor Johnson cleared charts, graphs, and wine catalogues off the glass showcase he'd been using as a desk. "Any sign of Fancy?"

Titan shook his head sorrowfully. Professor Johnson didn't know what else to say. He wondered what Dymphna would do. He guessed she might hug Titan. Should *he* hug Titan?

Probably.

Professor Johnson steeled himself. He walked over to the big man and put his arms clumsily around him. Titan seemed surprised, but within seconds, he was crying uncontrollably. Professor Johnson patted Titan's muscular, heaving back, trying to quiet him, but the sobs brought Fernando and Polly running in from the kitchen.

"What have you done?" Fernando asked Professor Johnson accusingly. He reached for Titan, who turned and collapsed into Fernando's embrace—not an easy feat, since Fernando was a foot shorter.

"I was only trying to help," Professor Johnson said. "He's upset about Fancy."

At the mention of the buzzard's name, Titan's weeping escalated. Polly threw herself into the Titan-Fernando tangle. Thud struggled to his feet and leaned against Titan's legs. For something to do, Professor Johnson took off his glasses and wiped them on his shirt.

"Thank you." Titan sniffled as he disengaged from the group hug. "I've been holding that in all day."

"Come on over to the café," Fernando said. "I'll make us some tea. Would you like that?"

Titan nodded and trailed miserably behind Polly and Fernando. Thud followed the group. Professor Johnson hesitated, not sure if he was invited or not. He wished he had Thud's social skills. Polly suddenly turned around and gestured that he should come with them. She rolled her eyes, but Professor Johnson didn't care. He tried to keep the gratitude out of his step as he walked into the café and joined everyone at the table.

"It's been over two months," Titan said, using his napkin to dab at his eyes. "I'm beginning to give up hope."

"That's probably realistic," Professor Johnson offered. Everyone at the table seemed to freeze and Professor Johnson quickly reversed course. "To *begin* to give up hope. Not to actually *give up* hope."

"That's a very subtle distinction," Titan said.

Fernando sniffed. "Very."

"Maybe we should change the subject," Professor Johnson said. "Take your mind off . . . things."

"OK," Titan said. "But I don't want to talk about the road."

"Or wine," Fernando said.

"What else is there to talk about?" Professor Johnson said.

"I could tell you about the new guy I met," Polly said.

"That's perfect," Titan said, as Fernando poured more tea. "Let's hear all about him."

Professor Johnson looked through the archway at his papers stacked haphazardly over in the Boozehound. But there didn't seem to be any way to escape.

"His name is Poet, and he—"

"His name is *Poet*?" Titan's eyes widened. "How fabulous!"

Professor Johnson was about to say that the man's name was probably not Poet but a pretentious moniker he'd thought up to impress impressionable girls like Polly—and apparently grown men like Titan—but he decided to keep quiet. Titan was distracted and that was all that mattered.

"He's staying over at the Rolling Fork Ranch with his cousin," Polly said.

"Oh," Professor Johnson said. "His cousin, Laureate?"

"No," Polly said, looking confused. "His cousin Herman. Who is Laureate?"

"Never mind," Fernando said. "Professor Johnson is just being tiresome."

"Anyway, you'll never guess what he does for a living," Polly challenged.

"My money is on him being a poet!" Titan said.

Titan beamed at Professor Johnson, who just nodded. He'd gotten himself in enough trouble.

"I don't get to guess," Fernando said. "I already know."

"Tell us already," Titan said.

Polly looked each of the men squarely in the eye. Professor Johnson could barely keep from running out of the room. How could he be business partners with this group? He had to find a way to get Dymphna back here. He couldn't manage this sort of interaction alone. Mercifully, Polly finally spoke.

"He runs a wagon train in Nebraska," she said.

"Excuse me?" Professor Johnson said, assuming his mind had wandered and he misheard.

"She said he runs a wagon train in Nebraska," Fernando said, daring Professor Johnson to say anything snide.

"What does that even mean?" Professor Johnson asked.

"I thought you were the smart one," Polly said. "Don't you know what a wagon train is?"

"Yes, I do," Professor Johnson said. "I also know you're talking about the Oregon Trail and that the last wagons went through in the 1880s."

"He works in Nebraska, not Oregon," Polly said hotly. "Shows what you know."

Professor Johnson rubbed his temples. Perhaps he should spend his last dime rebuilding the engine of the Outback. To hell with the centrifugal de-stemmer. These people were impossible.

"Anyway," Polly said, glowing, "he's here to learn how to ride horses and stuff."

"Wait." Professor Johnson held up a hand. "I'm going to take a leap of faith here and accept that Poet runs a wagon train. But how can a man run a wagon train and not know how to ride a horse . . . and stuff?"

"That *is* a good question," Titan said softly.

"OK, maybe he doesn't exactly run the wagon train," Polly said, a hint of petulance creeping into her voice. "But his best friend's family owns a wagon train reenactment company and he wants to make a career of being a wagon master, so he's here to learn. He's just super lucky he has a cousin already in the business."

"That is super lucky," Titan said.

"We have a stellar career guidance center back at the university," Professor Johnson said. "I could make a few calls . . . you know, in case this wagon master dream falls flat."

"You don't take anything seriously, do you?" Fernando asked Professor Johnson, an edge to his voice.

"Aren't you usually accusing me of being *too* serious?" Professor Johnson shot back.

"This isn't even about you," Polly said to Professor Johnson.

"Please don't fight," Titan said. "Why is everyone always fighting these days?"

It was as if Titan had dealt them all a collective slap across the face. It might as well have been a banner over Main Street: WHY IS EVERYONE ALWAYS FIGHTING THESE DAYS?

"I think I better get up to the farm," Professor Johnson said. "I have animals to take care of."

Thud heard the change in Professor Johnson's tone and struggled to his feet. The two of them walked out the door together. Powderkeg was standing in the middle of Main Street, trying to get a signal on his phone.

"I give up," Powderkeg called out to Professor Johnson. "I was trying to get a quote on gravel, and I think the place closed while I was trying to get a signal."

"Gravel?" Professor Johnson said. "For extending the road down Main Street?"

"Of course," Powderkeg said. "We need a layer before we put down the asphalt, right? And the city isn't going to pave this place."

"I think perhaps we should wait. We don't have a consensus on this—not even close."

"Who cares?" Powderkeg said. "The road will be good for the town. Some of our neighbors are just too romantic for their own good. I say we pave the street and get it over with."

"I do not want to antagonize anyone any further."

"You just don't want to piss anybody off right now 'cause you're saving up for the big fight."

"The big fight?"

"There's gonna be some tough, expensive choices coming up in the next year about the grapes, right?"

"Right."

"My point exactly. How does it feel to be on the unpopular side of everything?" Powderkeg said.

"I thought we were both on the same side."

"I stand corrected. How does it feel to be the spokesperson for the unpopular side of everything?"

"Not good, actually," Professor Johnson said. "But, as you said, these people are too romantic for their own good."

"Well, I got your back." Powderkeg slapped Professor Johnson on the back and disappeared into the last of the twilight.

Professor Johnson stood looking up and down the street. He felt like an utter failure. He had the best interests of the town at heart. Why couldn't his fellow townspeople see that and just let him do what needed to be done?

"At least we got Titan's mind off Fancy," he said to Thud as they headed down Main Street to the cutoff that led to the farm. They passed the Creakside Inn, where Pappy and Old Bertha sat on the front porch, rocking in chairs Powderkeg had made. Thud ran up the walk, startling Patsy, Old Bertha's miniature mule. Patsy was a gift from Pappy in the love-struck early days of their relationship. Dymphna would often say that she hoped when she and Professor Johnson were old, they'd still be in love like Pappy and Old Bertha. These discussions always confused Professor Johnson. Pappy and Old Bertha bickered more than any two people in Central Texas. Even more than Pappy and Dodge.

Professor Johnson darted up the path after his dog, but he was too late. Thud had jumped onto the porch and was begging for attention. Old Bertha peered into the dark.

"Professor Johnson?" she called. "You out there?"

"Yes, ma'am," Professor Johnson said, his boots crunching up the walkway.

"Don't 'yes, ma'am' me," she said. "Come get your dog."

Professor Johnson tested the bottom step, decided it would hold, and climbed up on the porch. He grabbed Thud's collar.

"How's the car?" Pappy asked.

"What car?" Professor Johnson asked.

"Your car that's with Dymphna," Pappy said. "Heard it threw a rod."

"How did you hear that?"

"Who knows?" Pappy said.

"There aren't any secrets in Fat Chance," Old Bertha said.

Professor Johnson wanted to ask if they'd heard if Dymphna had decided when she was coming back, but decided against it.

"We were just talking about Main Street," Pappy said, nodding toward Old Bertha. "Looks like we gotta start courting this little lady."

"Pardon me?" Professor Johnson said.

"Well, you, me, and Powderkeg are for paving Main Street, and Dymphna, Fernando, Polly, and Titan are against it. To even tie the thing up, we need Old Bertha on our side."

"Suppose I say I don't care one way or the other," Old Bertha said.

"I'd say I don't believe you," Pappy said.

"You calling me a liar?" Old Bertha snarled.

"Either that or you're losing it," Pappy said. " 'Cause only a damn fool would be against paving that street."

"So you're calling me a damn fool?" she snapped.

"Nothing wrong with your hearing at least," Pappy said.

Professor Johnson gave Thud's collar a hefty yank. The two of them scrambled back down the walkway.

Has everyone in town gone mad?

As they made their way up the hill, Professor Johnson saw a light was on in the farmhouse. His heart started to pound. Was there an intruder? He looked down at Thud, who seemed oblivious. As usual, Professor Johnson was on his own.

He kept off the trail, treading as lightly as possible through the grass. Was he overreacting? Why would someone break into the farmhouse? Or rather walk into the farmhouse, since the door was never locked. Professor Johnson made a mental note to start locking the door from now on. Of course, first he'd have to get some keys made, but after that, the farmhouse was going to be the Fort Knox of Fat Chance. Which actually wasn't saying much.

Professor Johnson knelt in the high grass, staring at the farmhouse. He wondered if he should tie Thud in the barn so he wouldn't get hurt. He reached for the dog's collar, the battered snakeskin rough to the touch. The collar was a gift from Powderkeg, a trophy to commemorate Thud's battle with Big John the rattlesnake.

"I guess you can be heroic if the situation calls for it," Professor Johnson said to himself. He stood up as a silhouette passed in front of the kitchen light. There was someone in there, all right.

"You be quiet," Professor Johnson hissed at Thud as they climbed the step to the tiny front porch. The night was full of shadows, but it was still light enough to make out the entire yard. Whoever was in there had come on foot; there was no car or truck anywhere. It occurred to Professor Johnson that it would have been hard to sneak up on the farm in a vehicle anyway, as someone in town would have heard an engine.

As Old Bertha said, there were no secrets in Fat Chance.

Thud let out a muffled *woof* and strained at his collar. Professor Johnson thought that might be a sign that Thud was on the case, but closer inspection revealed a wildly wagging tail.

"I mean it, Thud," Professor Johnson said. "Be quiet!"

The front door creaked open, something it always did when anyone was on the porch. Professor Johnson took a deep breath and silently made his way into the living room. He held tightly to Thud as he adjusted to the darkened room. The only light was coming from the kitchen. He approached the doorway that separated the two rooms. Flattening himself against the wall, he peered into the kitchen.

Even with her back to him, he could tell it was Dymphna standing at the sink washing dishes. He would know those wild curls anywhere.

He stared at her in silence, trying to gather his thoughts. He had refused to allow himself to think she might not come back, but in his heart, he worried that she might actually decide to stay in Los Angeles, where people were sane. Where *some* people were sane. Where more people were sane than in Fat Chance.

He knew he should say something, but he didn't want to startle her. Thud was quivering with excitement, but was miraculously keeping his promise to be quiet. Professor Johnson kept hold of him, just in case. He smiled at the sight of Dymphna standing there. She was like a vision. He squinted at her. Had she put on some weight in the week she was gone? Dymphna was always slender and delicate as a leaf, but the behind in front of him was pert and rock solid, packed into black yoga pants. The muscles in her butt cheeks shifted as she put a pan in the dish rack. It was mesmerizing.

Thud suddenly couldn't take it anymore and bounded into the kitchen. Her face was still covered by her wild hair, but he heard her laugh as she knelt down and kissed the dog.

Professor Johnson reached for her, lifting her to her feet. He enveloped her, kissing her with a passion that unnerved him.

She was back. She was in his arms. And boy, was she kissing him back.

He reached down her back, hands traveling to that hypnotizing butt. He squeezed.

Nobody's ass could change that much in a week.

This is not Dymphna's butt.

Professor Johnson pulled the woman away from him. Was he going insane? The woman in front of him looked strikingly like Dymphna, but this woman vibrated with an intense energy where Dymphna radiated calm. Her eyes, so much like Dymphna's, snapped with life, as if she were enjoying a private joke. And the hair!

They stared at each other.

"You're one hell of a welcome committee," the woman said. "You must be Professor Johnson."

"Who are you?" Professor Johnson heard himself ask, although he felt as if he were having some sort of out-of-body experience. The woman smiled and stepped toward him. He stepped back.

"I'm Mary Magdalene," she said. "Dymphna's sister. You can call me Maggie."

Chapter 7

"You need to be in my office in one hour," Wesley said into the phone as he paced his Century City corner office.

The pacing was business as usual, but he was using his cell phone rather than the speaker phone. This conversation could not be overheard.

"One hour?" Cleo replied. "That's impossible! I'm getting my chakras balanced."

"Cancel it."

"One doesn't cancel chakras, Wesley," Cleo said. "That's not how it works."

"I don't care how it works," he said. "You have one hour to get over here—balanced or unbalanced chakras are up to you."

He hung up.

Cleo was in the morning room, already dressed for Madam Molly's Chakra Cleansing Canteen. Most of her friends had the chakra reader come to their houses, but Cleo liked to hit the streets of Beverly Hills every now and then, just to make sure she was keeping in touch with real people. She looked down at her vintage Diane von Fürstenberg wrap dress, truly the most remarkable piece of clothing ever designed. In it, Cleo could be dressed and quickly undressed for any occasion. The fact that the most exciting undressing she was doing these days was for her chakra reader was mildly depressing, but perhaps she would feel better once one or more chakras had been unblocked.

She wasn't sure what she should do. She certainly couldn't make it a habit of letting her lawyer order her around like she was a . . . a . . . *person*. On the other hand, Wesley had never been so . . . commanding.

Do I like that?

Jeffries was standing by with a pot of coffee. She felt her cheeks redden as she realized her butler had witnessed this humiliating phone call. She thought fondly of the days when she thought servants didn't register the dramas of their employers' lives. But *Downton Abbey* and *The Butler* had certainly put an end to that little flight of fancy.

Jeffries stood silently. If movies and TV were actually depictions of life, then Jeffries must have an opinion about what she should do.

"Well, Jeffries, what would you do?"

"Ma'am?"

"You heard Wesley," she said. "He's insisting I show up at his office in an hour. Would you go?"

"He hasn't asked me to go."

"If you were me," she said. "Would you go if you were me?"

"Has he ever steered you wrong?"

"No!" she said, shocked at the idea. "Never."

"All right, I'm here," Cleo said, storming past Ruth Ann, Wesley's latest gorgeous receptionist. "What's so damn—Oh, hello, Dymphna! What a surprise!"

Nobody could handle caught-off-guard better than Cleo. Cleo smiled her dazzling $20,000 smile and sailed to Dymphna, who stood to greet her.

What can my nephew possibly see (kiss to one cheek) *in this little ragamuffin* (kiss to the other cheek)*?*

"Hi, Cleo. I was hoping I'd get a chance to see you while I was in Los Angeles," Dymphna said softly before settling back on the sofa. "I just didn't expect it to be under these circumstances."

"I'm so glad to see you, too," Cleo said, taking in the stern-looking woman sitting next to Dymphna. Cleo turned to Wesley. "What *are* these circumstances?"

"Have a seat, Cleo," Wesley said. "Can I have Ruth Ann get you anything? Coffee? A sparkling water? A diet soda?"

No bourbon? We are on our best behavior.

"I'm fine, darling," Cleo said as she lowered herself, straight-backed, into the low chair.

Cleo kept her eyes averted from the woman across from her. She had learned the hard way that Wesley gathering people she didn't know rarely— if ever— worked in her favor. She would never forget the day seven strangers had met in her living room to view the video of her father explaining his will. She was grateful for the way Wesley handled that meeting, but he hadn't managed to come up with some spectacular loophole that kept her out of Fat Chance either.

He may have never steered me wrong, but he hasn't done me any favors either.

"This is Erinn Wolf," Wesley was saying. "She's a friend of Dymphna's."

"I'm sure you remember me telling you about Erinn," Dymphna said.

Cleo quickly looked Erinn up and down. Erinn's wild hair was pinned up in a haphazard up-do, a non-ironic homage to Bernadette Peters. And her clothes were ghastly! She was wearing a blue faux-linen blazer over a white blouse that gapped slightly under her bra. The ill-fitting pants and Toms slippers completed the disaster. Cleo supposed Erinn must be one of those women with such vivacious personalities, they didn't need to work on their looks.

"Vaguely, yes." Cleo half rose and shook Erinn's hand. "Pleased to meet you."

"And I, you," Erinn said solemnly.

So much for that theory.

"Now that we're all here," Wesley said, "I won't hold everyone in suspense any longer."

"Actually," Erinn said, "only Ms. Johnson-Primb is in suspense. The rest of us already know why we're here."

"I stand corrected," Wesley said. "All right, Cleo. I won't hold *you* in suspense any longer."

"I hope this is okay with you, Cleo," Dymphna blurted.

"We'll find out, won't we?" Cleo answered.

"As you know," Wesley said to Cleo, "Dymphna came back to Los Angeles to pick up her rabbits . . ."

"And Elwood's car broke down," Cleo said, relaxing. "That's no problem at all. I can supply a car. Would you like a red Bentley Flying Spur or a blue BMW M6?"

"I need space to bring the rabbits," Dymphna said. "Are either of them four-doors?"

"They both are," Cleo said. "But they really aren't suited for transporting rabbits."

"We're getting a little ahead of ourselves," Wesley said. "As I was saying, Dymphna is here to collect her rabbits and is staying with her friend Erinn, in Santa Monica."

"Now I remember," Cleo said. "You're Erinn Elizabeth Wolf, the playwright. You used to be the toast of Broadway when you were younger. Correct me if I'm wrong."

Erinn flinched. "You aren't wrong. Now I'm a documentarian."

"Are you now?" Cleo said. "I thought I remembered Dymphna saying you were the brains behind a series about wine and junk food. But again, correct me if I'm wrong."

"Again, you are not wrong," Erinn said. "But I am pretty solidly entrenched in the documentary world now, which is why—"

"Which is why," Wesley cut in. He took a deep breath and continued. "Which is why we're here today. Erinn has decided to do a documentary about Fat Chance."

"Oh?" Cleo said. "Why?"

"It's really an incredible story," Erinn said. "A billionaire leaves a ghost town to a bunch of strangers whose lives he somehow ruined—at least in his own mind—and the town improbably becomes successful. It's compelling television."

"The press has already covered all this," Cleo said.

"The press covered the story years ago," Erinn said. "The fact that your nephew discovered a patch of historic grapes, the fact that the artisans have started to make names for themselves, and the back stories of why and how all those people flourished in Fat Chance, will all be new avenues to explore."

"I don't think anyone will find this interesting in the least," Cleo said.

"I disagree," Erinn said.

"What if I say no?" Cleo asked.

"That isn't up to you," Erinn said. "Since you are Cutthroat's daughter and part of the story, I'd like you to be part of the process. But I'm going to Fat Chance with or without your approval. This is more of a courtesy call."

"Really?" Cleo said. "This is your idea of courtesy?"

"Cleo is just getting used to the idea," Wesley said, patting Cleo's arm. She jerked it away.

Wesley stood up, signaling the end of the meeting.

"I hope you'll like this idea once you've had time to think it over," Dymphna said. "And thank you for the offer of a car, but—"

"No buts!" Wesley said heartily. "You've got rabbits and camera equipment to move! We'll just use the stretch limo!"

"That's very kind, but I think we've been enough trouble," Dymphna said, shooting Cleo a sheepish look.

Wesley was already escorting them to the door. Cleo stayed in her seat, giving the women a bright smile and index-finger wave. She stared out the window as Wesley ushered the two women out. When he returned, Cleo's demeanor had changed.

"I don't understand the urgency of all this . . . or what it has to do with me," she said. "I cancelled plans to be here!"

"You might have noticed that the timetable isn't up to us," Wesley said. "That woman is making a documentary—and we need to keep an eye on her."

"And what is this 'we' business? 'We need to keep an eye on her' and 'we'll just use the stretch limo'?" Cleo asked. "Are you going to Fat Chance, too?"

She turned to face Wesley, who was now pouring two hefty snifters of brandy. He handed her one.

"Yes. We're all going together in the limo," he said.

Cleo choked on her brandy. "Have you lost your mind? You and I are going in a limousine to Fat Chance with Dymphna and that hideous woman? Why would we ever do that?"

"Remember your father's favorite saying," Wesley said. "'Keep your friends close but your enemies closer.' That's why."

"Why can't we take the private jet, like normal people?" Cleo tried to keep the whine out of her voice.

"Because I don't want the press to get hold of this," Wesley said. "And they watch that plane like a hawk."

"And you think no one is going to suspect a thing as the whole gang of us sneaks off in a stretch limo?"

"If Jennifer Aniston can pull off a secret wedding, I think we can get away with it—at least for a while," Wesley said. "I'll plant an item that Brad and Angelina are in town registering some of their brood for school. That should keep the paparazzi busy."

"All right," Cleo said. "If you're sure."

"Really? I thought this was going to take much more persuading."

"Don't I always take your advice?"

"Actually, no."

"Well, I'm taking it this time, so don't push your luck."

"Deal."

Cleo took a sip of bourbon to hide her smile.

So I get another shot at my ex-husband after all.

Chapter 8

Dymphna sat in the back of the white stretch limousine that took up the whole of Erinn's driveway. She couldn't believe that her rabbit cages fit perfectly across the backseat. Spot, Blanche, and Earrings were going to have a cozy ride to Fat Chance. She took comfort in that—and that alone. Doubts buzzed around her head like gnats. The rabbits were so trusting. And they were happy in Santa Monica, weren't they? Would their lives be happy in Fat Chance? Which led to the bigger question: Would *her* life be happy in Fat Chance?

While she'd told Professor Johnson she was going to Los Angeles to pick up her rabbits, that was at best a half-truth. She also wanted to think about her future without the responsibility of being a girlfriend. She wanted to breathe. The fact that she was heading back to Fat Change so soon after she left had her reeling. She'd gotten so swept up in Erinn's plan for the documentary that she forgot her own reasons for leaving town in the first place.

Dymphna realized this was the story of her life. She'd get caught up in other people's ideas and realize she wasn't where she wanted to be. She was never one for confrontation, so instead of speaking up, she'd move on and the whole thing would start over again.

No matter where she went, there she was, as the old saying goes.

She'd had only one conversation with Professor Johnson, when she first arrived in Santa Monica. She'd promised to let him know she'd arrived safely. She wished she'd never made that promise because she'd had to add that she'd blown up his car. In his usual fashion, Professor Johnson took the news stoically. She knew he was confused by her request to have some time to sort out her feelings. She knew she loved Professor Johnson, but he had changed over the last year while taking a leadership role in town. She was proud of him, wrestling the free spirits of Fat Chance into action when it came to the grapes and the road. But there never seemed to be an end to his ideas.

There was no doubt life was different now.

She just wasn't sure if she liked the difference.

She reached through Earrings' cage and stroked her soft hair, calming them both. Dymphna couldn't remember how Erinn had convinced her that they needed to head to Texas as soon as possible. The story could not wait, according to Erinn. Erinn's ability to persuade was almost a superpower. Here they all were, Erinn, Wesley, Cleo, and—much to her surprise—Jeffries, Cleo's butler and driver, in the final preparations of their journey.

"I'll get that," Erinn said to Jeffries as he lifted the camera bag into the stretch limo's cavernous trunk. "This stuff is expensive."

"Ms. Johnson-Primb entrusts me with all her valuables," Jeffries said stiffly. "I have yet to disappoint her."

Dymphna thought about intervening but decided not to. Wasn't that why she was annoyed with Professor Johnson? Because he was always intervening? Always solving things? She took a deep breath and decided everyone would be better off if she just settled into the backseat with her rabbit cages and left Jeffries to duel with Erinn on his own.

When Cleo and Wesley had arrived in the limo from Beverly Hills, they had decided to go for a walk in Palisades Park while Erinn and Dymphna made their final preparations for the trip. Wesley returned to the limo first, and now was settled in the backseat with Dymphna, Erinn, and the rabbits, looking at his iPad. He had the air of a man used to waiting.

The back door of the limo suddenly opened and Cleo leaned in.

"Hi, Cleo," Dymphna said.

Cleo looked around the interior as if she'd never seen it before. Her head popped out of the stretch like a champagne cork from a shaken bottle.

"There are rabbit cages on the backseat!" Cleo said accusingly.

"Yes," Dymphna said. "But only three. The rabbits will be no trouble, I promise. They'll be quiet and stay in their cages most of the time."

"*Most* of the time?" Cleo said. "How about *all* of the time?"

"That hardly seems fair." Wesley's voice boomed from inside the limo. "How would you like to be locked up for three full days?"

"I am going to be locked up for three days?" Cleo said, poking her head back inside. "Fat Chance is only twenty hours away! Why do we have to spend three full days on the road?"

"We don't," Dymphna offered. "I can drive part of the way. So can Erinn."

"Have you ever driven a stretch limo?" Cleo asked.

"No," Dymphna said.

"I thought not," Cleo snapped.

"Have you?" Wesley asked.

"Of course not," Cleo said. "But I'm not offering to drive, am I?"

"If it makes you feel any better," Wesley said, patting the armrest, "I happen to know how to drive this baby. So if you really want to get to Fat Chance sooner, I can give Jeffries a break from time to time."

"And what will people think if they see you?" Cleo asked, aghast.

"'There's Wesley Tensaw driving a bunch of rabbits'?" he offered. "Or are you thinking something more along the lines of 'Oh, how the mighty have fallen'?"

"No one is driving the limousine but the driver," Cleo said.

Dymphna knew Cleo well enough to understand the conversation was at an end. But Wesley's eyes were gleaming with mischief.

"Don't you want to know why I know how to drive a limo?" he asked.

"I don't know," Cleo said. "Do I?"

"Probably not," Wesley said, grinning at her. "Let's get out. We can't appear to be hiding."

But I am hiding, Cleo thought.

Wesley glided out of the backseat, looking much less intimidating in his khaki slacks, polo shirt, and Timberland hiking boots than he did in one of his dark suits. Dymphna wasn't sure if she was included in Wesley's statement that they couldn't appear to be hiding, but she climbed out after him, just in case. She wondered why he chose hiking boots for a three-day drive, but she had learned that the rich had their peculiarities.

"I'm not sharing the backseat with rabbits," Cleo said as Wesley stood beside her.

Out of nowhere, Dymphna found herself enveloped in a one-armed maternal hug. It was Virginia. Already tearing up at the thought of Dymphna leaving. Virginia's other arm was cradling Piquant, the Chihuahua, who wanted nothing to do with messy goodbyes.

"This visit was much too short," Virginia said.

"I know," Dymphna said, meaning every word.

"When Erinn comes back, you can always come back with her," Virginia said. "You're family."

Dymphna nodded. She felt a twinge of guilt. The thought of family always inspired a flight response—even when everything was perfect.

After Erinn and Dymphna had said goodbye to Virginia, Piquant, and Caro, Erinn's cat, the limo pulled onto Ocean Avenue, dodging jaywalkers on their way to Palisades Park. Dymphna sat nestled between two rabbit cages, facing Wesley and Erinn. Cleo opted to sit in the front with Jeffries, insisting that she was not sharing a backseat with rabbits. Dymphna watched the window between the front and the back rise. She could barely make out Cleo in the front passenger seat, saying to Jeffries:

"Another trip to Fat Chance, Texas. Can you believe it?"

"Actually, ma'am—" Jeffries replied.

The screen between the sections locked into place.

Dymphna could only imagine what Jeffries might have said.

Professor Johnson gathered the morning eggs. He'd promised Dymphna that he'd keep the farm running in her absence. Although she hadn't said when she'd be back, he took it as an unspoken promise that she *would* be back. He thought back to when he'd had to leave Fat Chance at the end of their initial six months. Every fiber of his being wanted to stay, but he'd had obligations in Los Angeles that needed to be fulfilled. Leaving Thud was his unspoken promise that he would return. A few months ago, he would have bet money he and Dymphna were on the same page. But she had seemed so withdrawn lately, it was hard to tell. He took comfort in the fact that while she might leave him in the lurch, she'd never abandon her goats and chickens, not to mention her fruit trees.

Am I pathetic in taking comfort in that?

He wondered if he should ask Maggie about Dymphna. He wanted to ask Maggie about herself as well. Why was she here? He assumed the answer was more complex than "I came to visit Dymphna, my sister who never mentions me." But just the thought of talking to Maggie made him break into a cold sweat. After their initial encounter, he'd bundled her off to the Creakside Inn. He sure couldn't have her stay at the farm with him—just looking at her, he realized she was too hot to handle.

That night Old Bertha and Pappy had both come to the door of the inn, Old Bertha primly tying her pink flannel robe.

"This better be important," Pappy scowled, but spotting the woman peering out from behind Professor Johnson, he brightened. "Dymphna! You're back!"

Maggie stepped forward. Old Bertha let out a gasp.

"I'm Mary Mag—" Maggie began, but Professor Johnson cut her off.

Introducing yourself as the most famous fallen woman in the history of the world was probably not going to go over well with Old Bertha.

"This is Maggie," Professor Johnson said. "Dymphna's sister."

"Well, I'll be damned," Pappy muttered.

Maggie stood with her fingertips resting lightly on her hipbones as she looked around the parlor. The room seemed to heat up several degrees just having her in it.

What were your parents thinking? Professor Johnson thought. *Dymphna and Mary Magdalene Pearl.*

Mary Magdalene was currently enjoying a restored reputation among scholars. She was now being touted as one of the apostles, formerly consigned to history as a tarnished tart because men feared the power of women. Professor Johnson thought this was a reasonable interpretation from a scholarly perspective. But a sideways glance at *this* Mary Magdalene made it hard to think anything but that she was living up to the stereotype.

Old Bertha gave her the fisheye, as Pappy appeared to be holding in his stomach.

"Welcome to Fat Chance, Texas," Pappy boomed when he finally found his voice.

"Thanks, handsome," Maggie said. "I can't believe I'm finally meeting a real cowboy."

Old Bertha and Pappy both reddened. For different reasons, Professor Johnson suspected.

"What's going on?" Polly said as she came down the stairs, yawning. She started at the sight of Maggie.

"This is Dymphna's sister," Pappy said, a goofy grin on his face.

"No shit?" Polly said. "Wow, you look just like her! Are you guys twins?"

"I'm eighteen months younger," Maggie said. "We're Irish twins."

"I didn't know Dymphna was Irish," Old Bertha said suspiciously.

"You didn't know she had a sister, either," Maggie said, and then added playfully, "That Dymphna is full of secrets."

Is Dymphna full of secrets? thought Professor Johnson.

As if he'd summoned her by just thinking of her, Maggie suddenly appeared in the barnyard out of the dawn fog. She was wearing a pair of jeans so tight, they were more like a nod to the concept of pants rather than an actual garment. Her blue T-shirt had lace sleeves. It was something Dymphna might wear, but on Dymphna, it wouldn't have that come-hither look. Part of him wished Maggie would go back to wherever she'd come from—or at least back to the Creekside Inn. He could see her at breakfast at the café, where he'd feel safe. He did not want to acknowledge what the other part of him wished.

"Good morning," he mumbled. "You're up early."

"I couldn't sleep," Maggie said. "Thought maybe you'd be up, too."

Did she just wink?

"I need to get these eggs to Fernando," Professor Johnson said.

"Do you want some help?" Maggie asked, moving closer to him.

"No, no . . . no-no-no," he stammered. "I've got this."

He tried to appear calm, holding up an egg, which promptly plopped onto his foot. Thud loyally raced in and gobbled up the mess.

"This is a sweet spread," Maggie said as she looked around the barnyard. "All this is Dymphna's?"

"Ever since Cutthroat deeded it to her," Professor Johnson said.

"It seems to be in better shape than the rest of the town."

"I think I heard that Pappy lived up here in his hermit days, but moved into town, such as it was, when he heard we were coming."

"That was nice of him."

"I don't think he had a choice," Professor Johnson said.

"I don't suppose you ever asked him?"

"Asked him what?"

"If it bothered him that he had to move into town."

"I'm not inclined toward that kind of dialogue and neither is he," Professor Johnson said, trying not to look at her.

"What kind of dialogue *are* you inclined to?"

Professor Johnson's hands started to sweat. He was never going to collect enough eggs if Maggie didn't leave.

"Powderkeg offered me a job yesterday," Maggie said, propping herself on a hay bale. "What do you think?"

"About what?"

"About me taking a job here in town."

"What would you be doing for Powderkeg?" he asked. "Do you know anything about carpentry or leather?"

"I've had some experience with leather, you could say." Maggie leered. As Professor Johnson's face colored, she smiled. "He said he needed some help around the place. He's getting so many orders that he can't do everything himself. He bought a really intense sewing machine for working on saddles and boots. He figures we can learn how to use it together."

"I'm sure your sister would be happy to have family around."

"Then you don't know my sister," Maggie said with a slight snort.

Chapter 9

A t Dymphna's request, Wesley knocked on the partition between
the front and back of the limo. Dymphna knew there was a
fancy intercom system, but liked the fact that Wesley was comfortable just rapping his knuckles on the window. The partition slowly
lowered. Wesley, who was riding backwards, turned around to face
front.

"We've got carsick rabbits back here," Wesley said.

"They're not running around willy-nilly, are they?" Cleo looked
into the back. "I don't want any animals throwing up on the seats."

"Calm down," Wesley said. "They're still in their cages and the
seats are leather anyway."

"The carpet isn't leather," Cleo huffed as Jeffries pulled the stretch
limo over to a rest stop.

"And rabbits don't regurgitate," Erinn offered over Wesley's
shoulder.

"Then how do you know they're carsick?" Cleo asked. "Oh, never
mind."

"The rabbits just need a break," Dymphna said to Wesley. "They're
freaking out. It's their version of carsick."

Jeffries expertly swung the limo into a parking spot.

"Dare I ask," Wesley said to Dymphna, "how you can tell they're
freaking out? They look the same to me."

"She just knows," Erinn said. "There's an impressive amount of
rabbit knowledge going on in that head."

Dymphna smiled shyly at the compliment. She'd been thinking
how much rabbit knowledge of her own Erinn had picked up over the
three years she'd been guardian of the Angoras. She smiled gratefully at Erinn as she harnessed all three rabbits. Cleo got out of the

limo, slammed the door pointedly, and walked toward the ladies' room.

"Do you want to walk them with me?" Dymphna asked Erinn.

"You go ahead," Erinn said as they stepped out of the car for the first time in hours. "I'm sticking close to Wesley."

Dymphna sighed. She knew Erinn thought she was going to get some juicy information from Wesley about Cutthroat Clarence, but Dymphna had her doubts. Wesley J. Tensaw did not get where he was by falling into traps set by filmmakers—even filmmakers as smart as Erinn.

"I'll help you with the rabbits, miss," Jeffries said.

Dymphna didn't really need help, but she welcomed the company.

"You know Cleo tried to kidnap me once," Jeffries said in his studied, bored voice.

"I remember," Dymphna said sympathetically. "When you drove her to Fat Chance three years ago. You said you'd stay if she knew your first name. I thought that was quite a gamble on your part."

"It wasn't really," Jeffries said. "I'd been working for her family for over twenty-five years, but I knew she'd never even thought about me having a first name."

"I can still see you standing there, at the turnout above Fat Chance, waiting for Cleo to come up with the answer," Dymphna said. "And you were right, she didn't remember your first name. But all of us who witnessed that scene remember! Your name is Donald."

"Thank you, miss," Jeffries said.

"Please call me Dymphna. And should I call you Donald?"

"No, thank you, miss," Jeffries said with a whisper of a smile. "But I appreciate the gesture."

A tiny bead of sweat formed on her upper lip as she realized she was running out of conversation. She suddenly brightened.

"Remember when you dropped Cleo off at the turnout, we had to carry all the bags down the hill because the trail was so messed up?" Dymphna said. "Well, we have a new road!"

"Do you, now?" Jeffries said, his voice returning to its flat timbre.

"Yes! You can take the limousine all the way into town now."

"That will be very convenient."

"Main Street still isn't paved. Just the trail. But that should be enough. Right?"

"I'm not sure Ms. Johnson-Primb would appreciate four-wheeling in the limousine," Jeffries said.

Dymphna was a little hazy on the details, since neither Cleo nor Wesley felt obliged to tell her their plans, but Dymphna had pieced together that the limo was going to replace Professor Johnson's Outback and stay in Fat Chance. Dymphna almost broke her own rule about radio silence to Fat Chance. She thought it only fair to tell Professor Johnson that his replacement car was a forty-foot land whale. But she respected the fact that Professor Johnson had abided by her wishes and she didn't think it fair to change the rules mid-hiatus. Besides, the limo would carry an awful lot of supplies from Spoonerville. Pappy's VW bus with the canvas roof—the vehicle they called the Covered Volkswagen—wasn't getting any younger.

From snippets of overheard conversation, Dymphna had divined that Jeffries was going to take the private jet back from Austin and return when summoned to drive Cleo and Wesley home. Dymphna wasn't sure what plans Erinn had made about leaving. She would be very interested to find out, just in case she wanted to hitch a ride.

I'm not even back and I'm planning to leave?

"I think I'll wash the windows as long as we're taking a break," Jeffries said with a small bow.

Dymphna looked for the rest of their party. Cleo appeared to be staggering, but Dymphna realized she was just talking into her cell phone while marching up and down the curved walkway. Erinn and Wesley were standing by the vending machines. The limousine was stocked with imported bottled water, alcohol, and mixers, but Erinn had a bottle of soda while Wesley had purchased a bag of chips. She knew Erinn and Wesley were playing a mental game of chess, and Dymphna would be interested to see who would win. She nudged the rabbits closer to them.

"You took over the firm very early in your career," Erinn was saying to Wesley. She wasn't wasting any time.

"I was young," Wesley said. "But I was being groomed by Sebastian Pennyfeather, the senior partner. When he died in a boating accident, I took over the firm."

"That isn't my understanding of how large law firms work," Erinn said.

"When Cutthroat Clarence is your premiere client and he suggests that a junior partner take over . . ." Wesley shrugged.

"Understood," Erinn said. "But there must have been some hostility? Some resentment?"

"That was years ago. I don't think anyone still resents it," he said, pointing to his hair. "I certainly am the right age now. Mr. Pennyfeather always said people want their attorneys to have gray hair. It makes them seem wise."

"Well, you do appear to have very wise hair," Erinn said.

"Why do you want to know all this?" Wesley asked. "I thought the documentary was about Cutthroat. I don't see what my legal career has to do with that."

"Neither do I," Erinn said. "Yet."

"One for the road?" Wesley asked, pointing to the vending machine.

"This should hold me," Erinn said, raising her soda in a toast.

As if by telepathic message, everyone returned to the limo at the same time.

"Are the rabbits feeling any better?" Cleo asked, as Jeffries opened the front passenger door.

"Yes," Dymphna said. "Thanks for asking."

"I was joking," Cleo said, getting in the front seat. Jeffries closed the door and raised an eyebrow at Dymphna.

"Interesting sense of humor," Erinn said as she helped Dymphna scoop up the rabbits and climb into the backseat.

Dymphna dozed, lulled by the smooth ride of the limousine and the murmur of Wesley's and Erinn's voices.

Chapter 10

"I just don't understand why he won't ask me to marry him," Old Bertha said. "I mean, we aren't getting any younger!"

Polly was heating soup in the tiny Creakside Inn kitchen. The sun had recently set and it was Polly's turn to cook.

"You want to get *married*? To *Pappy*?" Polly said, tapping some salt into the pot.

"Of course I do," Old Bertha said. "Just because I don't go around begging the man . . ."

"So you want him to put a ring on it?" Polly asked in surprise. "Does he know you want to get married?"

"I've given him a few hints," Old Bertha said. "Easy on the salt. I've got high blood pressure."

"What kind of hints?" Polly said, putting the saltshaker down. "What have you said?"

"Oh, I don't know," Old Bertha said. "Hmmm, maybe I have been playing my cards a little too close to the vest."

"Maybe," Polly said. "I don't think anybody in town—and that includes Pappy—thinks you've been all that interested."

"A woman can't be too obvious," Old Bertha said. "Men lose all respect if you seem too anxious."

"You know what I'd do?" Maggie said, taking the kitchen by storm. "I'd make him jealous. Start dating other men."

"What other men?" Old Bertha said. "The only other man in my age bracket is forty miles away."

"GU?" Maggie said, taking a chocolate chip cookie from the cookie jar.

"GU?" Old Bertha repeated.

"Geographically undesirable," Polly interpreted. "It means you won't date a guy who isn't conveniently located."

"That sounds snooty," Old Bertha said. "It's not that. It's just that at my age, I don't commit to a long novel, let alone a date with someone who lives far away. Besides, I hate to say it, but Pappy is the one for me."

"How long has it been since you've—" Maggie began, but one look at Polly and she changed gears. "Since you've been in love?"

Old Bertha flushed. "Oh, maybe since Clarence . . . back in 1955."

"In 1955?" Maggie said. "That's impressive."

"There have been other men since then, but nothing like what I had with Clarence Johnson, that's for sure."

"Clarence Johnson?" Maggie almost choked on her cookie. "You mean Cutthroat Clarence?"

Polly and Old Bertha exchanged a look.

"Don't you know that it's because of Cutthroat Clarence that we're all here?" Old Bertha asked.

Maggie shook her head.

"I have no idea why you're all here, to tell you the truth," Maggie said. "Seems like a pretty weird existence, if you ask me."

"Then how did you end up finding Dymphna if you didn't know the story?" asked Polly, bringing mugs of soup to the table.

"What story?" Maggie said. "All you guys have *one* story?"

Old Bertha quickly ran through the particulars of Cutthroat Clarence's last will, including details of how each person fit into the billionaire's sweeping mea culpa. From choosing a young hoodlum named Wally Wasabi because Cutthroat had swindled a store from a Japanese family during their internment during World War II, to Old Bertha's own broken engagement.

"I'm telling you Wally's part of the story 'cause he's not here, and I'm telling you mine 'cause I am," Old Bertha said. "You'll have to ask the others if you want to know how they fit into Fat Chance. It's not my place to say."

"Fair enough," Maggie said. "So, Polly, what's your deal? Why did Cutthroat Clarence want you to come here?"

"My father was a first responder during 9/11," Polly said, putting her cookie, which was on its way to her mouth, down on the table. "Cutthroat said he backed Big Oil when he knew there would be trouble. He said he couldn't make amends to all the firefighters' families. He kind of just picked me out of a hat, I guess."

"So, you just stayed?" Maggie said. "This seems like a pretty dead town for somebody who's not even twenty-five yet."

"Things can get slow," Polly said. "But I love it here."

"Are you going to stay, like, forever?" Maggie asked.

"Now, how is she supposed to know that?" Old Bertha asked. "Forever is a long time."

"Your turn," Polly said, picking her cookie back up. "If you didn't know any of this, how did you know Dymphna was here?"

"I didn't," Maggie said. "I was googling random stuff a few years ago and typed in 'Dymphna Pearl.' That podcast she did about knitting came up. When that went off the radar, I kind of checked online every once in a while to see if any of her knitting ever showed up. I found her stuff for sale online from a store in Dripping Springs. So I called. The lady at the store told me Dymphna lived on a farm in a place called Fat Chance, which isn't even on the map."

"We know," Polly and Old Bertha said simultaneously.

"I finally got here," Maggie said, "but all I found up at the farm was that strange professor dude. Dymphna had left. In typical Dymphna Pearl fashion."

Polly and Old Bertha both looked surprised.

"Dymphna was always pretty private," Old Bertha said. "We never even knew she had a sister."

"Well, she does," Maggie said. "But I'm all there is. No other siblings, no parents."

"What's your plan now, if you don't mind my asking?" Old Bertha asked.

"I don't mind. And I don't have a plan," Maggie said. "Dymphna would probably say 'in typical Mary Magdalene Pearl fashion.'"

Maggie got up from the table and headed toward the back door.

"Are you going out?" Old Bertha said. "It's after eight o'clock."

"Yeah," Maggie said, flipping her hair. "I thought I'd go up to the farm and see what Professor Johnson and Thud are up to."

Maggie was heading up the hill toward the farm when she spotted Titan down by the creek. It hadn't taken her long to get to know everyone in Fat Chance. That was the beauty of hanging out in a small town.

She glanced up at the farmhouse. Whatever plans were formulating in her head could wait. She turned toward the trickling stream.

"Hey, Titan," she said. "No luck with finding Fancy?"

"Nothing yet," Titan said as he looked up, sorrow etched in his face.

"I'll bet she was quite a girl," Maggie said, sitting on a rock that projected out of the water.

"She was," Titan said. "She is. I know this sounds crazy, but I think I'd know if she was gone. Do you know what I mean?"

"Yeah," Maggie said. "But you can be wrong, you know. I thought my sister would come back when she first left. But she didn't. I don't want to stop you from hoping. But our feelings sometimes don't have anything to do with reality. They just jack us up."

"I think Fancy is alive," Titan said. "And I think if she's gone, she must have had a good reason to go."

"She might have had a good reason to go," Maggie said. "I'll give you that." She stood up and leapt gracefully off the rock.

"Good luck," she called, without turning around.

Powderkeg and Pappy sat with Fernando in the café. Pappy poured a dark red liquid into three jelly jars.

"I made this wine with the grapes from my arbor," Pappy said as he held the liquid up to the light and swirled it. "This isn't the swanky stuff we'll be getting once the vines start producing. But I gotta say, I don't think it's bad. We could start generating wine right out of the gate."

"Have you joined the 'drink it now' camp?" Fernando said, sniffing gingerly at the wine.

"I'm not in any camp," Pappy said. "I just thought I'd do some experimenting so I have a realistic idea of what to expect. Can we make a profit right away by selling young wines? Or will our wines need to be cellared before we can sell them?"

"It's not a question of selling young wines and making a profit," Fernando said. "We have an opportunity to make a good wine— maybe even a great wine. We're building a reputation in this town as a respected group of artisans. Now we're going to churn out a shitty wine? We're going to need patience."

"And money," Powderkeg said as he took a sip. "Tastes good to me."

"Do you know anything about wine?" Fernando said, taking a sip himself. He gagged. "This tastes like a footbath. You two have no palate whatsoever."

"Footbath, my ass!" Pappy said, as Fernando gathered the glasses and stormed into the kitchen.

Pappy and Powderkeg watched him go. Powderkeg turned over two coffee mugs sitting on the table and Pappy poured them more wine. They toasted each other.

"To young wine and old women!" said Pappy.

Professor Johnson jumped to his feet as the porch floorboards groaned. His head no longer filled with hope that every sound on the front steps meant Dymphna had come back, but his heart was slow to catch up. Thud stopped snoring and raised his head before deciding to go back to sleep. The front door creaked open. It was Maggie . . . and her pheromones.

"Am I disturbing you?" she whispered.

That's a loaded question, Professor Johnson thought.

Without waiting for an answer, Maggie made a show of sneaking in stealthily, a finger to her rounded lips, making an inaudible "shhh" gesture. She perched herself on the end of the lopsided couch. Professor Johnson looked around the room, wondering how far away from this woman he could sit and not be rude. He decided to stand.

"I was bored," she whispered. "I saw your light on and thought I'd stop in."

"That's fine," Professor Johnson said softly. "Why are we whispering?"

Maggie pointed to Thud.

"I don't want to wake the dog," she said.

"Thud is a very determined sleeper," Professor Johnson said in his normal register.

The sound of his voice seemed to ricochet around the room, surprising Thud, who scrambled to his feet and looked around, confused. Maggie burst out laughing. She knelt down on the floor and patted the dog.

"I guess your dog isn't the brightest tool in the shed," Maggie said, scratching Thud behind the ears.

Professor Johnson wanted her to leave. He was pretty sure she didn't care that she had just mixed a ridiculous metaphor or that she had just insulted Thud, who was an extremely intelligent animal, in his own way. But as he watched Maggie snuggling Thud, her breasts jiggling on either side of the dog's head, he lost his train of thought.

"How are things working out with Powderkeg?" Professor Johnson asked when the blood had returned to his brain.

"At the shop?" Maggie said. "It's fine. That machine he bought to sew boot leather is pretty scary. I might ask Titan if I can hang out at the forge instead."

"You've only been working at Powderkeg's for less than a week," Professor Johnson said. "Don't you think you should give it more time?"

"I don't know. Maybe," Maggie said, looking up at him through her double row of eyelashes. "But have you seen that fairy-tale carriage Titan is building? I'd love to work on that."

He chastised himself. He'd been so preoccupied with the nuts and bolts of getting the wine business off the ground that he hadn't stopped in at the forge to see how Titan was getting along. He knew the man was grieving for his lost buzzard, but a little moral support wouldn't have hurt. He needed to correct that.

"I'll go see it tomorrow," Professor Johnson said.

"Cool. I'll go with you. Unless you don't want me," Maggie said, a small smile forming on her lips. "Do you want me?"

"Want you?" Professor Johnson was starting to sweat.

What is this woman talking about?

"Do you want me to go with you to Titan's?"

"I . . . I hadn't thought about it."

"Well," she said, giving Thud's head a final pat and curling up on the sofa as her voice grew husky, "think about it."

Professor Johnson looked at Thud, who seemed to be saying "I got nothin'."

"I suppose I don't really see what difference it would make."

Maggie's face fell. In that moment, she looked soft and vulnerable, like Dymphna. She put her hands over her face.

Is she crying?

"I'm sorry," Professor Johnson said, coming over to the couch and placing a hand on her shoulder. "Of course you can come to see Titan with me. Please don't cry."

"I thought you liked me." Maggie snuffled into her hands.

"I do like you," Professor Johnson said, stroking her hair. He realized now was not the time to quantify that statement. "I'm just not very good at these things."

Maggie must have had some ninja training. Her arms were suddenly around Professor Johnson. She pulled him on top of her and they tumbled backwards onto the couch. Thud started barking uproariously. Professor Johnson tried to yell at the dog to be quiet—the last thing he wanted was to alert the whole town—but Maggie's tongue was in his mouth as soon as he parted his lips. He tried to get a grip on the sofa to push himself off her, but Maggie's breasts seemed to be everywhere. Thud's barking suddenly stopped. Maggie and Professor Johnson looked up from their tangle.

Dymphna stood in the doorway.

PART TWO

Chapter 11

Dymphna wasn't sure if the woman had pushed Professor Johnson or he just lost his balance, but either way he landed on the floor. He jumped to his feet and straightened his glasses. Thud rushed to Dymphna. He was standing with his massive bloodhound's head against her hip. She absently rubbed the soft fur while taking in the scene in front of her.

"I guess I should have called," Dymphna said.

Her canvas bag sat at her feet. She went to pick it up, but Professor Johnson got there first.

"Let me explain," he said, clutching her bag to his chest.

"I think the situation is fairly self-explanatory," she said, trying to retrieve her bag from him.

"It isn't, I promise," Professor Johnson said.

"So I didn't just catch you on my sofa on top of another woman?" Dymphna asked.

"Well, yes," Professor Johnson said. "I suppose that part is, indeed, self-explanatory, but . . ."

"Hey, Dymph," Maggie said, sitting up and draping her arm around the back of the couch as if she'd just been invited to watch a movie on Netflix. She patted the seat beside her and Thud leapt up to join her.

Dymphna gave up the wrestling match over her bag. Professor Johnson stood there, not sure what to do with the prize from the tug-of-war.

"You're right," Dymphna said to Professor Johnson, who handed her the bag. "It is self-explanatory."

"It's been a long day," Dymphna said, grabbing the bag from Professor Johnson and turning toward the bedroom. "I guess I'll go to bed and we'll talk about this in the morning."

"I see you haven't changed at all," Maggie said without facing her. "Five years and you're still avoiding problems."

"And I see you haven't changed either," Dymphna said. "Five years and you're still causing them."

"I thought you were in California," Maggie said.

"I thought you were in Maine."

"It gets cold there," Maggie said. "I wanted a little heat."

"Mission accomplished," Dymphna said, glaring at her sister and boyfriend.

Thud whimpered, sensing the tension in the air. Dymphna stopped at the door.

"May I ask what the sleeping arrangements have been?" Dymphna asked. "I certainly want to avoid any problems in my own bedroom."

"You'll be happy to know that your uptight boyfriend made me sleep at that damn hotel since I got here," Maggie said hotly.

"Really?" Dymphna's posture relaxed. She looked at Professor Johnson and blinked back tears. "I guess that should have been self-explanatory, too."

She bit her lower lip and Professor Johnson took her in his arms.

"I guess that's my cue," Maggie said to Thud. "See you in the morning."

Maggie slammed the door behind her. Not even Thud reacted to the noise. Dymphna and Professor Johnson stood, locked in an embrace. Dymphna wasn't quite sure why she'd left or why she'd returned. Nothing was settled, but she was grateful that fate had brought her back. The sight of Maggie had inspired a tidal wave of feeling. The accusation that Dymphna ran from her problems hit home.

Maybe I'll stick this one out.

Dymphna finally broke the embrace to go put her bag on the bed. The old springs let out an exhausted creak. She turned to Professor Johnson in the bedroom doorway.

"I have a question," Dymphna said.

"Just one?"

"What is my sister doing in Fat Chance?"

"The whole town is wondering that. She hasn't exactly been full of information."

"That's Maggie."

"It seems to be a family trait."

Dymphna reddened. She couldn't very well dispute the accusation. "I can't stay," she said. She watched Professor Johnson stop mid-step.

"I mean, I can't stay *this minute*," she continued. "We need to get the rabbits out of the limousine."

"The rabbits are in a limousine?"

"Yes. But the limo can't get up the hill to the farm. Jeffries says it's too long or something . . ."

"Jeffries is here?"

"Of course," Dymphna said. "Who do you think drove the limo?"

"I'm still processing all of this."

"Anyway, your aunt is trying to talk Old Bertha into giving all of them rooms and—"

"All of whom?"

"It's a long story," Dymphna said.

Professor Johnson hurried out the door behind Dymphna, shutting the door firmly behind him. Thud howled in indignation at being locked in the house, but who could say what kind of a greeting committee a bloodhound would make for three domesticated rabbits?

The moon was only a sliver in the sky, but the path from Main Street to the farm was lit by the limousine's headlights. Its two bright eyes beamed up at them like a startled animal. Dymphna took Professor Johnson's arm and filled him in on the details.

As they passed the Creakside Inn, Dymphna saw Pappy hurrying into the building. With the exception of Maggie, and now Pappy, everyone in town was circled around the limousine. Apparently whatever negotiations Cleo had engaged in with Old Bertha were concluded. Even in the dim light provided by the limo, Dymphna could see Polly, Old Bertha, Powderkeg, Titan, and Fernando. She smiled to herself, surprised at how happy she was to see everyone. The addition of shell-shocked Wesley, Erinn, and Jeffries almost made her burst out laughing. Dymphna could see that Cleo was already giving orders. Dymphna realized in surprise that she wasn't the only one straddling two worlds. Cleo had gone and come back, too.

"Hey, Dymphna," Polly called out as Dymphna and Professor Johnson stepped onto Main Street.

There were hugs and kisses and shouts of "Welcome back!" While encased in Powderkeg's bear hug, Dymphna looked up at the second story of the Creakside Inn and could see Maggie's silhouette in one of the windows. Dymphna wasn't proud of it, but she was happy to have her sister witness this show of affection.

See? There are people who love me.

Dymphna turned away from the window. Titan stood holding two of the enormous rabbit cages as if they were boxes of cotton. Powderkeg was pulling the last cage out of the backseat. He started to put the cage on the hood of the limo, but a squeak from Cleo stopped him.

"If you were worried about getting a scratch on this thing, you shouldn't have brought her down the hill," Powderkeg said to Cleo. "Or better yet, you could have mentioned you were coming in the first place and we could have told you!"

Cleo sniffed. "We're doing a documentary. We don't announce ourselves."

Dymphna saw Erinn's startled reaction at Cleo's use of "we."

"You?" Powderkeg said. "You're doing a documentary? With Wesley? And Jeffries?"

"We're facilitating a documentary," Cleo clarified.

"How are they going to turn this big tub around?" Old Bertha whispered to Powderkeg.

"Maybe Jerry Lee can pull it backwards?" Powderkeg whispered back. "Pappy?"

They looked around. Pappy was nowhere to be seen.

"That old mule of his couldn't pull a little Fiat, let alone a stretch limo," Fernando added solemnly.

Jeffries stepped in, positioning himself between Powderkeg and the limo.

"I wasn't expecting a dirt road," Cleo huffed. She turned to Wesley. "I thought you said this godforsaken place was paved."

"I—" Wesley began helplessly, but Powderkeg cut him off.

"Nope," Powderkeg said. Dymphna could hear the teasing tone she knew Cleo hated. "Just the godforsaken dirt street."

"We're in discussions about paving the street," Professor Johnson said.

"Discussions?" Cleo said shrilly. "There doesn't need to be a discussion. Just do it."

"Right now?" Powderkeg asked in his maddeningly mocking tone.

"Don't start with me, Marshall," Cleo said, using her ex-husband's real name.

"Powwwwderkeg," Powderkeg corrected her, using his best pirate voice. "I left 'Marshall Primb' back at your place."

"I think the debate about the road can wait until morning," Professor Johnson said, taking the rabbit cage from him.

Dymphna could feel the collective surprise of the townspeople at this statement. Professor Johnson usually seemed ready to talk about the road or grapes anytime, anyplace, anywhere.

Maybe he has had time to reflect, thought Dymphna.

"We can take up the topic at breakfast tomorrow," Professor Johnson added. "It will be good to have some fresh opinions."

Or maybe not.

"Jeffries," Cleo said. "If you can get all the bags into the . . . hotel."

"No way, Cleo." Polly stepped in and picked up a bag. "It's late and this isn't Beverley Hills. We can all carry bags."

Polly pulled out her cell phone, snapped on the flashlight app and looked at the luggage tag. "Wesley Tensaw." She looked up in surprise, finally recognizing the lawyer. "Oh! Mr. Tensaw! What are you doing here?"

"I've been asking myself the same question," Wesley said, looking around him in a daze.

"I guess that can wait till morning, too," Polly said. "Anyway, here's your bag."

Titan, already carrying supplies, including the rabbits, headed for the farm.

"I know you have a lot to organize," Titan said to Dymphna. "I'll wait with the rabbits until you come up."

Dymphna gave Titan a grateful look and returned her attention to the chaos around the limo. Professor Johnson was trying to help Erinn with her camera gear, but Erinn seemed determined that no one should touch the equipment but her.

"What would you like to do about the limousine, Ms. Johnson-Primb?" Jeffries asked.

"I don't know," Cleo said wearily. "Turn off the lights and lock it up, I suppose."

"Lock it up," Polly said, snorting under her breath. "Like somebody might steal this whale."

The group moved toward the Creakside Inn. Loaded down with suitcases and duffel bags, they looked like a drunken caravan. Dymphna turned and saw Erinn still standing by the car.

"Erinn!" Dymphna said. "You've been so quiet!"

"I'm here as an observer," Erinn said.

"As Mahatma Gandhi said, 'Speak only if it improves upon the silence,'" said Professor Johnson.

"Or as Pierre-Joseph Proudhon said," Erinn added, "'When deeds speak, words are nothing.'"

"Or as Martin Lomasney said," Professor Johnson retorted, "'Never speak if you can nod, never nod if you can wink.'"

Dymphna stiffened. The two most intelligent people she knew seemed to be in a quoting contest. Dymphna could feel the brain cells flying through the night air.

"Touché," Erinn finally said. "Any room for me up at the farmhouse?"

Chapter 12

The next morning, Dymphna was first out of bed.

After they'd lugged the rabbits up the hill the night before, she had decided to put the cages in the tiny bedroom and locked Thud outside the room to minimize the trauma to all the animals. The chickens would cope, but she wasn't sure how the Angora goats and Angora rabbits would feel about each other. An introduction at midnight seemed a bad idea, so she, Professor Johnson, and Titan had wrangled the cages into her bedroom while Erinn settled herself and her camera gear into the closet-sized guest room.

Dymphna had wanted desperately to ask Titan about Fancy. She could tell by his defeated posture that the news was not good, but she wanted him to know she cared. She turned to Professor Johnson, who was trying to get Earrings' cage to sit straight.

"Do you think you could find some large towels to cover the rabbit cages for the night?" she had said to Professor Johnson.

"We have large towels?" Professor Johnson asked, looking at her in surprise.

The farmhouse was 320 square feet with a pencil-thin linen closet. There really wasn't anywhere for large towels to hide.

"I'll go look for large towels," the professor had said and left the room.

Titan didn't seem to hear. Dymphna reached out a hand and touched his shoulder. He turned around and stared at her. She could tell he was struggling to keep his emotions under control.

"Do you want to talk?" she asked, sitting on the sofa and patting the place beside her.

Out of nowhere, Thud had bounded up onto the sofa, his tail thumping the cushion. He had found a way to sneak back into the house. Titan let out a quick bark of a laugh. It was good to hear Titan laugh. He scooted Thud out of the way and took a seat. Thud rebounded and settled in the spot between them. The springs in the old sofa were so terrible that once Titan sat, Dymphna's feet left the floor as the cushion tilted violently to one side.

"Sometimes, people . . ." Dymphna began. "Sometimes people . . . including buzzards . . . just need a break to clear their heads."

"Are you talking about Fancy or you?" Titan asked without looking at her.

"Both, I guess," Dymphna said with a small smile.

"Well?" Titan asked, looking at her. "Did you?"

"Did I what?"

"Clear your head? Are you happy you came back?"

"I am glad I came back," Dymphna said, realizing for the first time that she was. "As far as clearing my head, I don't know."

"I didn't know you had a sister," Titan said.

Dymphna wasn't sure where to begin. So she'd simply said, "I do. I have a sister."

"She isn't like you at all."

"Thank you," Dymphna said, then realized that was an extremely unkind thing to say. "I mean, I know. We're very different people."

"When my mother died," Titan said, looking down at Thud and rubbing the bloodhound's fur in long, absentminded strokes, "I didn't have anybody. I would have given anything to have a sister. We could have shared everything. I wouldn't have had to be so alone."

Dymphna had known that it was not the time to burden Titan with the story of Maggie. Titan had got one thing right: Maggie was the queen of sharing. She shared Dymphna's clothes, her toys, and when they got older, her men. Sharing wasn't all it was cracked up to be as far as Dymphna was concerned. "Sharing" in Dymphna's mind meant "taking."

Professor Johnson was suddenly in the porch doorway, holding a pile of faded cloth.

"What do you know?" he said. "We do have towels."

Now, in the early morning light, Dymphna blushed as she pulled on a robe and tied it at the waist. It had been a strange homecoming for Dymphna and Professor Johnson with Erinn in the guestroom, but they'd managed. She looked over at him, sound asleep with one arm flung over his eyes. Her soft smile hardened as she thought of her sister, encamped at the Creakside Inn. Why was Maggie in Fat Chance? What did she want?

Maggie always wanted something.

Dymphna lifted the ends of the towels and checked on the rabbits. She reached in each cage and scratched each one of the rabbits in turn. While they were quiet, she sensed their tension. Was it the new surroundings? Fatigue from the trip? In the next room Thud let out a loud crescendo of a yawn and she felt Blanche skittle away from her touch to the edge of her cage.

"It's OK, Blanche," Dymphna whispered. "Thud would never hurt you."

Was that true? He was a bloodhound, after all. She didn't want to assume that Thud would overcome his baser instincts. Suddenly Maggie crossed her mind again.

Never assume someone will overcome her baser instincts, Dymphna thought.

She covered the rabbits back up, opened the bedroom door carefully, and signaled Thud to follow her to the kitchen.

Erinn straggled out of the guest room, rubbing her back. Dymphna winced.

"I know that bed isn't very comfortable," Dymphna said. "I'm so sorry."

"Don't apologize," Erinn said, bending down to pat Thud. "At least not for the condition of the mattress."

Dymphna was watering an assortment of herbs in the windowsill. She stopped short.

"Is there something else I should be apologizing for?" Dymphna remembered to whom she was speaking and corrected herself. "Is there something else for which I should be apologizing?"

Was that right?

"I thought we knew each other," Erinn said.

"We do know each other." Dymphna suspected where the conversation was going and went back to watering her plants. "What do you mean?"

"I mean, you never happened to mention you had a sister," Erinn said, sitting grumpily at the rickety table. "When I saw you two together last night I thought I must be hallucinating from fatigue."

"You know *now*," Dymphna said lamely. "Besides, don't you have things you don't talk about?"

"Many things," Erinn said. "We're not talking about me."

Professor Johnson peeked around the door. The two women looked at him. He gave a brief wave and headed to the shower.

"He seems like a very nice man," Erinn said.

"He is," Dymphna said.

Erinn seemed to be waiting for more, so Dymphna went on.

"He's very calm," she said. "And smart. And a godsend to have around the farm. Sometimes I don't think I could have kept the farm going without him."

"Oh, I'm sure you could have," Erinn said. "As Cher once said, 'Men are not necessities, they're luxuries.'"

"I don't believe it," Dymphna said.

"*I* didn't say it. I'm merely quoting."

"I know," Dymphna said, "That's what I can't believe—you quoting *Cher*."

Erinn sighed. "A life in reality TV will do that to a person. Next I'll be quoting Kathy Griffin. Let's hope this documentary saves me from a life of quoting the D-listers."

Someone had added a lopsided addition to the regular table in the center of the café to accommodate the troop from Los Angeles. Wesley, Titan, Jeffries, Cleo, and Powderkeg were already seated at the table. Polly had started making the rounds of the café with a pot of coffee, but had been sidetracked. She was standing at one of the smaller tables, chatting with a lanky young man with a ponytail and eyes so soulful, you could see them from the middle of the room.

"That's Polly's latest conquest," Powderkeg said to Cleo. "His name is Poet."

"Oh, for God's sake," Cleo said.

"How do you like our town?" Titan asked Erinn.

"In a word," Erinn said, "unusual."

"That's a good word for it," Maggie said, coming in from the archway that separated the Boozehound from the café. "I mean, wouldn't you say it's unusual when someone doesn't have space for her own sister, but a friend can waltz right into the guest room at a moment's notice?"

"I'm assuming that's a rhetorical question?" Erinn asked.

"Is it possible to get some coffee?" Wesley asked, looking around the café. He signaled Polly, "Oh, waitress . . ."

"Forget it," Titan said, getting up from the table. "I'll get us coffee. She's in love."

"Do they need to be mutually exclusive?" Wesley asked. "Coffee and love?"

"Here she comes," Cleo said, putting her hand on Titan's forearm and pulling him back down.

"Coffee, anyone?" Polly said, wagging the pot in the air.

Everyone held up their cups.

Cleo turned her gaze on Jeffries, who was holding out a chipped mug. "Jeffries, as soon as I find decent cell phone reception, I'll have the jet sent to pick you up."

"That would be fine, ma'am," Jeffries said, looking a little less confident as to his place at the table.

"Is Jeffries needed at home?" Erinn asked.

Dymphna could read the annoyance on Cleo's face.

"Is he needed here?" Cleo countered.

"I'm working on a documentary, as you know," Erinn said.

"Yes," Cleo said. "I believe that's why we're here."

"You're doing a documentary?" Titan asked, eyes widening. "On Texas?"

"On Fat Chance," Erinn said. "On Cutthroat Clarence and how you all have managed to exceed his expectations here."

"My grandfather was a multibillionaire," Professor Johnson said. "We've just started to make ends meet. I would hardly say we exceeded his expectations."

"You wouldn't say it," Erinn said. "But I would."

Cleo dipped her head modestly, as if Erinn was speaking about her specifically.

"I've got a show to sell," Erinn continued. "'Making ends meet' doesn't really sing, if you get my drift."

"What does any of this have to do with Jeffries?" Cleo asked.

"I could use some help," Erinn said. "He could be my assistant."

Everyone at the table suddenly added cream and sugar to their coffee at half speed, trying to casually listen in on the conversation. Dymphna looked around. The entire restaurant seemed to be studiously avoiding looking at the center table, but the crowd's collective body language made it evident everyone was paying attention to the newcomers' conversation.

"Why would Jeffries want to be your assistant?" Cleo asked, as if Jeffries wasn't there.

"Here's a crazy idea," Powderkeg suggested. "Why don't you ask him?"

"Jeffries," Cleo said, putting her coffee cup down on the table. "You don't want to stay here in Fat Chance."

"Cleo," Titan said, "that wasn't a question."

"He knows what I mean."

Dymphna thought back to when she and Maggie were kids, when the two of them would find themselves witnessing something funny or scary. They would exchange a look, almost involuntarily. Dymphna found herself looking right at Maggie without realizing it—and Maggie was looking right back. They both shifted their gaze immediately.

"I really don't need to return to the house, as long as you're in Fat Chance, ma'am," Jeffries said. "I'd be happy to stay, if I can be of use."

"Then it's settled," Erinn said.

"It is not settled," Cleo said. "I haven't given my permission!"

Everyone stared at her. She seemed to be holding her breath. She exhaled.

"Fine," Cleo said. "If you want to stay, stay."

"May we order?" Wesley asked.

"Order?" Polly rolled the word around in her mouth. "Order what?"

"Breakfast?" Cleo said through gritted teeth.

Dymphna snuck a look at Cleo. She wondered if Cleo was embarrassed by the weirdness of Fat Chance, looking at the town through Wesley's eyes. Dymphna shifted her gaze to Wesley, who seemed amused by the fits and starts of breakfast at the Cowboy Food Café.

"Nobody orders here," Maggie offered, proud that she was not one of the newbies. "Fernando just brings whatever he wants to serve."

"How novel," Wesley said. "All right, I look forward to chef's choice."

Cleo let out a sigh.

"Is there a problem?" Wesley asked Cleo.

"I was just wondering when you got so relentlessly cheerful," she replied.

Fernando burst through the kitchen door, carrying a tower of French toast in one hand, a platter of bacon in the other. Jeffries leapt to his feet.

"Allow me to help you with that, sir," Jeffries said.

"Sir?" Fernando said. "Better get over that notion, my friend. We're all the same in Fat Chance."

"Except Pappy," Powderkeg said. "He's the mayor."

"He is *not* the mayor," Professor Johnson said.

"Where is this Pappy?" Wesley asked. "I've heard so much about him. I'd like to meet the man."

"Where *is* Pappy?" Dymphna asked. "And Old Bertha? They're usually the first people at the table."

"Now that you mention it," Cleo said, "I didn't see either one of them this morning at the inn."

Old Bertha suddenly burst through the front door. Everyone in the café, regulars and visitors alike, looked up.

"Pappy's gone!" Old Bertha said. "I've looked everywhere."

Dymphna wasn't sure, but she thought she heard Wesley whisper "shit" under his breath.

Old Bertha threw herself into a chair and wailed.

Chapter 13

When cowboys gathered in a circle on the street, it was usually to look over a new horse, truck, or all-terrain vehicle. But after breakfast, the ranch hands from the Rolling Fork Ranch gathered around the limousine, still pointing up the hill toward Dymphna's farm. It was a testament to Fernando's cooking that even a stretch limousine in the middle of town wasn't more interesting than his French toast. Now Jeffries was at the wheel, but the wheels simply spun up dust when he pressed the accelerator. He refused to open the windows.

"What's your plan for her, ma'am?" one of them asked Cleo as she walked past the crowd on her way back to the inn.

"Talk to my lawyer," Cleo said, jerking a thumb toward Wesley.

The men turned to Wesley, who was sitting on a bench on Main Street. Although he was casually attired in jeans, a plaid shirt, and perfectly worn-in cowboy boots, Wesley looked more like an ad for a new Ralph Lauren line than one of the guys. He made his way to the stretch. Jeffries exited the driver's seat and stood by Wesley.

"I guess we'll have to find a way to move it . . . her," Wesley said. He looked toward the paved trail. "Do you gentlemen think a Triple-A tow truck can make it down that hill?"

The men guffawed.

"You don't need no tow truck," one of the men said, climbing under the limo. "We can move this baby ourselves."

"Really?" Wesley asked.

"Sure," the man's muffled voice could be heard from under the limo. "She's just stuck in a little ditch. My truck can pull her right out."

Jeffries almost collided with the man emerging from under the limo.

"I'm not sure this is the best idea," Jeffries said in a hushed voice to Wesley.

"It'll be fine, Jeffries," Wesley said. "This is a Texas version of a neighborhood activity."

Wesley gave the ranch hands the go-ahead. Seven men raced to the beat-up Ford truck parked in front of the café. Out came ropes and chains. By the time they had the chassis hooked to the back of the truck, a crowd, including Dymphna, Professor Johnson, Maggie, Erinn, and Powderkeg were watching from the boardwalk. Dymphna and Maggie stood as far apart as possible.

"Perhaps I should drive," Jeffries offered.

"We got this. Maybe you should wait up on the boardwalk," the man in the plaid shirt said. He turned to Wesley. "You too. Too many cooks."

"I haven't cooked in years," Wesley said, but he turned and followed Jeffries away from the fray.

"Isn't that Poet?" Dymphna asked Powderkeg, as she watched Poet blink his enormous eyes and jump in the driver's seat. "Polly's boyfriend?"

"Ah yes, the poet of few words," Powderkeg said. "He's the one."

"Where is Polly?" Dymphna said.

"She took Old Bertha back to the inn." Fernando's voice came from the doorway of the café. "Old Bertha is pretty upset."

"Well, I would be too," Maggie said. "I don't see why the rest of you aren't worried about Pappy. You seem more worried about that stupid bird."

The regulars looked around to make sure Titan was nowhere to be found. He would not take kindly to hearing Fancy referred to as "stupid."

"This isn't the first time Pappy has left without warning," Professor Johnson answered.

"You mean he just gets up and goes?" Maggie said, her eyes big as saucers. "Like Dymphna?"

Dymphna reddened, but the noise in the street diverted everyone's attention. The men were yelling in different directions, gesturing wildly with their arms, some pointing left, some right, some indicating that the limo should go straight back.

"I can't look," Maggie said to Powderkeg as she hid her eyes.

"Me either," Powderkeg said, pulling his cowboy hat over his eyes. "And I was in Vietnam."

"You were?" Maggie asked. "You look awfully young."

Powderkeg lifted his hat back into place and looked directly at Maggie. "Last—and youngest—recruit in the war," he said, a twinkle in his eye. "So don't erase me from your list just yet."

"Who says you were *on* my list?" Maggie asked with a little smile.

Dymphna rolled her eyes at Professor Johnson. Maggie was as shameless as ever.

"You might have been right about this," Wesley said to Jeffries.

"Thank you, sir," Jeffries replied.

Erinn raced past Fernando into the café and returned with her camera. She focused her lens on the scene in the street. The truck heaved. The wheels of the limo spun. Dust spread across Main Street like a curtain. The people on the boardwalk could see nothing but particles of street dirt flying so fast it was as if they were running for cover.

"I can't see a damn thing," Erinn said, covering her lens. "This dirt is murder on the camera."

"If we paved Main Street—" Professor Johnson began, but stopped when he caught Powderkeg's brief shake of the head.

Slicing through the dust, the truck suddenly shot into view, followed by the limousine.

"Holy hell," Powderkeg said. "It worked!"

"Awesome!" Maggie cheered.

She jumped into Powderkeg's arms. Powderkeg looked at Dymphna with startled eyes. Dymphna turned away.

Poet leapt out of the limo and joined the other ranch hands, who were all slapping each other on the back and shaking hands as if they'd won a lottery.

"I didn't think that monster was ever gonna budge," the leader of the effort said.

"Hey," someone else called out. "Look at that!"

The dust started to clear and the vague outline of a man stood where the limousine used to be.

"Titan?" Fernando said, straightening up in the doorway.

"What the . . ." one of the men said. "Did you *push* the limo?" A chorus of praise came from the assembled ranch hands.

"You're a mountain!"

"You're a forklift!"

"You're a monster truck!"

Titan stood, his brown skin covered in dust, muscles glistening with sweat. He was breathing heavily. As the men surged toward him, he turned and walked back to the forge. Everyone stopped and watched him go.

"That was impressive," Wesley said as he watched Titan recede.

"He's an impressive man," Jeffries added.

"I missed the whole damn thing," Erinn said, staring accusingly at her camera. She turned to Dymphna. "You know, if you just paved this street . . ."

Cleo couldn't help herself. She stood outside the kitchen of the Creakside Inn listening to Old Bertha sniffling while Polly tried to comfort her. She wasn't proud of herself for listening to a private conversation, but what else was there to do in this town?

"Don't you remember when Pappy left before?" Polly said.

"Of course I remember," Old Bertha said. "He was gone for almost five months!"

"But he came back!" Polly said. "He'll come back again."

"You sound like everybody reassuring Titan that Fancy is going to come back," Old Bertha said. "And we all know that's not happening."

"We do NOT know that," Polly said, sounding appalled.

Cleo bit her lip. Of course, she didn't think there was much hope Fancy would return, but she was certainly in the camp of lying to Titan. She also remembered when Pappy left last time. It was a few months into their tenure in Fat Chance. The neophytes were just getting the hang of things and were falling into some kind of rhythm, when Pappy suddenly announced he was leaving. He accused the newcomers of settling for just existing instead of pushing themselves to make something of themselves or at least the town. He came back as abruptly as he left, with not a word as to where he'd been. Cleo tuned back in to the conversation.

"Besides, we weren't a couple last time," Old Bertha said, bursting into a fresh wave of tears and hiccups. "You don't think he left because of me, do you? Too much pressure?"

"No!" Polly said with conviction. "Of course not."

Cleo couldn't believe this conversation. The Old Bertha she knew was a hardened, no-nonsense senior who had no time for romantic folly. And Polly! Cleo thought back to the Polly who had arrived in

Fat Chance with her Goth makeup and sullen disposition. Cleo could hardly reconcile herself to the mature and loving young person who had blossomed not only into a surprisingly nurturing woman, but a genuine artist. Polly's hats, jewelry, and now her quilts were true works of art. Cleo had decided that when she left Fat Chance—if her attempts at trying to rekindle something with her ex failed, or when Wesley got bored—she might bring Polly's creations back to Beverly Hills with her. She knew her friends would be wild for Polly's designs.

"You know what Poet would say about this?" Polly was saying in the kitchen.

Not everything had changed about Polly. She was still boy-crazy.

"I can't imagine," Old Bertha said. "Since I haven't heard him say more than two words strung together since he got here."

"He only speaks the truth," Polly said.

"Well, that'll keep a man quiet, that's for sure," Old Bertha said. "I don't see how that boy is gonna run a wagon train if he doesn't offer up some salesmanship."

Cleo lost interest in the conversation. She did a double take when she noticed a piece of folded paper stuck under a vase of flowers on the hall table. Cleo picked it up and studied it. The paper was folded in thirds but wasn't in an envelope. On one flap was written "Old Bertha," but the "Old" was crossed out. It looked as if it had been crushed and smoothed out again. Cleo wondered if the person who stuck it in the hall had rejected the idea of delivery, crumpled the paper, then rethought the rejection. She carefully pulled back one of the flaps and saw "Respectfully, Pappy."

She held the letter to her quickening heart. She closed her eyes and tried to catch her breath. She wanted desperately to read it, but knew she should race into the kitchen and hand over the letter. She also thought about all the changes Polly and Old Bertha had gone through as a result of living in Fat Chance, Texas. Was it possible she had changed, too?

No, it wasn't.

She opened the letter, the soft sounds of Old Bertha's sobbing fading away. When she finished reading, she peeked around the corner into the kitchen. She knew this letter was probably going to make things worse, not better. But withholding the information would be wrong. Even more wrong than reading it in the first place.

Cleo steeled herself for the upcoming drama.

I loathe drama.

She pasted on her bright, practiced smile and walked into the kitchen, waving the letter. Old Bertha had settled down. She and Polly were calmly drinking tea at the scarred table.

"I found this in the hallway," Cleo said, her tone so chirpy and chipper it might have left knife marks on the walls. She held the letter out to Old Bertha.

Chapter 14

Erinn stood in front of the Boozehound, camera equipment slung over her shoulder. She peered in the immaculate front window. Professor Johnson was in the far end of the saloon/museum, tools spread out around his feet. His head was deep inside a player piano. He reminded Erinn of a car mechanic, focused and searching for the perfect tool. Professor Johnson caught sight of Erinn. She waved and he waved back. She noticed he didn't signal that she should come in, but she decided, as a documentarian, she could not always wait for an invitation.

She opened the door and slipped inside.

"I see you're busy," Erinn said.

"Yes," Professor Johnson said.

Thud scrambled to his feet, came lazily over to her, received a pat on the head, and returned to the sun-warmed floor.

"I understand you are the one who discovered the mustang grapes," Erinn said, pulling up the piano bench.

"Yes," Professor Johnson said, as he continued to tinker with the piano.

"From what I hear, you're the driving force behind the town now," she said, knowing that modesty would prevent anything other than another one-word answer.

"Yes."

"Do you mind if I set up my camera while we chat?" Erinn asked.

"I'm a little busy right now," Professor Johnson said.

"That's fine. I'll just go interview someone else."

"I'd appreciate that."

"When would be a better time?"

"Never," Professor Johnson said. "Never would be a better time."

"I see," Erinn said. "Of course, I will honor that. But there is something to be said for being the first to be interviewed in a situation like this."

"A situation like what?"

"A documentary is not like a movie," Erinn said. "There is no script, no agenda."

"Oh? I'm to believe Michael Moore has no agenda when he's at work on a new documentary?"

"Point taken. Let's put it another way. *I* have no agenda."

Professor Johnson stopped working on the piano and looked at Erinn.

"I can't imagine you can possibly uncover anything new about my grandfather and his empire."

"My goal isn't a story about Cutthroat Clarence's empire," Erinn said. "My goal is to explore his human side. And to see what has become of Fat Chance, Texas, since he decided to leave it to all of you. What have you achieved? Have you been successful? Would Cutthroat Clarence think you were successful? What defines success in society today as opposed to his day?"

"And you think people will find that interesting?"

"I have a nose for what people will find interesting," Erinn said. "A few years ago, I created a show about pairing wine with junk food. Huge success. Huge."

"You must be very proud."

"If you let me interview you, you'll be able to lay the groundwork for my investigation. Your interpretation of events will set the rest of the story in motion. If you know what I mean."

"I do know what you mean. I remember a class in comparative religions at Georgetown," Professor Johnson said. "The professor asked the class to discuss what they thought about children choosing their own religion."

"As opposed to ... ?"

"As opposed to being raised with the traditional beliefs of the family. Even if a child were to investigate other religions as an adult, the core belief system of his or her family would always—for good or ill—be there for comparison. The child's early religious training would be the basis for any comparative investigation."

"In other words," Erinn said, "the child would always compare what she was learning against what she already knew."

"Exactly."

"I agree that would be the outcome."

"So then how do you suggest we proceed with this interview?"

Erinn mounted the camera on a tripod and set two chairs facing each other. While she insisted it would only take her a few minutes to prepare her notes for the interview, her ministrations were so comprehensive that Professor Johnson went back to working on the piano. Erinn set up a small monitor, but changed her mind, fearing its presence would be too distracting for the interviewee and took it down. With one final look through the eyepiece to assure herself that her choice of a soft-focus background of the player piano was the way to go, she asked Professor Johnson to take a seat.

Professor Johnson took in a breath, then let it out slowly. He rubbed his hands on his jeans and glumly took the chair opposite Erinn.

"Please say your name," Erinn said.

"My name is Professor Johnson."

"Do you have a first name?"

"Elwood."

"Would you spell that, please?"

"E-L-W-O-O-D."

"And you would like to be referred to as Professor Johnson."

"I would."

"Please spell that."

"Which don't you know how to spell? 'Professor' or 'Johnson'?"

"It's not for me," Erinn said. "It's for the editor."

"You've hired an editor who doesn't know how to spell 'Professor' or "Johnson'?"

"No," Erinn said, finding herself a little flustered. "Actually I haven't hired anybody yet. But . . . never mind. Let's move on."

"All right."

"I understand that you have taken on the mantle of overseer of Fat Chance."

"Not intentionally," Professor Johnson said. "All of us in this town are dedicated to making something of it. It's a lot of hard work and even more focus. The people here . . . are better at the hard work part."

"But you're the one rolling the stone uphill?"

"I certainly don't embrace the Sisyphus analogy. I expect to get the stone over the hill—eventually."

"But it's still a thankless task," Erinn pressed.

"Right now it is," Professor Johnson admitted. "But somebody has to keep things moving, and I guess that's me. My grandfather always said, 'I'd rather be admired than loved.'"

"And you?"

"Unlike my grandfather, I don't really think I have a choice in the matter."

Erinn felt a wave of sympathy. She knew what it was like to be in the role of thankless leader.

"What is your earliest memory of your grandfather?"

Professor Johnson took off his glasses, wiped them on his shirt-tail, and deposited them back on his nose. Erinn had trained herself to wait out these silences rather than move on. She suspected that Professor Johnson would have incredible insights once he started talking. She prided herself on having an instinct about these things.

"I was almost two," Professor Johnson said. "I was being potty trained and went into my grandfather's study to use the toilet. He poked his head around the door and asked if I needed any toilet paper."

"Uh . . . ," Erinn said, suspecting her instincts were getting a bit rusty. "I meant . . . what is your earliest *profound* memory?"

"Profound memory?"

"Of your grandfather," Erinn added, just to be clear.

"I suppose you would have to define 'profound.'"

"*You* define 'profound,'" Erinn said. "This is about you and your grandfather, not me."

"I thought you said this wasn't about my grandfather."

The momentary twinge of compassion she had for the man passed.

How can Dymphna put up with such a pompous, bombastic know-it-all?

"Oh," Professor Johnson continued, "I have it. Here is an early profound memory. I can't guarantee it's the first. I suppose I can't even guarantee it's profound. You'd need to be the judge of that, I suppose."

"Why don't you just tell me," Erinn said though gritted teeth.

"It was my fourth birthday. My parents were still alive, but my birthday party was at my grandfather's house. Aunt Cleo and Uncle Marshall were there, too. And Uncle Sebastian."

"Do you mean Sebastian Pennyfeather, your father's attorney?"

"Yes. Although at four I didn't think of him as an attorney. He was just Uncle Sebastian."

"Since he wasn't a relative," Erinn said, "why did you refer to him as 'uncle'?"

"I was four. I suppose some adult suggested it."

"Go on with your story."

"My grandfather had bought me a child-sized train set, complete with engine, two cars, and a caboose. He had bought engineer hats for us and he and I rode around the grounds. Every time we came by the adults, Grandfather would toot the ridiculous horn and everybody would wave to us. Even as a small child, I knew the difference between a real train and this contraption. The whole thing was embarrassing. Not just for me, but I felt the grown-ups were embarrassed, too, and were just humoring my grandfather."

"What happened next?" Erinn asked.

"Grandfather finally turned the engine off. My mother mercifully lifted me off the train and my grandfather looked at me and said, 'You are too damn serious, boy. You need to learn how to have some fun.' Then he stomped into the house."

"That's a very detailed memory for a four-year-old."

"I was very precocious."

"No doubt."

"Besides, after my parents died and I went to live with Aunt Cleo and Uncle Marshall, my grandfather put me in therapy. So my memories have been analyzed within an inch of their lives. If memories have lives."

"What did you and your therapists conclude, if you don't mind my asking?"

"That I'm not a fun guy."

What could Dymphna possibly see in this man?

The door flew open. It was Wesley. At the sight of the newcomer, Thud sprang up.

"Be careful," Erinn said as Thud came hurling past her.

Thud rocketed past Professor Johnson and knocked into the tripod. Erinn screamed as the tripod wobbled. It appeared to topple in slow motion. Erinn reached out, but the camera was tilting the other direction. She covered her face and waited for the sickening crash.

And waited.

"You can open your eyes," she heard Professor Johnson say. "Crisis averted."

She opened her eyes. Professor Johnson lay on the floor. One of his arms cradled the camera, which lay on his chest, the tripod legs sticking out at odd angles. His other arm was around the dog. Erinn approached them on shaky legs.

"Thank you," Erinn said. "Thank you so much for catching the camera." She felt a rush of gratitude and goodwill toward the professor. Perhaps there was something to this unusual man after all.

"I don't think there's any damage to the camera or tripod." Professor Johnson sat up and righted the equipment. "I'm so sorry. Thud is an acquired taste."

"That's been said about me more than once," Erinn said.

"Me too," Professor Johnson said, sitting up.

Did he actually smile?

Erinn stretched her hand toward the professor.

"I'm all right," he said. "I can get myself up."

"I was just going to grab the camera," Erinn said, righting the tripod.

She noticed the professor's glasses had flown off in the mêlée. She picked them up and handed them to him.

"One good turn deserves another?" Professor Johnson asked, straightening his glasses.

Erinn smiled. She noticed Wesley still stood frozen in the doorway.

"Good reflexes, kiddo," Wesley said to Professor Johnson. "That could have been a disaster."

The three of them stood looking at each other. Did Erinn detect a hint of disappointment in Wesley's voice that there *hadn't* been a disaster?

Chapter 15

Old Bertha walked along the creek that ran behind the stores. She walked past the table at the rear entrance to the Boozehound Museum and Saloon, where Professor Johnson restored artifacts for his museum. Currently, there was a dented brass spittoon, two arrowheads, and something that looked like a rusted wishbone that Professor Johnson thought was a boot spur.

She'd seen him in the drop-dead heat of summer, oblivious to the pelting sun, cleaning and polishing his treasures, preparing for the day when the grapes would be transmuted into wine and the crowds thronged to his saloon—his "tasting room"—and toured his museum.

Old Bertha admired his dedication to a vision that was not in the immediate future. Before she retired, she'd been in the business world. She knew that you couldn't always be Mr. Nice Guy when you had your eye on the prize and the prize was in the future. Professor Johnson seemed to know this better than the other inhabitants. He was often the odd man out, shaping his vision of the town's future.

Fernando was behind the café, tossing coffee grounds on his vegetable garden. Old Bertha was highly suspect that garbage of any sort was a boost to vegetables, but she couldn't argue with Fernando's cooking, so she held her tongue. She wondered if she should have held her tongue with Pappy.

"Hey, Bertha," Fernando said. "You okay? Is there anything I can do?"

"Do I smell brownies?" Old Bertha asked, sniffing the air.

"Yes," Fernando said. "Just whipped up a batch of Mississippi Mud Brownies. If it will put a smile on your face, I'll bring a plate of them over to the inn."

"I don't really have an appetite," Old Bertha said.

"I understand."

"But maybe by suppertime, I could have a bite."

"I'll have them there by nightfall."

Fernando went back into the café. Old Bertha stood behind Pappy's place, two buildings that made up the bank, the jail, and Pappy's living quarters. Old Bertha blinked back tears as she thought about Pappy caring for his mule, Jerry Lee, and tending his grape arbor, even though he'd practically moved in with Old Bertha months ago. Old Bertha went to the lean-to that served as Jerry Lee's stall. Jerry Lee looked at her with mournful brown eyes. She reached out and scratched his head.

"Hey, old man," Old Bertha said. "Your daddy left me a note asking me to watch over you while he's away.

She pulled Pappy's letter from her pocket. She opened it and started reading to the mule.

"My dear Bertha," she said, imitating Pappy's gravel-tinged voice, "I need to get out of town. I leave you in the care of Jerry Lee, and Jerry Lee in your care. Sorry I didn't have time to explain. Love, Pappy."

Old Bertha put the letter back in her pocket.

"Don't that beat all?" she asked the mule. "I mean, how are *you* supposed to take care of *me*?

Jerry Lee ducked his head and drank some water from his trough.

"I'll tell you one thing," she continued. "Your daddy had a hell of a nerve just walking away like that and assuming I'd take care of you. I mean, what if I said no?"

Jerry Lee looked up. Old Bertha backed down.

"Of course, that would never happen," she said. "You can count on me."

Jerry Lee bumped her with his muzzle. She leaned her face on the side of his broad, warm head.

"And I know you'll take care of me too. But you have to promise you won't walk out on me, too," she said softly. "You come on with me, now."

Jerry Lee followed her the rest of the way down the creek past Polly's milliner shop. Polly had an old trunk on a back stoop where she kept all her scraps of fabrics and ribbons. She told Old Bertha that she couldn't bring herself to get rid of any of these treasures. It was this overflowing trunk that gave Polly the idea that she should add quilting to her skill set, as she could use all her scraps as embellishments. Old Bertha didn't really understand the idea of taking a large piece of cloth, cutting it into little pieces and then sewing it back into a big piece again. But to each her own.

Old Bertha's own grocery store was next. Her back porch was spotless. She was diligent in her campaign against ants. Leaving out old jars and cans was just an invitation for trouble.

The last building on the boardwalk was Powderkeg's carpentry and leather shop. Powderkeg had an old barrel full of leather strips sitting against the lopsided wall. Old Bertha shook her head in disgust. There were huge pieces of different colored leathers and canvas scraps in the barrel. Powderkeg obviously wasn't as thrifty as Polly. Jerry Lee stuck his nose in the barrel and pulled out a long, thin strip of leather. He slurped it up like a linguini strand.

"Jerry Lee," Old Bertha said. "Stop that!"

Powderkeg stuck his head out the back door.

"I thought I heard something going on back here," he said. "How are you holding up, Bertha?"

"Pappy left me this damn mule to take care of," Old Bertha said. "Like taking care of my own little Patsy and all those new tourists from Los Angeles isn't enough."

"I'll take care of Jerry Lee, if he's too much for you," Powderkeg said.

"Did I say he was too much for me?" Old Bertha snapped. "Pappy wants me to look after him, and that's what I'll do. I've already got one miniature mule. One more regular-sized one won't make any difference."

Powderkeg put his hands up in surrender. Maggie squeezed by him and dumped more leather strips into the barrel.

"Hi, Bertha," Maggie said, squeezing Powderkeg's bicep. "I won't be coming back to the inn for dinner. Powderkeg is going to show me how to use the new machine. Tonight will be my first sewing lesson."

"Oh, please," Old Bertha said, giving Jerry Lee's rump a little swat to move him along. "Is that what they're calling it now? 'Sewing lessons'?"

Old Bertha walked toward the front of the buildings. The paved trail, to her right, let off waves of heat. Unpaved Main Street stretched out in front of her, dust devils playing tag up and down the road. She started toward the Creakside Inn at the far end of town, but she stopped in her tracks. She could hear clanging and banging coming from the forge.

"Jerry Lee," Old Bertha said, "you know where I live. You go over to the inn and see Patsy."

Jerry Lee turned and headed down the street, trotting toward the inn.

"I'll be damned," Old Bertha said as she watched him go.

She stood outside the forge. She felt a tinge of embarrassment at her hard-heartedness about Fancy. Now that she was dealing with her own huge loss, she felt she and Titan were kindred spirits, doing their best to make it through the day.

Old Bertha debated whether she should go in or not. She had never really cultivated a friendship with Titan. She found him a bit sensitive for her tastes. She had little patience with dreamers like Titan and Dymphna. Give her no-nonsense people like Pappy and Powderkeg.

And look where that got me.

She went in.

It took a minute to get used to the darkness and the heat. As soon as she could see, Old Bertha looked around nervously, forgetting for a moment that Fancy was gone. The noise was coming from out back. She knew that Rocket might be out there, but the giant bull never made her as uneasy as Fancy.

A shadow passed over the light filtering through the back door. When she turned to look, she could only make out the backlit outline of Titan filling the doorway. She'd known Titan for three years now, but the sheer size of him always startled her.

"Bertha?" he asked. "You all right?"

She found she couldn't trust her voice, but managed a tiny nod. She realized instantly that there was no way that Titan could see her nod in the smoky darkness of the forge. She tried again to speak, but again, no sound came out. Filling her lungs with whatever air there was to be had in the forge, she tried again. Titan crossed the forge in four long steps. He wrapped his arms around her.

"I know exactly how you're feeling," he said, his chin resting on top of her head. "It really helps to cry."

Old Bertha's shoulders shook. A little squeak escaped her. It sounded like a rusty faucet being used for the first time in years. But just like a rusty faucet, once primed, there was no stopping the water. The tears flowed.

Titan just waited. Old Bertha finally cried herself out and pulled away from him.

"I'm sorry," she said. "It's just . . ."

"Come with me," Titan said, taking her by the hand and leading her toward the back door. "I want to show you something."

When they got outside, Old Bertha let out a gasp. She had heard that Titan was making a full-sized metal rendition of Cinderella's coach, but she hadn't seen it yet. It was made of different colored metals, but appeared to have been spun from some otherworldly gossamer material. The coach was circular, with a crown on top. Vines with leaves and flowers climbed up the sides. The spokes on the oversized wheels looked impossibly thin, as if spun by a spider. A delicate stepladder perched against the center of the coach, leading into the interior.

"It's beautiful," Old Bertha said.

She thought about Titan's evolution as an artist. When they'd first come to Fat Chance and he'd been told he'd been left a forge, Titan didn't even know what that was. Within six months, he was not only making horseshoes, but turning out his first jewelry. Her heart squeezed when she thought about her first gift from Pappy. Pappy had first disappeared for five months, and when he returned he grabbed a pair of earrings from Titan on the way to the inn. Old Bertha had pretended not to be impressed, either by Titan's workmanship or Pappy's gesture. But she loved them both.

Will Pappy come back again?

"It's for Fancy," Titan said, breaking into her thoughts.

"Pardon?" Old Bertha said, sure she must have missed something.

"I'm making this for Fancy," he said. "I figure I can sit around worrying or I can put that energy into something . . . something as perfect as I can build. When she comes back, all the pain will have been worth it, because something beautiful came out of it."

Old Bertha was about to ask what happened if Fancy didn't come back, but she didn't.

After saying goodbye to Titan, Old Bertha continued her walk down Main Street. Wesley was helping Erinn carry camera equipment down the boardwalk. Fat Chance was already full of oddballs, but the two of them certainly upped the ante.

In the front yard of the inn, she could see Jerry Lee contentedly chomping grass alongside Patsy. Old Bertha smiled. She loved her miniature mule. When Pappy had first showed up with Patsy, he was brimming with pride. He thought a miniature mule was the greatest present ever. In her typical fashion, Old Bertha had pretended she found the mule annoying. She wondered where she'd picked up her inclination to never give Pappy an inch. She shook her head. She would take Titan's advice; she was not going to give in to worry.

Walking up to the gate of the inn, she saw Cleo sitting on the porch, reading. Cleo looked up when the steps creaked, announcing Old Bertha's arrival.

"You have any skills?" Old Bertha said, panting after climbing the steps.

"Pardon me?" Cleo asked.

"Any artistic skills?"

"No," Cleo said.

"Nothing? You didn't take pottery or stained glass at any of your fancy summer camps?"

"I know how to cook."

"Not what I'm looking for," Old Bertha said.

"I'm actually baking zucchini bread right now," Cleo said, defending her position. "You had too many zucchinis. They were getting too ripe."

"Is that what I smell?" Old Bertha sniffed the air. "Well, it's not much, but it's something."

Old Bertha made her way across the porch, but stopped before going over the threshold. She turned back to Cleo.

"I remember your zucchini bread from your café days," Old Bertha said to a surprised Cleo. "It was really good. It's still not what I'm looking for, but you should be proud you can cook the way you do."

"Thank you," Cleo said. "What are you looking for?"

"I'm not sure," Old Bertha said. "But I'll know it when I see it."

Old Bertha heaved herself through the front door, panting from the exertion of her day in town. She stood looking at the hall-tree, which was ablaze with Polly's hats. Each was a creation worthy of a Dadaist master after too much caffeine.

"Hey, Bertha," Polly called out from the sitting room.

Old Bertha went in and sat across from her. Polly was curled up on the settee, working a needle and thread quickly through a blue and white quilt. It was Polly's latest passion. Old Bertha envied Polly her artistry. Polly could go from hats, to jewelry, to quilts, without missing a beat.

"What are you doing down here?" Old Bertha asked, knowing Polly thought the light in the sitting room was less than optimal for crafting of any kind.

"Waiting on the zucchini bread," Polly said. "Fernando is a great cook and all, but nobody can make bread like Cleo."

Old Bertha peered through the window, hoping Cleo hadn't heard. Cleo Johnson-Primb didn't need any compliments going to her head. Old Bertha had to admit, though, Cleo could turn out a mean pumpkin or banana bread, along with her little zucchini number.

"What do you think of this?" Polly asked, holding up an unfinished blue and white quilt for Old Bertha's inspection. "It's called a nine patch."

Old Bertha studied the geometric shapes in front of her. Five dark blue squares attached to four light squares, resulting in a checkerboard. Her accountant's brain was perfectly at ease with the concept of the pattern.

"It's very pretty," Old Bertha said.

"Thanks," Polly said. "Do you think it's manly enough? I want to give it to Poet, so he can take it back to the wagon train with him."

"As quilts go," Old Bertha said, "I'd say it's manly enough. I mean, it's blue. But I'm not sure the white part is gonna hold up. I'm no wagon train expert, but I bet a quilt is gonna get mighty dirty."

"I never thought about that," Polly said, looking at the half-finished quilt.

"But I'm sure he'll love it," Old Bertha said. "Who cares if it gets a few grass stains? It's the love behind it that matters."

"Do you really mean that?" Polly asked suspiciously. "'Cause, well, that doesn't really sound like you."

Old Bertha thought back to her visit with Titan. She visualized the beautiful carriage being spun from love. Who cares if it wasn't practical?

"I've had a change of heart," she said. "You think you could teach me how to make one of those?"

Chapter 16

Dymphna walked down the hill, carrying several knitted shawls and gloves she'd made during her brief absence from Fat Chance. Everything was knitted from the Angora goat hair she'd been harvesting from her farm animals, but she was already dreaming about the creations she'd be turning out with rabbit mohair in a few short months. The rabbits seemed content in their new habitat and their presence on the farm created nary a blip on the other animals' radar—if goats and chickens had radar.

Dymphna passed by the Creakside Inn on the way to Polly's shop. From the trail leading from her farm, she could see Cleo on the porch, but by the time she'd gotten to Main Street, Cleo had gone inside. The porch door of the inn creaked open and Dymphna looked again, always happy to exchange a greeting with any member of the community.

Make that almost always.

Her sister, Maggie, was walking—make that bouncing—down the front steps. The two sisters froze in their tracks. Maggie was the first to thaw enough to start moving. She walked past Dymphna.

"I'm working at Powderkeg's," she said without turning toward her sister. "Don't know if your boyfriend told you that or not."

He had not, but if there was any time to put a spin on a situation, it was now.

"We were too busy getting reacquainted to talk about you," Dymphna said.

"Gross, Dymphna," Maggie said. "TMI!"

"You asked, Mary Magdalene," Dymphna said, proud she had gotten under her sister's skin.

"Maggie!"

"Sorry, Mary Magdalene," Dymphna said. "I mean Maggie."

Erinn was just leaving the Boozehound, but stayed in the doorway, a witness to the sisters bickering.

It's a shame I'm not still working in reality TV. I have a feeling those two have a great story, she thought.

Erinn watched Dymphna turn into Polly's shop and Maggie stalk past her on the boardwalk, heading to the other end of town.

"Let me help you with that tripod," Wesley said from behind her as Erinn finally stumbled out of the Boozehound.

"Where is Jeffries? I thought he was going to be my production assistant," Erinn asked as she looked up and down Main Street. "I can't afford you."

"You probably can't afford Jeffries," Wesley said, reaching for the tripod. Erinn snatched it away. "I gave him a shopping list and sent him to Spoonerville for a few incidentals. I told him I'd cover for him."

"All right, fine," Erinn said, relinquishing the tripod. "If you're going to help, you might as well learn the lingo. These are called 'sticks,' not a tripod."

"Got it," he said. "What else?"

"My guess is you are unaccustomed to taking orders," Erinn said. "Is that going to be a problem?"

"Not at all," Wesley said. "And you have me all wrong. I'm just an attorney. I'm always at the mercy of my clients. I make suggestions, but nobody has to do what I say. I'm always the one taking orders."

"And do any of your clients believe that?"

"Where are we going with these sticks?" Wesley asked, shouldering the tripod and ignoring her question.

Erinn turned on her heels and led the way past the café. Fernando suddenly yanked the front door open.

"Erinn," Fernando said. "We have to talk!"

"Does it have to be now? I really have to get a few of these interviews done."

"Yes! Now!" Fernando said. "It can't wait."

"Will you excuse me for a minute?" Erinn said to Wesley.

"He can come, too," Fernando said, beckoning them both inside. "In case I need to sue somebody."

The three of them sat at the long center table. Fernando set out three tiny glasses and a mason jar full of a mahogany-colored liquid. He poured each of them a thimbleful.

"This is my cherry brandy," Fernando said. "I'm making fruit brandies until the grapes come in and we can start making real wine. Have a sip."

"It's a little early for brandy," Wesley said as he stared at the liqueur.

"This isn't 'it's five o'clock somewhere,'" Fernando said. "This is business. Drink."

Erinn and Wesley picked up their glasses and drank.

Wesley's eyes widened. "This is good," he said in amazement. "I can't believe it."

"Why can't you believe it?" Fernando asked. "Has Professor Johnson already turned you against me?"

"Why would Professor Johnson try to turn me against you?" Wesley asked.

"Because he wants to convince everybody that I don't know what I'm doing," Fernando said. "He wants us to concentrate on making a serviceable wine that we can get out to market as soon as we have enough product to bottle."

"What has that got to do with cherry brandy?" Wesley asked.

"I want to make small-batch, award-winning wine that will bring people to Fat Chance, just like they come to Napa Valley now," Fernando said, wagging the brandy bottle. "If I can do *this* with cherries, just imagine what I can do with grapes."

"But aren't you at least two years away from making wine?" Wesley asked.

Erinn tried to figure out how she might turn on her camera, but couldn't think of anything.

"Yes," Fernando said.

"But I thought you said we had to discuss this now," Erinn added.

Fernando stared at Erinn as if he had unmasked a traitor.

"We do have to discuss it now," Fernando said. "This all has to be decided before the first grape harvest. You grew up in Napa Valley just like I did, Erinn. I would think you would understand. We don't want a commodity. We want perfection."

Erinn thought about reminding Fernando that her parents were college professors, not winemakers. But she felt the point would be moot. She of course had opinions—she had opinions about everything—but she reminded herself that, as a documentarian, she had to be impartial.

"So," Wesley said, "who are you planning to sue?"

"Production assistants are to be seen and not heard," Erinn said hotly.

"I agree with Professor Johnson about paving Main Street," Fernando said. "But if he doesn't come around, I might withdraw my support."

"That's just silly," Erinn said.

"Actually, it's a solid business tactic," Wesley said.

Erinn glowered at him.

"We really need to be going," Erinn said, standing up. "But we'll certainly keep all of this in mind."

"That sounds like you're blowing me off," Fernando said with a little pout.

"I'm just taking in all the facts," Erinn said. At Fernando's hurt look, she added, "But keep the faith, Fernando! You know what they say. 'Perfection is not attainable, but if we chase perfection, we can catch excellence.'"

Once outside, Wesley said, "Vince Lombardi. I'm impressed."

"Pardon me?" Erinn asked.

"That quote about perfection. Lombardi said that. Didn't expect you to be quoting football coaches."

Erinn was pleased with herself. She always knew a good quote when she heard one.

"OK, boss, whom do we interview next?" Wesley asked.

"I thought I might pop in on Powderkeg."

"Sounds good. He probably has some great stories."

"That's the general idea," Erinn said, trying to tamp down her annoyance at Wesley's exuberance. "Don't you have somewhere else to be? Something else to do?"

Wesley looked up and down Main Street. "No," he said.

"Lawyers always seem to have work on which to catch up," Erinn suggested. "I can handle this, if you're pressed for time."

"What?" Wesley said with a grin. "And give up show biz?"

Erinn took a deep breath and stalked toward Powderkeg's shop. Wesley did not seem the type to be enamored of a shot at show business. *This man has to have an agenda, but what is it?* she wondered.

She walked into Powderkeg's shop. Wesley followed her carrying the sticks. Erinn was surprised to find Maggie sweeping furiously, tears in her eyes. Maggie's face instantly became a mask when she recognized Erinn, the woman who had managed to snag her sister's guest room.

"May I help you?" Maggie asked.

"I'd like to see Mr. Primb," Erinn said.

"Come on, now," boomed a voice from the back of the shop. "We're all in this together now. Call me Powderkeg."

Powderkeg walked into the shop, carrying a saddle. He tossed it effortlessly on the counter.

"Hey, Wesley," Powderkeg said, eyeing the tripod. "So, I guess Cleo was telling the truth—you *are* making a documentary."

"Always trying to help when I can," Wesley said.

"Too bad you weren't the family attorney when Cutthroat was deciding I wasn't good enough for his little girl," Powderkeg said. "Maybe I wouldn't be divorced now."

Wesley shrugged. "Wasn't Mr. Pennyfeather's fault. He was just taking orders."

"Water under the bridge," Powderkeg said. "Cleo and I have been ships passing in the night more than once. Hell, we've been ships sinking in the night more than once."

Erinn heard a noise coming from the back of the shop, but Wesley and Powderkeg were caught up in their conversation and didn't notice. But Maggie did. She put down her broom and headed to the back of the shop. Erinn tried to keep one ear on the discussion between Wesley and Powderkeg and one ear toward the back room.

A loud grunt came from the back room. This time the men heard it too, and the three of them ran into the back of the shop, past Powderkeg's little living quarters and out the back door.

"I caught her red-handed!" Maggie said.

She was sitting on Old Bertha, who was sprawled out on the ground, clutching scraps of leather and heavy canvas in both fists.

"Get this nut-job off me!" Old Bertha bawled.

"Nut-job?" Maggie said. "I'm not the one stealing worthless scraps."

"When I get up, I'm gonna tan your hide," Old Bertha said.

"If you get up, you mean," Maggie said. "Besides, you probably don't know the first thing about tanning hides."

"Like you do?" Old Bertha said. "Now that you've worked with Powderkeg for five minutes you're some kind of expert?"

Powderkeg jumped off the back porch and took Maggie by the arm. He pulled her off Old Bertha. "That's enough," he said.

He reached down and offered a hand to Old Bertha.

"Get me up so I can teach this kid some manners," Old Bertha said.

"Calm down, Bertha," Powderkeg said, withdrawing his hand. "I'm not going to help you up until you promise you won't cause any trouble."

"Don't you threaten me!" Old Bertha said.

"Your call," Powderkeg said.

Old Bertha tried to get herself up, but appeared as helpless as a turtle rolling around on its back.

"Fine," Old Bertha said. "I'll be quiet. Get me up."

Powderkeg heaved Old Bertha to her feet. Her white hair had come loose from its bun and floated around her head like a crown of demented cotton balls. She pushed her hair back into a facsimile of its former glory.

"You should fire her," Old Bertha said, peering at Maggie, who stood behind Powderkeg.

"You should give me a raise," Maggie said. "I saved you from being robbed by this crazy woman."

"Don't start now," Powderkeg said, turning Maggie around by the shoulders. "Go back in the store."

Maggie shot Old Bertha another look and then trounced into the store.

"I'm not crazy, you know," Old Bertha said to the assemblage of Powderkeg, Wesley, and Erinn.

"Of course not," Powderkeg said. "But, um, do you mind telling me why you were . . ."

"Collecting scraps?" Wesley offered.

"Well, they're your scraps, so I guess I owe you an explanation," Old Bertha said. "I'm going to make a quilt."

"Out of leather and canvas?" Powderkeg asked.

"Yeah," Old Bertha challenged. "You got a problem with that?"

"Not at all," Powderkeg said, hands raised as if in surrender. "You're welcome to all the scraps you can carry."

"I don't have to carry them," Old Bertha said. "Polly's sewing machine won't sew this tough material. I gotta use your heavy-duty machine."

"You know that machine isn't a toy, Bertha."

"Do I look like a child? I know it's not a toy. All I need is for you to teach me how to use it."

Powderkeg sighed. "OK, if it will keep your mind off... If you want to make a leather and canvas quilt on my machine, I'll be happy to help."

"That's better," Old Bertha said.

"You're welcome," Powderkeg said.

"And you better find a place for your girl Maggie at the shop," Old Bertha said. "She's no longer welcome at the inn."

"Awwww," Powderkeg said. "That's just not fair, Bertha!"

"Don't talk to me about fair," she said. "Nothing in life is fair."

She handed Powderkeg her stack of scraps, turned on her heels, and walked away.

"Don't get rid of those," Old Bertha commanded from the doorway. "I'm going to start working on them in the morning."

"You need to remind me," Erinn said to Wesley. "I have *got* to keep my camera with me at all times in Fat Chance."

Chapter 17

After dropping off her knitwear at Tops, Hats and Tails, Dymphna stopped at the Boozehound and poked her head inside.

"I'm making vegetables and rice, if you and Thud want to come up for lunch," she said.

Thud was at the door immediately. Dymphna knew the dog responded positively to the word "rice" and hoped Professor Johnson did, too. Professor Johnson joined the bloodhound and Dymphna, carefully locking the door behind him. Nobody but Professor Johnson locked his or her shop. He said that the historic artifacts were too valuable not to keep under lock and key. Dymphna thought the more practical items at Polly's shop, the grocery store, the café, or Powderkeg's leather and carpentry store might be of more interest to potential thieves, but Professor Johnson was not to be swayed. Most of the time, Dymphna found his dedication to his artifacts charming. On the trip back to Fat Chance from Los Angeles, she had to remind herself every now and then about his endearing traits, instead of finding them annoying. She was so different from Professor Johnson. Sometimes the thought scared her.

"How are the rabbits doing?" he asked as they trudged up the hill.

"Fantastic, as far as I can tell," Dymphna said. "You and Powderkeg did a great job making them a home."

"I want the rabbits to be happy here," Professor Johnson said.

"I know," she said.

Dymphna took his hand. She knew he meant, "I want you to be happy here."

"Erinn interviewed me for her documentary," Professor Johnson said.

"That must have been fun."

"Not really. I already lived through my childhood once. And my aunt made me go over it again and again in therapy after my parents died. I'd be just as happy never to look back on the past again."

Maybe we aren't so different after all.

Dymphna watched Thud bound ahead of them. When Thud first came to live on the farm, he'd experimented with different methods of opening the gate himself. He'd finally settled on sticking his nose between the gate and the post and rocking the gate back and forth. Usually on the third try, the gate would swing open and Thud would leap forward before the gate snapped shut again. In triumph, he'd race into the yard, scattering the chickens. She realized that, after three years, Fat Chance still felt new to her but had been Thud's home for almost half his life. She wondered if he even remembered being a Los Feliz dog.

"Do you like Erinn?" Dymphna asked after watching Thud's successful mission.

"She is not what I expected from a TV person," he said. "She's very smart."

"Well, she mostly does History Network shows," Dymphna said, trying not to sound defensive. "I know she's had to compromise a few times in her career, but don't we all?"

"No," Professor Johnson said, stopping and looking at her. "Isn't that why you and I are here in Fat Chance? Because we won't compromise?"

Dymphna thought about it. It was true that she stayed dedicated to her craft, even when times got tough and cash got short. Her only compromise now was making jams from her fruit trees instead of focusing entirely on yarns and knitwear. She had never made much money, but Professor Johnson had not only turned his back on the family fortune but also left a safe, tenured, well-paying university job. He'd actually taken much more of a gamble than she. She realized that all the inhabitants of Fat Chance stubbornly clung to their independence, refusing to give up and pack it in. Was there a chance in hell that they would ever come to terms on the road, or the wine? Before she'd left for Los Angeles, she and Titan had started working on a plan for the whole town to unite, a project of a less contentious nature than grape production or road construction, which would get everyone working together again. Of course, that was before Fancy and Pappy disappeared. But maybe those disappearances made the plan even more pertinent. She decided that after lunch she'd go visit Titan. Maybe it was time to revisit their scheme.

"Erinn said she isn't sure where this story will take her," Professor Johnson said. "I don't think I could work that way. No structure!"

"Well, it's like life," Dymphna said. "You don't know where life will take you. If Fat Chance has taught us anything, it's that life has no structure."

"That doesn't mean I like it. But Erinn seems to know what she's doing. She's an interesting woman."

Dymphna knew she shouldn't ask, but she couldn't stop herself.

"Do you think she's more interesting than . . . my sister?"

They walked in silence for a few moments. Professor Johnson opened the gate, which creaked open in welcome. He finally broke the silence.

"Your sister is interesting in a different way," he said.

Dymphna resisted asking for more. She knew that the problem lay with her own relationship with Maggie, not whether her boyfriend found her sister interesting or not.

Professor Johnson and Thud looked in on the farm animals while Dymphna prepared lunch. She was struck by the gender-defined roles they lived by on the farm. The thought of Professor Johnson doing the heavy lifting while she scooped rice and sweet peppers onto plates made her feel guilty. Her face flushed when it occurred to her that when she left for Los Angeles, Professor Johnson had to do the lifting *and* the scooping.

And it isn't even his farm!

Dymphna had never met a man she could rely on the way she could rely on Professor Johnson. He could be infuriating and single-minded, but, if she was honest with herself, he did more than just the heavy lifting on the farm. He did the heavy lifting in town. Looking out the tiny window above the sink, Dymphna saw the fledgling grapevines marching across the hills. Even though it was a town effort, Professor Johnson kept everything—and everyone—on track. Even when it made him unpopular.

And as far as Maggie went, Dymphna resolved to put her petty jealousy aside. She was going to be a better girlfriend. She would let the little things go.

Professor Johnson and Thud stood in the kitchen door just as she was carrying the plates to the table.

"I'll wash up and be right back," he said.

Despite her good intentions, Dymphna felt a twinge of irritation. Professor Johnson was never one to say something along the lines of "That smells wonderful" or "You look beautiful, glistening with perspiration over a hot stove." She stared at him. He stared back at her, wearing the look of confusion she had come to know so well. She loved that look.

He tried so hard. He tried harder than she did. She put the plates down and walked over to him.

"The rice can wait," she said, taking him by the hand and leading him down the hallway.

Professor Johnson looked back toward the kitchen.

"Thud is eating our lunch," he said.

"He's welcome to it," Dymphna said, pulling him into the bedroom.

Chapter 18

"You don't really need to stay during the interview," Erinn said to Wesley.

"Sure I do," Wesley said. "Besides, where else am I going to go?"

She couldn't argue with that.

"All right," Erinn said. "But you have to be quiet."

"I'll be an absolute mouse," Wesley said.

Erinn doubted Wesley's ability to be a mouse on any level, but she needed to be interviewing Powderkeg, not arguing about where Wesley was going to spend his afternoon. She could see Powderkeg, sitting in the chair, eyes scanning the room, getting restless. This was not a peaceful man. She took her seat opposite him and put her earbuds in. She could hear a scratching sound. Erinn cupped her hands over her ears. Sometimes the earbuds gave her a false sense of the ambiance of the room, but the scratching sound continued.

"No sweeping," she heard Wesley say.

She looked up to see Maggie, broom in hand, the other hand over her mouth as if caught doing something wrong. She mouthed the words "I'm sorry" to Wesley. Erinn brushed off the indignity that if there was apologizing to be done it should be to *her*, not Wesley. She shifted her attention to Wesley. Was this her mouse, talking within five minutes of being told to be quiet? She glared at him.

"Maggie was sweeping," Wesley said to Erinn by way of his defense for speaking.

"I could hear that," Erinn said. Did Wesley think this was her first rodeo? OK, she didn't actually know what the scratching sound was, but she'd have gotten there. "Let's everyone settle down. We need the room to be very quiet."

The door to the shop swung open and a cowboy filled the door-frame.

"Herman!" Powderkeg said, getting up from his chair. "I've got your saddle right here."

The big man smiled and entered the store. He was followed by a smaller man, whom Erinn recognized as Polly's new flame, Poet. She also noticed Maggie's entire demeanor change, now that there were younger men in the place. Did Maggie actually unbutton one of the tiny pearl buttons on her sweater?

"You can go back to sweeping," Erinn said to Maggie. "Looks like we'll be awhile."

But Maggie had put down her broom. She had her eye on bigger things.

"I can ring them up," Maggie said to Powderkeg.

"Nah," Powderkeg said. "I want to go over the saddle."

"It's a beauty," Herman said, running his hand over the leather and admiring the workmanship.

"I included a replacement horn wrap and some latigos," Powderkeg said.

"Sounds good," Herman said, studying the saddle. "Those do tend to go first."

"Yup," Poet said.

The saddle, like everything else Powderkeg made, was a work of art. Texas wildflowers were carved deeply into the leather. The seat and cantle were also cut and shaped, but with a geometric design that complimented the rest of the carvings.

"Powderkeg took a lot of care with this saddle," Maggie said.

"I can see that," Herman said, looking down at the diminutive Maggie. "Aren't you the lady with the goats up at the farm?"

"No." Maggie's flirtation dwindled down a notch. "That's my sister, Dymphna. My name is Maggie."

"Well, you could have fooled me," Herman said.

"Yup," Poet said.

"You're Poet, right?" Maggie asked the younger man.

"Yep," Poet said.

"Polly says you're going to work on a wagon train," Maggie said. "That sounds fascinating."

Erinn thought Maggie was laying it on a little thick, but she had to admit, the job did sound interesting. Poet just shrugged. It occurred to Erinn that Poet was going to have to up his game if he was going to spin the illusion of a wagon train reenactment in the twenty-first century. She waited impatiently for the business to be concluded.

"Here you go," Herman said, putting a large battery-powered lantern on the counter. "Gotta love the barter system."

Poet and Herman lugged the saddle out of the shop. Powderkeg returned to his seat and Erinn to hers. Maggie gave up all pretense of keeping herself busy and sat down on a sawhorse.

"You took an old lantern in exchange for that beautiful saddle?" Erinn asked.

"Yeah," Powderkeg said, looking over at the squat lantern on the counter. "I'm still working on my designs and the kid needed a saddle. And this lantern is a classic."

"A classic what?"

"A World War II electric navy lantern," Powderkeg said. "Don't see too many of them around."

"No," Erinn said, "I suppose not. Shall we get started?"

"I thought we had," Powderkeg said.

"Please introduce yourself and spell your name," Erinn said.

"Powderkeg," Powderkeg said. "P-O-W-D-E-R-K-E-G, just like it sounds."

"I meant your given name."

"Powderkeg is my given name. I gave it to myself."

What is it with these people and their names? Erinn thought.

"Correct me if I'm wrong," Erinn said. "But aren't you Marshall Primb, decorated war hero from the Vietnam era? You were married to and subsequently divorced from Cleo Johnson-Primb, making you the ex-son-in-law of Cutthroat Clarence Johnson."

Powderkeg just stared at her.

"Well?" Erinn said, breaking the silence.

"You said to correct you if you were wrong," Powderkeg said. "You weren't wrong."

Erinn thought she heard a snort from Wesley, but when she looked at him, he was as poker-faced as ever.

He was a very distracting production assistant.

"I understand that Cutthroat's motivation for resurrecting Fat Chance was to make amends for taking the American Dream away from several of the people here . . . but not you," Erinn said. "Cut-throat didn't feel he owed you a shot at the American Dream."

"Is that a question?" Powderkeg asked.

This time the tittering came from Maggie, who was not as adept at hiding her mirth as Wesley.

"If Cutthroat didn't feel he owed you a chance at the American Dream, what did he owe you?" Erinn asked.

"Don't think I haven't asked myself that many times," Powderkeg said, suddenly turning serious. "Maybe he felt he owed me a chance to get back with my wife."

"Do you feel as if he ruined your marriage?" Erinn asked.

"He sure didn't help," Powderkeg said. "I wasn't exactly what he had in mind for Cleo, I can tell you that much. I never had a dime—and never wanted one. I sold hand-tooled belts at craft fairs across the country. He didn't see that as a life for his little girl. And you know, he was right. Cleo couldn't take the ups and downs of real life. She stuck it out with me for a while, but once her brother and his wife died, Cutthroat saw to it that Cleo would be taking care of Elwood. He pretty much circled the wagons on his family. He just wanted me gone."

"Did you go?"

"After 'Nam, I recognized a losing battle when I saw one. I knew I couldn't fight Cutthroat Clarence. Besides, Cleo was pretty much done with me by then."

"So Cutthroat paid you to divorce his daughter?"

"He did," Powderkeg said. "Which was pretty funny when you think about it."

"Why is that?"

"Because all he had to do was ask. Cleo could never live the life I wanted to lead and I couldn't live the life she was forced to lead."

"And you just moved on?"

"I managed," he said. "But the whole thing never set easy on me. I haven't made much of myself, but I'm not a quitter. I feel like I quit on Cleo—and even though he wasn't my kid, I quit on Elwood . . . Professor Johnson. I don't mind telling you, he was a weird little guy. He could have used a father figure. All he had was Cutthroat and his henchman."

"His henchman?"

"His right-hand man," Powderkeg said. "Sebastian Pennyfeather. You know, I always thought Cutthroat reveled in his own bad publicity. I swear he's the role model for Donald Trump. Wanted to look like a total badass. But he never did the actual dirty work. He left that to Pennyfeather. Pennyfeather always cut the checks. But I guess somebody had to."

"No hard feelings?"

"Oh, plenty of hard feelings." Powderkeg smiled. "But what are you going to do? When I got my divorce papers, I sent Pennyfeather a hand-tooled belt with a copper buckle. It was the exact color of a penny. I etched the design of a quill feather into it."

"As a gesture of goodwill?" Erinn asked, surprised by the turn in the conversation.

"As a gesture of surrender," Powderkeg said. "Like I said, the thing didn't set easy on me."

"As William Booth once said, 'The greatness of a man's power is the measure of his surrender,'" Erinn said, admonishing herself for getting personal during an interview. She saw herself more as an Anderson Cooper rather than a Barbara Walters. But this man's story touched her. She knew all about having to surrender.

Powderkeg nodded.

"What happened when you and Cleo both found yourselves in Fat Chance three years ago?" Erinn asked, getting the interview and herself back on track.

"Let's just say I think old Cutthroat would be proud of me, if I gave a rat's ass what he thought of me anymore. I tried to give Cleo and me a second chance and for a while it looked like it might work. But I was dreaming. We just repeated all our same mistakes. In the end, she hightailed it back to Beverly Hills."

Just then the door to the shop crashed open. Cleo staggered inside with two large duffel bags. She was panting from the strain of carrying the bags.

"Hey!" Maggie said, jumping up from the sawhorse. "That's my stuff."

"I know it's your stuff," Cleo snarled. "Old Bertha said you're not staying at the inn anymore and demanded I bring it down here."

"Old Bertha is being a damn fool," Powderkeg said. "But fine. Maggie can stay here with me."

"Like hell," Cleo said. "She's young enough to be our daughter."

"Our daughter?" Powderkeg grinned.

"Come with me," Cleo said, dumping the bags at Maggie's feet.

"Where are we going?" Maggie said, picking up her belongings.

"To jail," Cleo said.

"Jail?" Maggie squeaked. "That old woman was stealing the scraps, not me! Put *her* in jail."

"You're not under arrest," Cleo said. "For one thing, Pappy was the sheriff—"

"I thought he was the mayor," Maggie said.

"That too," Cleo said. "But he was also the sheriff, so he was in charge of the jail. It's empty now, so you can make yourself right at home there."

Maggie waited for someone to say something, but when she was met with nothing but silence, she slung her bags over her shoulders and stormed out.

"Wait for me," Cleo said, racing after her. "I've got the keys to the cell."

"Interesting that Cleo doesn't want Maggie bunking with you," Erinn said. "Proprietary interest? Any thoughts you might rekindle the flame?"

"Nope," Powderkeg said. "Not really in the mood for that flame to burn me one more time."

Erinn and Wesley packed up the gear while Powderkeg went back to work. When she was done, Erinn paused at the door and turned back to Powderkeg.

"One more question," Erinn asked, acutely aware that the camera was packed and she was asking this solely for her personal edification.

"Go ahead," Powderkeg said, looking up from the pair of boots on which he was working.

"Why send a gift to Pennyfeather instead of Cutthroat?"

"Couldn't think of a polite way to carve a 'Johnson,'" Powderkeg said with a twinkle in his eye.

Chapter 19

When Dymphna and Professor Johnson had returned to the kitchen, and Dymphna served new plates of rice and vegetables, she made a vow that she was going to be more patient with the lovely man who was her partner. She felt she was making progress. Having Maggie show up in Fat Chance made Dymphna want to run. Running away was always her answer. But as she got older, she began to realize running probably was not the answer. No matter where you went, the one constant would be yourself. It shouldn't have come as a surprise that everywhere she went, there she was. Now with Maggie up close and personal, Dymphna had to make up her mind. Stay and face the music—and Maggie—or get out of Dodge.

"We need to teach Thud to stay off the table," Professor Johnson said, eyeing the dog, who had bits of rice in his whiskers.

"He's fine," Dymphna said. "I always make extra."

They ate in contented silence, touching hands across the table. Dymphna wished it could always be like this. Professor Johnson looked at her over his glasses.

"Thank you for lunch," he said. "This is very tasty."

Was that a compliment? Even if he'd used the goofy word "tasty," she was pretty sure that was a compliment. Maybe Professor Johnson was doing his own soul-searching.

"Thank you." Dymphna beamed. "Everything OK in the barn?"

"Everything seemed fine."

"Rabbits fine?"

"Yes, fine."

Dymphna pushed the broccoli around her plate. The last few

months had been full of heated arguments at the dinner table. Was it possible that if they weren't debating, there was nothing to talk about?

"The ranch hands have been saying there might be a few storms moving in," Professor Johnson said.

Really? We're going to talk about the weather?

"I'm sure we'll be fine," Dymphna said. "This town has been here a long time."

"The town has been flattened twice by twisters," Professor Johnson reminded her. "And now we have the grapes to worry about."

Dymphna pushed her plate away. She knew he was right, but why did every conversation have to circle back to the town? She waited for him to mention the road. She silently dared him to mention the road.

"And then there's the road," he said. "A big storm won't do us any favors if Main Street turns to mud."

Later, as she headed down the hill with Thud at her heels, she told herself that storming out wasn't really leaving. She was just cooling off. She almost ran to the forge. The front door was open a crack. Titan was using the anvil, working on a pair of horseshoes, when she slipped through the door.

"I think it's time to head over to Spoonerville," Dymphna said.

"Oh no," Titan said. "Are Professor Johnson and Fernando fighting?"

"No," Dymphna said. "Professor Johnson and I are fighting."

"Even worse," Titan said. "But I'm not sure our plan will help you guys."

"I think any distraction will help. Anyway, it can't hurt."

Titan whacked the iron horseshoe a few more times, concentrating on his work. Dymphna waited. She spotted Fancy's lair in a darkened corner of the shop. One of the first pieces Titan had forged was a metal tree for Fancy. It had branches she could maneuver, even with her bad wing and eye. It made Dymphna's heart hurt to see it. She was suddenly a little ashamed of herself for being annoyed with Professor Johnson. At least he didn't just disappear.

Like I did. Like I always do.

Her cheeks burned. She never really thought about the pain she caused other people when she moved on. Maybe Maggie had her reasons for being resentful.

Titan moved methodically from one situation to the next and she didn't rush him. He tapped lightly on the anvil with the hammer. Dymphna knew this was a sign he was finished with his project.

When Titan was first bequeathed the forge, he knew nothing about the art of blacksmithing. Pappy showed him the ropes. Pappy told him that it wasn't necessary to tap on the anvil in order to cool down the tools, but there was a legend about the devil, hobbling lamely into a forge. He demanded the blacksmith make him some shoes for his hooves. The blacksmith recognized his visitor and purposely shod him poorly and painfully. The devil never returned. The tapping is supposed to discourage the devil from entering the smithy.

"Better to be safe than sorry," Pappy had said, landing one final tap on the anvil.

After Titan was satisfied the forge was clean and the fire put to rest, he opened the front door. Sunlight streamed in, giving the place a more welcoming look. The two of them left the forge, planning to walk to Spoonerville, when Jeffries pulled up in the limousine. He rolled down the passenger window and asked for directions to Spoonerville.

"This whole area seems to have stumped the GPS satellites," Jeffries said.

"We were just heading over there ourselves," Dymphna said.

Jeffries stared straight ahead, squinting into the sun. Dymphna wondered if he had the authority to offer them a ride. She suspected he was asking himself the same question. He turned back to face her.

"Why don't you come with me?" he asked. He started to get out of the limo, but Dymphna called him off.

"You don't have to open our doors," Dymphna said. "We can just climb in."

She opened the passenger door, but Thud beat her to the shotgun seat. She and Titan exchanged a look and a shrug and got in the back.

After determining that no other townspeople wanted to hitch a ride, the limo was on its way. Jeffries carefully maneuvered the limousine up the trail, onto the highway and across to the dirt road leading to the majestic entrance to the Rolling Fork Ranch.

"Spoonerville is on a ranch?" Jeffries asked, as he drove under the elaborate archway that announced they had arrived.

"That threw all of us, too," Dymphna said. "The ranch is huge and Spoonerville is the supply town. Until we resurrected Fat Chance, there wasn't anywhere else to shop for twenty miles."

"The ranch hands must have been glad to see you succeed," Jeffries said.

"Some were," Titan said. "Anybody looking for a decent meal, for one thing. But they now have competition from Powderkeg's carpentry work and leather shop."

"Not to mention your horseshoes," Dymphna added.

"Just keep on this road," Titan said to Jeffries, deflecting Dymphna's compliment. "You'll see a couple of buildings that make up about as much of a town as Fat Chance does. The store is at the end of the street."

The general store sat above the road, up a steep set of stairs. A few ranch hands were sitting on the long, wide porch. Dymphna could see them sit up as the limo pulled up.

Jeffries got out of the driver's seat and started toward the back of the limo to open the doors for Dymphna and Titan, but they were already getting themselves out. Dymphna pulled the front passenger door open and Thud bounced out, heading up the stairs to meet and greet.

"Hey, Thud," a ranch hand named Jake said. "How are ya, buddy?"

Dymphna and Titan exchanged a look. Since Fernando had started feeding the cowboys, trips to Spoonerville had become much more pleasant. But this was a recent development and they were still on their guard. The three of them climbed the steep stairs.

"Hey, little lady," Jake said to Dymphna, as he tipped his hat. "I heard you left town."

"I'm back . . . Jake," Dymphna said. She knew his face and name from breakfast at the café. She was surprised that news from Fat Chance was of any interest to the Spoonerville crowd.

"We knew that! Remember, she came back with a bunch of rich folks from Los Angeles. That's where the limousine came from," another cowboy, Freddy, said to Jake. Then, turning to Dymphna for validation, he asked, "Isn't that right?"

"Yes," Dymphna said. She wondered if she needed to protest the "rich folks" comment, but decided against it, considering they had just pulled up in a limousine.

"This limo your new ride, now that Pappy left with the Covered Volkswagen?" Jake asked, looking down from the porch at the limo, which gleamed despite the dust.

"For now," Dymphna said. "Until Pappy gets back."

Cowboys and ranch hands, both male and female, wandered in and out of the store, or sat on the few chairs and the railing that skirted the porch. Dymphna was always amazed how many people the porch could hold. The porch could be a hotbed of gossip, but gossip Texas-style. Just a comment or two, said in passing, about the latest goings-on on the ranch. She remembered the first time she and Powderkeg had stepped up onto the porch after Powderkeg learned that his sweetheart, Lacey "Mikie" Carmichael, had been offered—and taken—a job as a pilot in New Mexico.

"Sorry to hear about Mikie," one of the old-timers had said.

Powderkeg had wheeled on the man, expecting to see a smirk on the weather-beaten face. But all he saw was concern.

"There's a lot of work in New Mexico right now," another cowboy had offered. "But you never know, she might come back."

"Yeah," Powderkeg said. "Thanks."

Dymphna had followed Powderkeg into the store. She knew Powderkeg was not about to explain why Mikie really left—and she suspected the men on the porch didn't want to hear it. She knew that Lacey sensed Powderkeg's devotion to his ex-wife, no matter how valiantly he fought against it. The day she left, Mikie took Dymphna aside and confided in her.

"I know Powderkeg is going to go all macho-idiot and clam up about us, the way men do," Mikie had said. "But I want you to know why I'm bailing."

Dymphna suspected what was coming. Mikie poured out her heart, saying that Powderkeg would never love her the way he loved Cleo. Mikie couldn't accept being second place, but loved him too much to hang around. When the offer came from New Mexico, she jumped at it.

"I actually love him enough to hope he'll be happy someday," Mikie had said, her eyes filling with tears. "But I'm selfish enough not to stay around and see it happen without me."

Gossip about the Rolling Fork Ranch and Spoonerville now officially extended to Fat Chance. Dymphna knew it would be rude to just walk past the men, into the store. Everyone had worked hard to make and maintain this détente, and she didn't want to damage it. But she did not want to talk about Pappy. It made her feel disloyal to Old Bertha. The cowboys were now scrutinizing Jeffries, who stood out in his khakis and blue dress shirt.

"You the driver?" Jake asked Jeffries.

"I was the driver," Jeffries said. "Now I'm the drover."

Seconds passed while the two cowboys stared at him. Jake narrowed his eyes. "You even know what a drover is?"

"Someone who drives livestock to market," Jeffries said, pointing to Thud. "I just drove that bloodhound to this market, so, I'm now the drover."

Dymphna stiffened. It had been awhile since there'd been a newcomer in their midst and she wondered how this was going to play out.

Freddy looked thoughtful for a moment, then his face split into a grin. "Works for me," he said, shaking Jeffries's hand. "Welcome, drover."

"Hey, Titan," Jake said as Titan headed toward the screen door. "Any word from your bird?"

Titan just shook his head and walked into the store.

"Poor guy," Jake said. "Pappy and Fancy. Those old buzzards will break your heart every time."

Dymphna and Jeffries followed Titan into the store.

"I'll find Dodge," Titan said.

Dymphna turned to see Jeffries strolling the few aisles, a frown on his face. She smiled to herself, remembering the first time all the Fat Chancers had laid eyes on the store. Most of the inhabitants of Fat Chance were big-city dwellers, and the idea of going without their particular brand of paper towels or fresh bagels took some getting used to. Of course, there was an upside: The Spoonerville store stocked three kinds of chicken feed, and there was always someone with whom to discuss goats. One look at Jeffries told her that the upside would fall on deaf ears.

"Can I help you with anything?" Dymphna asked, placing a hand on Jeffries's shoulder.

"I have a list from Mr. Tensaw," Jeffries said, looking helplessly at her. It took Dymphna a second to remember Mr. Tensaw was Wesley. "He wants fresh-squeezed orange juice and Babo Botanicals sunscreen."

"Well," Dymphna said, handing Jeffries a sack of oranges, "this is our way of getting fresh-squeezed juice."

He took the bag and followed Dymphna to another aisle. She popped a bottle of Coppertone in his hands.

"This is as fancy as we get around here with sunscreen," Dymphna said. "But you should also tell him to stop by Polly's and get a hat. A cowboy hat was the original sunscreen—and is still the best."

"I'll do that," Jeffries said. "Thanks."

Dymphna thought Jeffries seemed a little distracted. She followed his gaze. He was looking at Titan, who was at the counter, talking to Dodge.

"Who is that?" Jeffries asked.

"That's Dodge Durham," Dymphna said. "He's the one who tried to steal the town from us when we first got here. He runs this store, so we have to deal with him, but be careful around him."

Jeffries seemed to relax.

"Anything else I can help you with?" Dymphna asked.

"No, I think I get the idea," Jeffries said. "Basic stuff only."

"You got it!" Dymphna said.

Jeffries went back to shopping and Dymphna went to stand with Titan. Dodge tended to keep his distance from Dymphna, having relegated her to the role of "Professor Johnson's girl." There was an uneasy peace between the two men after Professor Johnson flattened Dodge after a fight about Thud. Dodge acknowledged her with a quick nod, but didn't stop his exchange with Titan.

"You want to buy whitewash for the whole town?" Dodge was saying. "Why?"

Dymphna put her hand on Titan's wrist, hoping to stop him from answering. If Dodge found out they were trying to keep this a secret, he'd find a way to alert the whole county. But Titan was oblivious to the signal.

"Dymphna and I think it would be a unifying activity," Titan said. "Everybody's fighting over extending the asphalt and what we're going to do with the grapes when the harvest comes in."

"Really," Dodge said. Dymphna could practically see his antennae go up. "Y'all are fighting, huh?"

"Fighting is much too strong a word," Dymphna said.

"I don't think it is," Titan said miserably. "Professor Johnson and Fernando are at each other's throats about the grapes." Turning to Dymphna, he added, "And you left town because you were so sick of hearing about the road! Besides, why are we here spending our own money if we aren't trying to unite the town?"

Dodge turned his eager glance toward Dymphna.

"Now that Cleo's back," Dymphna said, knowing that just the sound of her name put Dodge on high alert, "we just thought it would be nice to spruce the place up."

"What are you—" Titan started to say, but Dymphna's grip on his arm got firmer and he quieted down.

"Well, I can get you a nice deal on some real nice paint," Dodge said. "It'll be about a thousand dollars."

Titan gasped. "A thousand dollars?"

"You're lucky Main Street is full of false-front buildings. If you had real buildings, it would be more."

"We have real buildings," Dymphna said, brows furrowing.

"Tell you what—I'll even throw in delivery. So you don't have to worry about getting paint on your limousine," Dodge said. "You want this on your tab or Titan's?"

Dymphna's breath caught. She shared an account with Professor Johnson, and she didn't want him to get wind of this. But she couldn't really ask Titan to take on the financial burden. Neither of them had bargained for this price tag.

"You can put it on mine," Titan said.

"Are you sure?" Dymphna asked. "It's a lot of money. Maybe we should rethink this?"

"Or ask Cleo," Dodge said. "She's probably got more money in her purse than I make in a year."

"This is a gift from *us*," Dymphna said, annoyed with herself for answering him. She knew he was baiting her.

Thud nosed between them.

"Looks like Thud needs to go out," Dymphna said.

"That's fine," Titan said. "I'll finish up here."

"OK." Dymphna put a bottle of shampoo on the counter. "May I pay for this, please?"

Dodge picked up the bottle and studied it. "That's funny," he said. "Your sister bought this same bottle."

Dymphna looked up in surprise. When had Maggie come to Spoonerville?

Dymphna shook her head. Maggie was a free agent. As long as she wasn't causing trouble, she could come and go as she pleased.

She paid for the shampoo, stowed it in her canvas shopping bag, and headed to the front door. She glanced around for Jeffries, who once again seemed transfixed by Titan and Dodge. Thud butted her leg. She held the door open and she and Thud went outside.

Chapter 20

"Let me buy you lunch," Wesley said to Erinn.

"You're my PA," Erinn said. "In the real world, you wouldn't have any money."

"Look around," Wesley said, sweeping his arms to include all of Fat Chance. "What about this place says 'real world' to you?"

"Even so," Erinn said, "I don't think the PA buying the director lunch is . . . seemly."

"Seemly?" Wesley said, furrowing his brow. "Interesting word. Would you consider it *un*seemly? Or just not seemly?"

"I don't think there is much difference," she said.

The fact that this man dared to play word games with her made Erinn very nervous. She could usually count on being the smartest person in the room, yet here in Fat Chance, with a population of more or less ten people, she found herself having to contend with both Professor Johnson and Wesley Tensaw. She needed to stay on her game.

"I disagree. If you find it *un*seemly, I can't talk you into lunch. But if you only find it *not* seemly, I still have a chance."

They walked by the Cowboy Food Café. Erinn couldn't tell what Fernando was making, but whatever it was smelled divine.

I don't have to be hungry while staying on my game, she thought.

"All right," she said. "But next time it's on me."

"Oh, there's going to be a next time?" Wesley said. "I'll look forward to it."

Erinn found heat rising from her collarbone. She was trying to sound casual—not her strong suit—but Wesley made the suggestion seem absolutely lurid.

He held open the door to the café and Erinn walked in. Lunch patronage at the Cowboy Food Café was smaller than the breakfast crowd. Erinn chose a table for six, stacking her camera equipment in all but two of the chairs.

Polly came over with two glasses of water. "Hey, Erinn. Mr. Tensaw."

"Please," Wesley said, "call me Wesley."

"OK," Polly said. "I'll try, but you seem like a Mr. Tensaw, even in Fat Chance."

"Your call," Wesley said.

Erinn stared at the chalkboard menu on the counter. She really needed her glasses to focus on Fernando's cursive, but her vanity wouldn't allow her to rummage in her pocket for them. The ease she felt when she was wrapped in her professional persona continued to melt away.

"Did Old Bertha settle down?" Wesley asked, referring to the mayhem of the morning.

"I guess so," Polly said, shrugging. "Pappy leaving town has kind of freaked her out. She's got this crazy idea of making a quilt out of canvas and leather. I told her I had plenty of good cotton fabric, but she won't listen."

"What's anyone going to do with a quilt made of canvas?" Wesley asked.

"Your guess is as good as mine," Polly said. "But if that's what she wants to do, I'll help her. That's the great thing about this place. You can run with every crazy idea and see what happens. Nobody judges you."

Erinn nodded. She couldn't imagine what Old Bertha hoped to achieve by sewing up an incredibly uncomfortable quilt.

"Today's special is shepherd's pie," Polly said.

"It has potatoes," Polly offered. "Do I need to say that?"

"Not to us," Wesley said, smiling.

Those are very white teeth, Erinn thought. She wondered if he had veneers.

"Erinn?" Polly prodded.

"Fine," Erinn said, relieved to find she didn't need to read the board. "That sounds fine. And coffee."

"I'll have the same," Wesley said. "Decaf with soy."

"We don't serve decaf," Polly said. "Or soy."

"Herbal tea?" Wesley asked.

"Dr. Pepper is really popular," Polly said. "It makes Fernando crazy, but what are you going to do?"

"I'll just have water," Wesley said, defeated.

Fernando appeared at the table. He slapped down an herbal tea bag.

"From my private stash. Glad to share," Fernando said, returning to the kitchen as quickly as he had appeared.

Polly brought over a pot of hot water for Wesley and a steaming mug of coffee for Erinn. They drank in silence. Erinn always felt trapped in social situations. A one-on-one conversation with an attractive man was the worst.

"Are you happy with the footage you've gotten so far?" Wesley asked.

Erinn was instantly on guard. There was something about the timbre of his voice that made her wary. This was not the conversational tone of a fellow filmmaker, or even a bright subordinate's attempt to ingratiate himself. This was a man who wanted to know something.

But what?

"I think we have a few interesting moments," Erinn hedged.

"Like what?"

"You tell me," Erinn said. "As an insider, what do you think of the footage we've gotten?"

"I would hardly qualify myself as an 'insider,'" Wesley said, looking around the room. "Not in a town that doesn't serve decaf."

"But you know everyone involved in Cutthroat's will," Erinn said. "And you knew Cutthroat."

"I didn't really know anyone besides Cleo and Elwood," Wesley said. "And as far as knowing Cutthroat, we had a strictly business relationship."

How convenient.

"The man with all the dirt on Cutthroat would have been Sebastian Pennyfeather," Erinn said. "Am I right?"

"Yes," Wesley said. It was as if they were in a poker game now, the cards being played very close to the vest.

"Did he have any family, this Pennyfeather?" asked Erinn.

"No."

"He sounds like he was an interesting man."

"He was," Wesley said. "He was a brilliant man."

"Was there a thorough investigation into his death?"

"What do you think?"

A non-answer.

"It wasn't his fault he died in a boating accident," Wesley continued. "The world lost a great mind that day."

Erinn folded. They returned to silence as Polly arrived with the shepherd's pies.

"Anything else I can get for you?" Polly asked.

"We're fine," Wesley said. "Thanks."

Used to friendly banter with the customers, but sensing this was not the time, Polly extricated herself.

"This is amazing," Erinn said after taking a bite of the pie.

She was relieved to be changing the subject, although she felt a twinge of disloyalty to her sister back at the tea shop in Venice. When Fernando had been the chef at the Rollicking Bun, his shepherd's pie had customers lining up on the boardwalk an hour before opening. When he went to open his B & B on Vashon Island, he kindly left behind all his recipes, but Suzanna didn't really ever get the hang of the pie.

"I never eat anything this rich at home," Wesley said.

"Don't you like it?" Polly was unexpectedly at his side, like a ninja waitress, one hand on the back of his chair, the other on her hip.

"I like it very much," Wesley said, startled. He slapped his taut stomach. "I just better not get used to it."

Polly beamed and left again. Wesley watched her. When he was sure she was out of earshot, he said, "Of everyone whom I met at the reading of the will, Polly has changed the most."

Erinn relaxed. Anything that was fodder for the documentary was safe ground.

"How so?" she asked.

"The last time I saw Polly, she wore vampire makeup," Wesley said. "And I didn't see her smile once. I'm sure her life here has been harder than it ever was in New York City, but she's blossomed here."

"Blossomed?" Erinn said, arching an eyebrow.

"I know, I sound like I'm ninety," Wesley said. "But I hated to see somebody so young with such a chip on her shoulder."

Erinn was surprised someone with the reputation of Wesley Tensaw would even notice a young Goth-girl's chip.

"Why do you suppose she changed?" Erinn said.

"Support? Love? Acceptance?" Wesley offered.

"I hope not," Erinn said. "Support, love, and acceptance do not a documentary make."

"What if that's the secret?" Wesley asked. "What if that's all you find?"

Erinn could see that he was trying to appear casual, but the grip on his fork told her otherwise.

The more I talk to you, the more I doubt that is all I'm going to find, she thought.

Polly came back to clear their plates when they were done.

"What time are you finished here?" Erinn asked her. "I'd like to interview you, if you have the time."

"Cool," Polly said. "But you'll have to interview me over at my shop. I have a hat order for a store in Galveston and I need to work on it."

"No problem," Wesley said.

Erinn shot him a look. Wesley smiled back sheepishly.

"Overstepping my production-assistant bounds?" he asked.

"Massively," Erinn said.

"*Pardonnez-moi*," Wesley said.

To Polly, Erinn said, "We'll see you over at the store this afternoon."

"Amaze-balls," Polly replied.

As Polly walked away, Erinn stared after her in amazement. "Did she just say 'amaze-balls'? What does that even mean?"

"It means 'amazing' or 'awesome,'" Wesley said. "All the kids are saying it."

"Thanks for the translation," Erinn said, embarrassed that she'd asked. She gauged that she was at least five years younger than Wesley.

"It's good to keep up," he said.

Chapter 21

Now loaded with gear, Wesley preceded Erinn into the store. Blinking to adjust from the harsh outdoor glare of Main Street to the softer light of the interior of the shop, Erinn found she could hear Wesley and Polly chatting before she could see them. When her eyes finally adapted, Erinn looked around. She gasped. If the shopkeepers at Disney ever needed a lesson in excess, a field trip to Tops, Hats and Tails would be just the ticket. One entire wall was lined with cowgirl hats decorated with elegant, whimsical, or outrageous originality. Another wall held the men's selection. The hatbands featured Titan's graceful metal embellishments and Powderkeg's hand-tooled leather.

The store was packed with ribbons of every color, pattern, and texture. Lace in every width, some so fine it appeared to be spun by Arachne herself. Bolts of hand-dyed fabrics were crammed into every corner, and traditional-design quilts hung from the rafters. In the center of the store were two cabinets. On one, a display table held earrings, which were another collaborative effort of Titan and Polly's.

The other cabinet was newer, brighter, and steadier. Erin suspected it to be Powderkeg's handwork. Six mannequin head forms, three female and three male, sat disembodied on the cabinet. The effect of six heads sitting in the middle of the store was a bit unnerving. The heads all wore unfinished cowboy hats, so Erinn suspected that this was Polly's workstation.

Erinn was stunned by the artistry. She stole a glance at Polly, who was showing Wesley around the store. What a surprise to find that this girl, who only seemed interested in the breakfast crowd of cowboys, possessed such talent. Erinn admonished herself for her earlier impression of the girl.

Bad attitude for a documentarian. Don't assume anything.

While Erinn and Wesley picked a location for the interview, Polly worked on a cowboy hat at her workstation. Erinn found herself distracted by Polly's process. The cowboy hat before her was a dappled fabric, gray to dusty black. Polly first fitted a simple black leather hatband, which Erinn thought complimented the hat exactly. Polly stood back, biting her bottom lip in concentration. She swapped the hatband for a thicker model with carved roses on it. Erinn watched Polly walk around the cabinet, studying the hat from all angles. When she returned to her starting point, she snatched the hatband off and replaced it with a third. The change in the hat was remarkable. The new hatband was a thinner black leather but was accessorized with flattened studs that appeared to have been antiqued with some sort of stain. The gradations in the color of the studs picked up the gradations in the color of the hat. It was perfect. Polly looked up, catching Erinn's eye.

"Yeah?" Polly asked, indicating the hatband.

"Yeah," Erinn said.

Erinn and Wesley finished prepping for the interview. When they were all set, Erinn insisted that Polly flip the Open sign in the window to Closed. Polly obliged, then took a seat opposite Erinn.

"Please say your name and spell it," Erinn said, bracing for the inevitable questions that seemed to follow whenever she requested this information from an inhabitant of Fat Chance.

"Polly Orchid," Polly said, asking no questions. "P-O-L-L-Y O-R-C-H-I-D."

"Really?" Erinn asked. "Your name is Polly Orchid?"

"Yes. Something wrong with that?"

Erinn caught a glimpse of the Goth girl she'd been told about. A steely defensiveness appeared suddenly in Polly's eyes.

"No no," Erinn said. "It's just that . . ."

"Just what?" Polly's tone was getting more and more defensive.

Erinn chided herself. She needed to stay completely neutral in these situations, and she'd now put herself in the position of having to explain.

"In Latin, polyorchidism is a medical condition," Erinn said.

"What kind of medical condition?" Polly asked.

"It means . . ." Erinn looked at Wesley. Surely he'd studied Latin in school. He must know.

"It means a person with more than two testicles," Wesley said.

Polly stiffened. Erinn was afraid the interview was over before it began, all because she couldn't keep her own mouth shut. She looked at Polly, whose fingers had flown to her mouth in surprise.

"I'm sure this is all just a fluke," Erinn began. "I mean, Polly is a lovely name and—"

Erinn was cut off by Polly's laughter.

"Dude! My father was a first responder," Polly gasped. "He knew medical terms. How awesome is that? "

"I'm glad to see you find the humor in it," Erinn said as she quietly clicked on the camera.

"Are you kidding?" Polly said. "My mom used to tell this story about when she was pregnant. When people asked if they wanted a boy or a girl, my dad used to say 'As long as it has balls, I don't care.'"

Erinn tried to smile, but this was not her kind of humor.

"I guess when he had a girl, this was his little joke on the world," Polly continued, wiping her eyes. "Wow. That is frickin' hilarious. Go, Dad."

Erinn wasn't sure how to segue into her interview, so she just plunged in. "Tell me about how you found yourself in Fat Chance."

Polly sobered immediately.

"Where do you want me to start?" she asked.

"Wherever you want to start," Erinn said.

"I guess . . . I guess it all started when I got that letter from Mr. Tensaw's office," Polly said, looking quickly at Wesley.

Even in the darkened room, she could see Polly was seeking Wesley's approval. Was this because he was a man or because he was the famed Mr. Tensaw of Beverly Hills? Erinn waited. Polly resumed only after Wesley nodded his assent.

He's just the PA! thought Erinn.

"You know the drill," Polly said. "We all got the same letter asking us to meet at Cleo's house. None of us knew why."

"Tell me about the meeting," Erinn said. "When you found out why you were there."

"Cutthroat was up on the screen, telling each of us why he was including us in his will," Polly said, her voice getting very small. "He said something about choosing me because he felt he should not have been backing Big Oil at the expense of our country, or something like that. He picked my name kind of randomly because my dad died rescuing people at the World Trade Center during 9/11."

"I wish I could thank—" Erinn began.

"Yeah, yeah, you wish you could thank my father for his service," Polly said, the bitter young woman reappearing for a moment. "Thanks. But you can't thank him, can you? Because he's dead."

Erinn sat and waited. She knew Wesley was trained to wait, too, so the room was very, very still for a long time. Finally Polly cleared her throat.

"Anyway," Polly said, "my mom never really got over my dad's death and I was just sort of wandering around New York. So I thought, 'What the hell, I'm not doing anything. I'll go to Texas and when the six months are over, I'll take the money and run.' Only, obviously, I didn't run."

"Why?" Erinn asked, leaning in. "Why did you stay?"

"It's hard to explain. I mean, partly it was because of *this*," Polly said, looking around the store as if seeing it for the first time. "I never knew I could design stuff. I don't know how he knew! But it was more than that. I could take this stuff anywhere, right?"

Erinn and Wesley didn't answer, just waited for Polly to continue.

"When I got in the RV to come here, I was already counting the days until I could leave," Polly said. "But I ended up loving it here. Loving the crazy town. Loving the feuds we get into with Spoonerville and with each other. It ended up being home, you know?"

It occurred to Erinn a theme was finally emerging. Fat Chance became the unlikely familial center for a bunch of wanderers.

"Do you think you'll stay here forever?" Erinn asked. "I mean, you're very young."

"I never really thought about it," Polly said. "But now . . . I can't see me ever leaving Old Bertha, especially now that Pappy dumped her. She needs me."

Is that the secret of Fat Chance? They need each other? wondered Erinn.

"Is that your supposition?" Erinn asked. "That Pappy is gone because he wanted to dump Old Bertha?"

"I can't see why else he would leave," Polly said. "I mean, you guys came in, but . . . that doesn't seem like it would drive Pappy away. He's used to weird people just showing up. Not, uh, that you guys are weird."

"But Pappy left before," Erinn said. "And he came back."

"He did," Polly said. "None of us ever found out where he went, but we knew why he went. He wanted to make sure we could stand on our feet without him. Now that I think about it that adds to my theory, right?"

"Your theory about Pappy dumping Old Bertha?"

"Yeah," Polly said, her voice rising. "Maybe he's sick or something and wants to make sure Old Bertha can stand on her own two feet. Do you think that's it? Do you think Pappy is sick?"

"I have no idea," Erinn said. "But I suppose it's a possibility."

"Man, that would just suck," Polly said, her fingers flying in front of her mouth again. Her voice dropped to a whisper. "I probably shouldn't say 'suck' on camera. I'm sorry."

"That's okay," Erinn said. "My camera has heard worse. Thanks. That's it for now."

Erinn clicked off the camera.

"Was that OK?" Polly asked.

"Yes!" Erinn said emphatically. "It was really good. We'll get out of your way."

Erinn turned to tell Wesley to start packing up the gear. Her voice caught in her throat. Wesley was staring into space. He had turned deathly pale.

"Wesley?" Erinn said softly.

Wesley snapped to, his color and relaxed demeanor returning instantly.

"Ready to go, boss?" he asked.

"We're wrapped at this location," Erinn said, teeth on edge at hearing "boss" yet again.

Wesley started to pack the tripod into its case. Erinn put the lens cap back on her camera and started to disassemble the light stand, but she kept her eyes on Wesley.

What was really on his mind?

Chapter 22

Polly went back to work, laying her gorgeous cowboy and cowgirl hats, one at a time, in mountains of tissue paper. She popped each cloud of tissue-covered hat into a hat box, closed the lid, and added it to a rising stack beside her work area.

Wesley stopped packing gear and watched the hats disappearing into the paper.

"Those are really great-looking hats," he said. "I should buy one."

"Not a problem," Polly said, pointing out the rack of cowboy hats on the wall. "See if there is anything you like over there. If not, I'll make you one to order."

Erinn put her hands on her hips, expecting Wesley to notice that his "boss" was getting more than a little annoyed with him.

Fat chance.

Erinn continued to wrap gear while Wesley tried on cowboy hats.

"What about this one?" he asked, facing Polly.

"It's too big," Polly said. "A cowboy hat should be snug, not just perch on your head. You don't want it to come off when you're riding fences."

Erinn snorted. As if Wesley were going to be riding fences any-time soon. She realized she didn't really know what "riding fences" meant. She was pretty sure Wesley didn't know either.

Wesley tried on another hat, this one winning Polly's approval. He put it on the counter.

"Do you want to wear it now or should I pack it up?" Polly asked as she rang up the sale.

"I'll wear it," Wesley said. He put it on his head and turned to Erinn. "Hey, Erinn, what do you think?"

"If you got one that's tight enough to stay on your head while you pack gear," Erinn said without looking up, "then I love it."

Wesley gave Polly a wink and began helping Erinn pack. Polly went back to packing her own boxes.

"I have a big order for hats from a hat shop in Galveston," Polly said. "Pappy used to take me there in the Covered Volkswagen. I guess I'll see if Poet can borrow a truck and take me."

Jeffries stuck his head in the door. "I noticed you packing up," he said to Erinn, "so I assume the interview is over. I've been standing outside. Shall I turn the Closed sign around to Open?"

Jeffries flipped the sign at Polly's nod.

"Look who's here," Erinn said, a little too heartily. "Jeffries is back from Spoonerville."

"Just in time," Wesley said.

Erinn was surprised. It hadn't occurred to her that perhaps he was getting bored with his role as underling. That thought annoyed her, but not as much as the idea of him tailing her any longer.

"Polly needs a ride to Galveston," Wesley said, cutting Erinn off before she could utter a word.

"Don't be crazy," Polly said, although Erinn could hear the excitement in her voice. "Galveston is four hours from here! It's an overnight trip."

Jeffries stood silently at the door.

"I'm not sure your boyfriend would be happy to see you going off with another man," Erinn said, desperately trying to circumvent this latest disaster initiated by Wesley.

"Oh, he wouldn't care," Polly said. "I mean, he never minded me going off with Pappy. Another old guy won't make a difference."

Erinn saw a slight twinge in Jeffries's cheek muscle. Jeffries was a good thirty years younger than Pappy, and while he clearly had no more interest in Polly than she had in him, the comparison probably stung.

"Let's not hear another word about it," Wesley said, digging out his wallet and handing a black American Express card to Jeffries. "I insist."

"Didn't you say you knew how to drive a limousine?" Erinn asked.

"I said I knew *how* to drive one," Wesley replied. "I didn't say I *intended* to drive one."

"I won't be leaving until tomorrow," Polly said, unsure of where she stood. "Is that OK?"

"That's fine," Wesley said. "I'm sure Jeffries can keep himself busy until then, can't you, Jeffries?"

"Maybe he can keep himself busy as my PA?" Erinn said.

"No need," Wesley said. "I've got you covered, boss."

"Well, cool," Polly said. "I'll see you tomorrow, Jeffries. Thanks."

"No need to thank me, miss," Jeffries said with a small bow. "Let me know if I can be of service in the meantime."

Jeffries was out the door as quietly as he'd entered.

Erinn wheeled on Wesley, who was blithely wrapping up the rest of the equipment. She could not remember meeting a more arrogant man in her entire life.

Dymphna carried the rabbits from their habitat to the grassy area of the yard she'd cordoned off for their use. She sat in the thick grass and looked around her farm as the Angoras hopped languidly around the yard. She'd made a life for herself here. It would soon be a busy fall. The goats' hair would need to be collected, as well as the rabbits'. In a few years, her farm and the vineyards would keep her busy all year long. Fruits would need to be canned and made into preserves starting in early summer, followed by the animals' hair being thinned in the fall and the garden mulched and prepared for the following spring. Winter would give her time to knit new creations from both the goat and rabbit mohair. As the weather warmed, she'd start a garden and make repairs to her farm buildings, in preparation for yet another spring. It seemed perfect, everything she'd ever wanted in life.

Blanche jumped in Dymphna's lap. She absentmindedly stroked the Angora's soft fur as she thought about Professor Johnson. In all her plans, Professor Johnson was front and center. She guiltily admitted to herself that although there were times when she pictured a future without Fat Chance, she never pictured her future in Fat Chance without Professor Johnson. She looked up at the hills that embraced Fat Chance, covered in their fledgling grapevines. She didn't know much about their timeline—when the grapes would be harvested, when they would be turned into wine, what would happen to the wine once it was made. The professor was interested in her every thought about the farm and she certainly wasn't returning the favor in terms of being interested in his passions. She felt guilty when she realized how much she took him for granted.

After returning the rabbits to their habitat, she let the goats and chickens back into the barnyard. Although she would never let the Angoras hop around the dirt barnyard, she always put the other animals in the barn when it was time to let the rabbits roam. The rabbits were used to tranquility, and a pen full of farm animals was anything but tranquil.

She stood up and looked down at the town. She smiled as she saw Professor Johnson coming out of the Boozehound with Thud by his side. She made a vow to herself that she would take more of an interest in Professor Johnson's passions. Even if she disagreed with his vision, his heart was in the right place.

Her smile faded when she saw Maggie pop out from inside the jail and stride over to Professor Johnson. Dymphna walked to the edge of the farm and leaned on the fence in the vain hope that the wind would carry the conversation up from the boardwalk. The professor and Maggie seemed oblivious to Dymphna watching them. But Thud turned his large square head in her direction and wagged his tail. Then he turned and followed Professor Johnson and Maggie into the jail.

Dymphna gripped the fence post. Maggie always accused her of running away from confrontation, but Maggie was always confronting her. Dymphna decided she was not going to run this time. She would just stay up here and keep herself busy. There was always plenty to do on a farm. Then she quickly changed her mind and ran down the hill as fast as she could toward the jail.

She was out of breath when she hit Main Street. She slowed her pace, refusing to arrive winded and wild-eyed at the jail. She walked briskly past the shuttered Boozehound and the café. She was in Pappy's domain now, passing the bank and city hall. She stood in front of the jail. Peeking in the window, she saw that Maggie and Professor Johnson were not in the room, nor in the cell. Thud was curled up inside, in a patch of sunlight.

Why aren't you guarding Professor Johnson? Dymphna thought irrationally.

She tested the door. It opened instantly and Dymphna crept inside. Thud scrambled to his feet and staggered sleepily toward her. She scratched his head while she listened. She couldn't hear any conversation coming from the back room, but since the door was slightly ajar—as all doors in Fat Chance tended to be—she made her way to the back room. No one was there.

Thud looked up at her.

"Where is Daddy, big guy?" Dymphna asked.

She hated referring to Professor Johnson as "Daddy," but refused to call a human being "master." She tried calling Professor Johnson Thud's "friend," but that just sounded cloying. Next, she gave "human" a shot. Nothing seemed to fit, so she settled on "Daddy."

Thud seemed to understand and scratched at the back door. Dymphna looked out the small window and saw the professor and Maggie, heads bent together. Before she knew it, she'd opened the door and Thud had rushed past her. Maggie bent to pat the dog, as if being in the backyard with her sister's boyfriend was the most natural thing in the world.

Of course, Dymphna thought, *for Maggie, it* was *the most natural thing in the world.*

Professor Johnson looked up when he saw Dymphna standing in the doorway. She worried she was going to have to explain why she'd barged in on them and was hoping to come up with something better than "I saw you two together and it sent me into a jealous fit." Professor Johnson spoke first.

"Maggie noticed a bug on the grapes and wanted to alert me," he said. "In case it's some sort of epidemic."

The three of them stared up at the grape arbor as if waiting for it to impart its wisdom. Dymphna noticed that Professor Johnson was holding a cluster of red mustang grapes in his hands.

"Is it some sort of epidemic?" Dymphna asked, although she already knew the answer.

This was just one of Maggie's ploys: pretending to be interested in Dymphna's boyfriend's passion. Dymphna flashed back to middle school, when Maggie suddenly took an interest in college football, which happened to be Dymphna's crush's favorite sport. Or in high school, when Maggie suddenly started learning how to play the guitar and ended up in Dymphna's boyfriend's band—and bed. By college, Maggie had taken up knitting and was presenting sweaters and scarves to anyone in whom Dymphna seemed to have a remote interest. Dymphna steamed inwardly, but had to hand it to Maggie; it was a damn good tactic. It had worked then and was apparently working now.

Maggie giggled. "I think I jumped the gun."

"Oh?" Dymphna said.

"Professor Johnson said it was just an ant."

"An ant," Dymphna said, as if she'd never heard of one before.

"Yes," Professor Johnson said. "Crisis averted."

Chapter 23

Dymphna loved Professor Johnson's naïveté. As they climbed the hill to the farm, he told Dymphna how Maggie had stopped him on his way out the door, sure there was a pest invading the grapes on Pappy's arbor. She said she'd heard about the brown marmorated stinkbug invading vineyards in the East and South and was afraid that if there were bugs on the arbor, they were probably on the vines as well.

"Of course, there hasn't been an outbreak of stinkbugs anywhere near Texas, but I was curious," Professor Johnson said. "Better to be safe than sorry."

"I couldn't agree more," Dymphna said grimly.

"Your sister is a very smart woman."

"Oh, I know that," Dymphna said. "Believe me."

Thud was already at the gate when they arrived hand in hand. Professor Johnson opened the gate and the three of them walked to the farmhouse, illuminated by one light glowing from the kitchen. Dymphna loved the sight of the farmhouse. It was tiny and mis-shapen, but in her eyes, it was perfect. She thought back to the day she arrived in Fat Chance and Pappy announced that Cutthroat Clarence had left her a real, working farm, with Angora goats, chickens, and fruit trees. She never knew Professor Johnson's grandfather, but he certainly knew her. She put her arms around Professor Johnson as she stood, taking in the beauty that was her home.

"By the way," Professor Johnson said, stopping in the quiet barnyard. "What brought you to town? I wasn't late, was I? You weren't worried about me, were you?"

"No, you weren't late," she said. "But, yes, I was worried about you."

They fell into their comfortable routine, Professor Johnson checking on the animals and Dymphna starting dinner. Thud was the only one without a pattern. He sometimes followed Professor Johnson around the farm, but was just as likely to stay in the kitchen with Dymphna.

Thud is quite the goodwill ambassador, Dymphna thought as she reached down to give his head a pat, happy that the bloodhound had favored her this evening.

Dymphna put last night's rice and vegetables in a bowl for Thud on the floor. The dog pounced. Dymphna loved Thud's appreciation of leftovers. She served stuffed cabbage for the professor and herself, and they ate quietly.

Dymphna rested her hand on Professor Johnson's arm.

It's a perfect night, Dymphna thought. *I need to remember times like this.*

After dinner, they sat on the porch, taking in the night sky. Dymphna was curled in Professor Johnson's arms. She looked at the house. Although it still looked remarkably like it had when she first saw it, she and Professor Johnson had made enough improvements to make it theirs. Professor Johnson had put new screens in the doors and made screen frames for the windows. Each window was slightly different, so the frames had to be custom built. Dymphna had scrubbed the porch, and Polly came up one summer evening and painted a "welcome mat" in front of the door. Dymphna had also hauled out an old chest she'd found in the barn and dragged it onto the porch. She'd filled it with various afghans. No matter what the weather, one of her knitted mohair afghans would be perfect. She was currently wrapped up in one of the first blankets she'd knitted from her goats' wool. It was whisper soft and almost snowy white. She sighed contentedly. The porch swing creaked softly.

"I should oil those," Professor Johnson said, looking up at the rusty chains that held the swing.

He started to rise, but Dymphna pulled him back down.

"Just leave it," she said. "Who cares if it creaks? Everything creaks here. You just have to listen in a different way. Hear each creak and groan as a song from another era. It's part of the history of the place."

"That's one way of looking at it," Professor Johnson said.

Dymphna sensed he was not convinced. But there wasn't any way to get all the creaks out of Fat Chance. And to her mind, you shouldn't want to. She looked up at him.

"I want to know more about the grapes," she said.

"What do you want to know?"

She felt terrible when she heard the guarded tone in his voice.

"Anything," she said. "Everything. I think I got tired of fighting you about Main Street being paved and kind of shut down by the time the great grape debate started. That wasn't fair of me. I want to correct that."

"I know I can be dry."

"You mean boring? You're not!"

"I am. In my student reviews, all the kids said so."

"Well, you don't thump your chest getting a point across. But you certainly make yourself understood."

Professor Johnson took her face in his hands and kissed her. She snuggled closer.

Maggie is not getting this one, if I have to hear every grape statistic in Texas, thought Dymphna.

Thud, who was lying at their feet, lifted his head. Erinn struggled up the front stairs with her camera and tripod. Dymphna and Professor Johnson straightened up. Professor Johnson leapt up and grabbed the tripod from her.

"Let me help you with that," he said.

Dymphna noticed that Erinn relinquished it gratefully.

"Hope I'm not interrupting anything," Erinn said.

"I was just about to explain to Dymphna why Fernando and I have differing views on how the wine should be handled," Professor Johnson said.

"But I thought there wasn't going to be any wine for at least one, maybe two years," Erinn said, leaning against the railing to catch her breath. "I don't quite understand why you're fighting about it now."

"The business plan has to be hammered out long before the first grape ripens," Professor Johnson said.

Dymphna smiled. Professor Johnson might be the only man in the world who could sound poetic while explaining a business plan.

"I made stuffed cabbage. Just picked the cabbage today," Dymphna said. "Are you hungry?"

"I'm starving, now that you mention it," Erinn said.

"I'll heat it up," Dymphna said, realizing that the prospect of a romantic evening had been killed with the first squeak of the gate.

Erinn sat on the rail with her legs crossed in front of her. She tilted her head back and closed her eyes. In the fading light, Dymphna could see the panic in Professor Johnson's eyes. If Dymphna left the porch, he would be obliged to make small talk. He was terrible at small talk. But so was Erinn. Dymphna hurriedly prepared the cabbage, in order to return and relieve Erinn and Professor Johnson of the burden of conversation.

She came back with a steaming plate of stuffed cabbage, pushing the screen door open with her backside. Erinn was no longer languidly relaxing on the porch railing. She was sitting bolt upright, tensed and ready for verbal battle. Dymphna had seen that body language before.

"If Theophilus hadn't died in 842, there wouldn't *be* an Iconoclastic Controversy," Erinn said.

"Because his widow restored icon veneration in 843?" Professor Johnson parried. "You can't seriously make that claim. Who knows what else might have transpired?"

Erinn counter-parried by dragging Dymphna into the conversation. "Dymphna, the Iconoclastic Controversy. Thoughts?"

Dymphna hated it when Erinn asked for her thoughts.

"There's no denying it's controversial," Dymphna said, calculating that the dates they were speaking of meant the whole thing took place in the ninth century. "But it seems as if that's old news. It is what it is."

Both Professor Johnson and Erinn looked pleased, as if Dymphna had come down firmly on both their sides. Dymphna handed over the cabbage and sat back on the swing with Professor Johnson.

"How was your day?" Dymphna asked, stuffing Erinn and Professor Johnson into a time machine and bringing them back from the Byzantine Empire.

"Exhausting. Slow going, with all the drama in this town. But that's good," Erinn said. She waved a fork of cabbage at Dymphna. "This is amazing, by the way."

"Thanks," Dymphna said, glad the night sky was dark and hid her flushed face. She loved compliments from Erinn, who only doled them out when she really meant them. "Is Jeffries back as your PA?"

"No," Erinn said. She stopped eating and put her fork down. "Professor Johnson, I know Wesley is a friend of your family's, but he is just impossible. I hope I'm not offending anyone."

"If by 'anyone' you mean me, then no," Professor Johnson said. "I hardly know the man."

"He insists on being my production assistant. I can't get rid of him."

"You're in charge," Professor Johnson said. "It's within your power to fire him."

"I can't fire him. I need someone to help, and he keeps sending Jeffries on errands. Tomorrow Jeffries is driving Polly to Galveston."

"In the limo?" Professor Johnson asked.

"Of course in the limo," Erinn replied. "It's the only car in town."

Dymphna and Professor Johnson became very quiet, missing Pappy and his Covered Volkswagen.

"Did you learn anything interesting?" Dymphna asked.

"Yes. It's been . . . actually, it's been fascinating getting information from those of you who were chosen to come here," Erinn said. "Although I'm only halfway through the interviews."

"That's right," Dymphna said. "You haven't interviewed me yet."

"But you guys are only half the story," Erinn said. "The scheme of getting you guys to Fat Chance must have taken Cutthroat months to formulate. That's a huge part of the story I want to tell and, as far as I can see, there's no way to tell it."

"He didn't do it alone," Professor Johnson said. "I mean, Wesley was the one who contacted all of us. He must have had a hand in it."

"Regardless," Erinn said, "Cutthroat was the mastermind. He's the one with the answers I want. And that Sebastian Pennyfeather, he could have answered all of my questions. Those two were the heavy hitters. And they're both gone. All I've got is Wesley. And, boy, do I have Wesley."

"You know, I just remembered something," Professor Johnson said. "Pappy knew Cutthroat, too."

"Oh, great," Erinn said. "I'm just batting a thousand."

Chapter 24

Dymphna couldn't sleep. She squinted at the clock on the side table. It was four o'clock—still several hours before dawn. She wondered if it was possible to get out of bed without waking Professor Johnson or Thud. She scooted sideways. Professor Johnson stirred briefly, rolled on his side, and settled back down. Thud let out a low moan, which morphed into a yowl. Dymphna put her fingers to her lips. The dog focused his rheumy eyes on her as she stood up, then flopped back to sleep.

Erinn was sitting in the living room, staring into the LCD screen hinged to her camera. She was frowning, but Dymphna couldn't tell if it was from concentration or consternation. Dymphna tried not to make any noise as she came into the room, but the floorboards would have none of it and sang out her arrival. Erinn looked up.

When did Erinn start wearing reading glasses? Dymphna wondered.

"Everything OK?" Dymphna asked as she went into the kitchen.

"Fine, I suppose," Erinn said. "I made some tea. Feel free to have some."

"Thanks." Dymphna took a mug from the shelf and poured herself some strong mint tea.

"Don't thank me," Erinn said absently. "It's your tea."

Dymphna came into the living room. She sat, silently watching Erinn's eyes move back and forth over the screen, the hum of the interviews too low to decipher. Erinn clicked off the camera and rubbed her eyes.

"I should have brought my F55," Erinn said.

"Oh?" Dymphna offered.

Dymphna worried that Erinn was about to mount a technological version of the obscure Iconoclastic Controversy discussion. Dymphna knew nothing about cameras.

"I didn't want to bring my expensive camera to a dusty old ghost town," Erinn said, pointing to the camera on the coffee table. "And now I'm paying the price."

"I'm sure it will be fine," Dymphna said. "Your work is always wonderful."

Erinn took a tiny chip out of the camera and slipped it into a slot on her laptop, which had been sitting beside her.

"What are you doing?" Dymphna asked.

"Remember when I used to shoot on digital tape?" Erinn asked, perking up at the prospect of camera talk. "Well, now all the media is on a little memory card. I just download it onto the laptop, delete what I've shot, and start over. Saves me from carrying boxes of tapes everywhere I go."

"What happens if you lose your laptop?"

"Don't even put that into the universe."

Since Erinn didn't believe in help or hindrance from the universe, Dymphna knew a lost computer would be a very serious consequence.

"Do I seem happy to you?" Erinn suddenly blurted.

"Happy?" Dymphna asked, startled by the randomness of the question. "I don't think 'happy' would be the first word that comes to mind when I think of you."

Dymphna saw a shadow pass across Erinn's eyes. Dymphna had learned over the years that, for all her bravado, Erinn was as insecure as everyone else. Dymphna hurried on.

"I would say 'brilliant,' 'motivated,' 'curious,'" Dymphna said. "And by 'curious,' I mean you have a lot of curiosity, not 'curious' like you're weird."

"I probably fit both descriptions," Erinn said, raising her mug of tea. "Why do you ask?"

"I've just been thinking a lot about happiness since I started these interviews. As I'm going through this footage, it occurs to me that all of you came to Fat Chance not for the money but for a chance to be happy. None of you, except for Cutthroat's family—"

"You mean Cleo and Professor Johnson."

"Yes. Except for them, none of you had really *landed* anywhere."

Dymphna lowered her eyes. She thought she had landed in Santa Monica with Erinn's family. Erinn's family thought so, too.

Did they feel betrayed when I told them I wasn't coming back? Did all the people I've run from my whole life feel betrayed or abandoned?

Did Maggie?

Dymphna shook her head. Her pattern of skipping town when things got tough may have started with Maggie. But Maggie deserved it. When she looked up again, Erinn was tapping on her computer. She pulled the chip out of the computer and reinserted it into the camera.

"I want this to be a hard-hitting documentary," Erinn said. "But I'm beginning to worry that I've got a nonfiction *Wizard of Oz*."

"'There's no place like home'?"

"Exactly," Erinn said dismally. "Not exactly award-winning stuff."

"You still have a lot more to shoot," Dymphna said, feeling defensive that Fat Chance wasn't proving to be more exciting. "You might still find the wizard who holds all the secrets."

"The way this is going, I'll find the wizard," Erinn said, "and he'll be dead."

"Is this you starting to work on being happy?"

Erinn snorted.

"As long as we're both awake, do you want to do my interview?" Dymphna asked, happy to change the subject.

"Won't we wake the gentlemen?" Erinn nodded to the bedroom. Dymphna assumed she meant Professor Johnson and Thud.

"I think we'll be fine."

"OK, good idea," Erinn said. "Let me start setting up and you go brush your hair. And change your T-shirt. Do you have anything light blue?"

"I do . . . not sure if it's clean though," Dymphna said.

"Don't worry about that," Erinn said. "Just put it on. If it's clean to your shoulders, we're good to go."

Dymphna got up, realizing she and Erinn were both more comfortable when Erinn was in control of the situation. When Dymphna returned in a wrinkled shirt and smoothed hair, Erinn had already set up two chairs, a tripod, and a light bar in the kitchen. Thud followed Dymphna as far as the living room and curled up in the only darkened corner he could find. Erinn's light bar had the kitchen looking as bright as daylight; the light was so strong that it lit the living room as well. Dymphna tiptoed back to the bedroom door and stuffed a towel under it. It wasn't an effective solution, as there were so many cracks in the door and gaps in the doorframe. However, Dymphna suspected that after years of trying to stay asleep while Thud moved around on the bed, pawed at him and barked for breakfast, Professor Johnson would most likely just pull the covers over his head and stay asleep.

Erinn motioned for Dymphna to take a seat.

"Please say your name and spell it," Erinn began.

"Dymphna Pearl. D-Y-M-P-H-N-A, like the saint, and P-E-A-R-L, like the oyster."

"Thank you."

"I was named after the patron saint of the insane," Dymphna offered, looking right into the camera.

She knew Erinn already was aware of this little factoid, but Dymphna was always asked "What kind of name is that?" so she decided to clarify.

"Don't look in the lens," Erinn said. "Talk to me."

"Oh. Sorry."

"Not a problem. OK, tell me about your experience with Cutthroat Clarence."

"I didn't have one."

"That is less than helpful, Dymphna."

"Oh. Right. Sorry. OK, let me think," Dymphna said, shaking out her hands. "OK. I'm ready."

"All right."

"What was the question again?" Dymphna said, her cheeks coloring. "I'm sorry, I'm really nervous."

"Don't be nervous. There is no right or wrong answer."

Dymphna's nervousness intensified. People often said that there were no right or wrong answers, but that wasn't true. Or maybe it was true—maybe there were just satisfactory or unsatisfactory answers.

"Let's try it this way," Erinn continued. "How did Cutthroat Clarence affect your life?"

"You already know that," Dymphna said. "Why don't you tell the story? You're so much better with words than me."

"Than I."

"See?"

"I think it would have more impact if you told the story yourself."

"All right." Dymphna took a deep breath. "I was trying to raise Angora sheep in Malibu. There was a plot of land I was leasing for very little money. It was really rough going, though. Everything in Malibu is expensive. But somehow, I was keeping my head above water. Little by little, I was making a name for myself in the little boutiques from Malibu to Santa Monica, selling the knitwear I made from the Angora mohair. That was one good thing about the area. Even my knitwear was overpriced."

"Go on."

"One day, I got a letter from . . . somebody. I don't remember who. But it said they were *tripling* my rent."

"Was that even legal?"

"I have no idea, but I didn't even have enough money to find that out. I sold the sheep, which broke my heart, and answered an ad on Craigslist about a guesthouse for rent in Santa Monica, which had a large yard. I thought maybe I could start over and raise Angora rabbits—you know, less overhead. It feels strange telling you this part, since the guesthouse was yours."

"Pretend I'm not here."

"But keep looking at you, even though you're not here?"

"Yes. Please go on."

"When I got my letter from Mr. Tensaw's . . . Wesley's office, I had no idea he had anything to do with my time in Malibu. But of course, once I got to Cleo's house and watched Cutthroat's video, I found out the truth."

"Which was?"

"Which was that Cutthroat was the guy who bought the land out from under me in Malibu."

"How did you feel about that?"

"Well . . ." Dymphna paused. "I wasn't happy about it, but I didn't really blame him. If he hadn't bought the land, somebody else would have. I didn't feel like he *owed* me anything. That's not how life works. If it wasn't for the fact that every single one of us had to go to Fat Chance before anybody could claim the inheritance, I might not even have come."

"Are you glad you did?"

Dymphna paused again. If she told the truth, that she *was* glad she had come, it meant that she was happy to have left her life in Santa Monica as Erinn's almost-sister. Talk about an unsatisfactory answer.

"It has its moments," Dymphna said truthfully.

"Let's talk about your sister."

"Why?" Dymphna asked sharply. "What has she got to do with this?"

"She's here," Erinn said. "And she certainly is impacting your time in this town. That much is obvious."

"What do you want to know?"

"How about the fact that all the time you lived in my guesthouse, I never knew you had another . . . had a family," Erinn said hotly.

"Clearly, I didn't mention it for a reason."

"Which was?"

"My sister and I never really got along. I don't like to drag negative energy with me, so I just . . . never mentioned her."

"Tell me about your upbringing."

Dymphna felt cornered. She would have accused Erinn of setting a trap for her, except she herself had suggested the interview.

"Nothing documentary-worthy about my family," Dymphna said. "My parents both worked in retail in Kansas City—Missouri, not Kansas. They were quiet. They went to work, came home, made dinner and saw that we did our homework."

"Would you say you had a happy childhood?"

What's with Erinn and her focus on the word "happy"? Dymphna thought.

"It was an adequate childhood," Dymphna said. "My parents weren't what you'd call warm."

"Where are they now?"

"My mother died seven years ago. My father died four years ago."

Erinn gasped. "Your father died since I've known you?"

"Yes, but I didn't know until after the funeral. Maggie didn't see fit to tell me."

"You'd lost touch with them?"

"Yes, years before," Dymphna said. "Maggie pretty much put everyone in the position of taking her side or my side. She was always a good talker and everyone always took her side. As soon as I was old enough to leave Kansas City, I did. And I didn't look back."

"Why do you think Maggie is here?"

Dymphna wanted to say "To make me miserable," but she knew she would sound childish. Instead she said, "Maybe she was bored. That happens a lot with her."

"I guess we've covered enough ground for now—" Erinn began, but Dymphna cut her off.

"May I say one more thing?" Dymphna asked.

"Certainly," Erinn said. Dymphna could hear the surprise in her voice.

"I know you have had your ups and downs with your own family," Dymphna said. "But you never felt unloved. It's different when you feel unloved. I won't say that my parents didn't do their best, but they were no match for Maggie. Maybe I shouldn't have shut them completely out of my life. You always think you'll have time to fix things. And suddenly, you don't.

"Here's the main thing I got from Cutthroat. He turned his back on his problems just like I did on mine. Cutthroat said in his videotape that each time he screwed somebody over, it got easier the next time. Each time I ran into a situation that would take some work to fix, I left. When I came back to Santa Monica—and wasn't sure I would return to Fat Chance—I started to think about that. I don't want to keep running. I don't want to end up like Cutthroat Clarence. I'm going to do the work this time."

"Does that include Maggie?"

As the sun came up, the two women sat looking at each other.

Erinn shut off the camera.

Chapter 25

Polly was pouring coffee for Poet. He always arrived before the breakfast crowd so they could have a few minutes together.

"Are you upset that I'll be in Galveston for a day or two?" Polly asked.

"Nope," Poet said, adding sugar to his coffee. He took a sip.

"I mean, I don't *want* to go; I *have* to go."

"Yep."

"I'll think about you every minute I'm gone. I'm really going to miss you," Polly said. "And I know you'll miss me."

"Yep."

"You're so sweet," Polly said, kissing the top of his head.

Fernando stuck his head out of the kitchen and glared at her. Polly scowled back at him.

"I don't know how he expects me to know what he's thinking," Polly said, but she followed Fernando into the kitchen. "What?" she asked.

Fernando blazed. "We might have other customers who want coffee."

"Really?" Polly looked into the dining room. "Where?"

Except for Poet, the room was empty.

"You have to be prepared," Fernando said. "You never know when the rush will start."

"Yes, I will," Polly said, pointing to the clock. "The rush starts in two minutes."

Polly left the kitchen, and in exactly two minutes, cowboys started pushing through the door. Polly caught Fernando's eye through the tiny pass-through window. When she first got to Fat Chance, she would have flipped him off. But then again, when she first got to Fat Chance, nobody would have hired her to work with the public.

By the time Polly had flirted with all the cowboys, gotten orders into the kitchen, and made a round with the coffeepot, the center table was full. Polly counted heads; all the regular suspects were at the table, except one.

"Where's Jeffries?" she asked.

"He's washing the limo," Cleo said. "He wants it to be clean when you head to Galveston."

"He shouldn't bother," Polly said. "I don't need a clean car."

"Don't worry," Professor Johnson said. "By the time he gets down Main Street, the car will be dirty again anyway."

Fernando was putting a platter of fluffy eggs on the table. "Not Main Street again," he said. "Don't you have anything else to talk about?"

"Yes, I do," Professor Johnson said, unruffled. "I can talk about grapes, if that's of any interest to you."

"Only if you've come to your senses," Fernando said before stalking away.

Jeffries appeared at the door. "The limo is ready anytime," he said to Polly.

"OK," Polly said. "Let me just finish my shift and . . ."

Maggie sprang from the table. "You go ahead," she said. "I've been a waitress. I can finish your shift."

"That's crazy," Polly said.

"No, seriously, I'm happy to do it," Maggie said, whipping the apron off Polly's hips and grabbing the coffeepot. In a low voice she added, "You'll be doing me a favor. I can't sit at that table any longer."

"OK," Polly said hesitantly.

"Besides," Maggie said, her voice a little more secure, "that cute guy in the corner looks like he could use a hot beverage."

Polly looked at the guy Maggie was pointing out. It was Poet.

"That's my boyfriend," Polly said.

"Husband?"

"No," Polly said. "Boyfriend."

"Just clarifying," Maggie said, putting the coffeepot down and tying on the apron. She reached back for the coffeepot, but Polly had picked it up.

"Let me tell you something," Polly said. "I'm not Dymphna. You go near Poet and I'll eat you for breakfast."

Polly handed Maggie the coffeepot and stormed out the door. She could hear Maggie explaining to Fernando that she was finishing Polly's shift.

"You're doing what?" Fernando said, his voice climbing an octave. "Dear sweet Lady of Fatima!"

As angry as she was, Polly couldn't help but laugh.

Poor Fernando.

Polly and Jeffries loaded the limousine with hatboxes.

"Can I ride shotgun?" Polly asked. "I'd feel stupid riding in the back."

"Certainly, miss," Jeffries said, opening the door for her.

"And none of this 'miss' stuff," Polly said. "Or opening doors, even. Too weird. We're a team."

"Yes, miss," Jeffries said as they started up the street.

Polly turned to look at him, wondering if he was joking. He was clearly distracted. She followed his gaze. Together they watched Titan returning to the forge as they drove out of town, up the newly paved road.

"Do you know Titan?" Polly asked.

"I only saw him at the mansion the day you all came up for the reading," Jeffries said.

"Do you remember me with all my makeup and studs?" Polly asked. "Up at the mansion?"

"I do," Jeffries said.

"Man, that was some day!"

"Yes, it was. That was some day."

Cleo stood on Main Street, pretending to be having one random conversation after another with people coming out of the café. As the crowd thinned, she looked in the window and saw Maggie clearing dishes. She calculated that she had at least an hour before Maggie showed up at Powderkeg's for the day.

She walked down the boardwalk and into Powderkeg's store. The smell of leather brought her back to their days as a young couple traveling the craft-fair circuit. She could hear Powderkeg in the back room. As she stood looking around the store, she realized she had no idea what she wanted to say to her ex-husband. They were past the point of any possibility of rekindling a romance, especially after he practically threw her out of Fat Chance the last time she was in town.

That wasn't exactly true, she told herself. But he did have the nerve to fall in love with somebody else. She'd had to leave with her tail between her legs, which was just as bad as being thrown out of town. Maybe worse! Just because things didn't work out with that long-legged Lacey, didn't mean there was any room for her. He'd made that clear. She turned to go.

"What's up, Cleo?" Powderkeg said.

She turned around to see him standing in the doorway between the front- and back rooms.

"I just came by to see how you were doing." Cleo could hear the false note in her voice and knew he could hear it, too.

"Can't complain," Powderkeg said. "Your old man ended up doing all right by me, I have to say. I never dreamed I'd ever have a shop like this with a clientele who appreciate quality workmanship."

"I appreciate quality workmanship," Cleo said, stung.

"Yeah." Powderkeg smiled. "For a belt that will last a season or a purse that might last two."

"I'll have you know, I have a Saint Laurent that looks as good as the day I bought it twenty years ago."

"I stand corrected."

Cleo sighed. "I don't want to intrude on your . . . quality workmanship," she said. "I'd better go."

She turned toward the door, but Powderkeg gently grabbed her forearm and spun her around.

"Don't go," he said.

She looked up at him, trying to gauge his feelings. Trying to gauge her own. He bent toward her and she closed her eyes.

The door banged open. They straightened and stared at the intruder.

It was Maggie.

"I hope I'm not interrupting anything," Maggie said. "I thought I might be, but then I figured you're a little old to be fooling around on a workday. Or fooling around at all!"

Maggie went into the back room. Cleo and Powderkeg smiled shyly at each other. Powderkeg dropped his gaze to the floor.

"Your boots could use some polish," he said. "Maybe I'll stop by the inn later and fix them up. Would that be all right with you?"

Titan stood back and looked over the Cinderella carriage. It was coming along nicely. He'd added burnished metal, shaped like leaves and corkscrew vines, to the top. He'd also added two side lanterns. The lanterns didn't actually work, but he thought Powderkeg might have some thoughts on that. He had plans to add a scallop of green-toned metal to the open door frames. He stood back, assessing the coach. He wanted to carry out the green somewhere else on the coach. Polly had taught him all about color and shading. He didn't use much of his new knowledge when he was making horseshoes, but when it came to the Cinderella coach, he could see that he had applied her lessons. He would have to thank her when he saw her.

His back was to the field behind him. He was so engrossed in his work that he didn't hear Rocket come up behind him. The large longhorn nudged him with his nose. Titan turned around and looked into the bull's huge brown eyes.

"Have I been ignoring you?" Titan said, scratching the spot between the immense horns. "I know I've been distracted about Fancy, but that doesn't mean I love you any less. You and I are family."

It wasn't easy to get his arms around the longhorn, but Titan hugged the bull awkwardly.

"You and I have had some bad luck lately," he said. "First Fancy and then Pappy taking off like that. I can't believe they're never coming back. They loved us. Fancy, well, you just had to guess, but Pappy told me a million times that I was like a son to him. Well, not in so many words. Pappy would never say anything that sentimental, but I knew what he meant. I mean, nobody can ever replace your mom, but Pappy really tried to be there for me."

Titan had stopped scratching the bull and Rocket nudged him.

"I don't know what it is about me that everybody is always leaving," Titan said, looking at the bull. "You're all I have left, big guy, so I'm begging you—don't leave me. I just don't think I could take any more."

Titan put his head on the bull's forehead and closed his eyes. Rocket held very still.

"I need to rethink this carriage," Titan said finally. "Right now, it's too heavy. I should get real wheels for this thing and then you could pull it down Main Street when we get it paved."

Rocket snorted.

"I know," Titan said. "Who knows if that will ever happen? But if it does, if Fancy comes home and Pappy comes home we'll have our own parade. I know Fancy will love the carriage. I'm not sure she'd be into a parade though. You know how she gets. Pappy will, though, being mayor and all. Can't you just see it? Pappy all dressed up, waving from his pumpkin coach? And I'd get Polly to make you a hat. How awesome would that be?"

Rocket snorted.

Chapter 26

"So. Dude," Polly said to Jeffries. "What's your deal?"

"My . . . deal?" Jeffries asked. "What do you mean?"

"Why are you here?"

"In Fat Chance?"

"Yeah."

"It's my job."

"Hmm," Polly said, looking out the passenger window as the Hill Country rolled by. "My father told me that if you pay attention, you can smell bullshit a mile away."

"Well," Jeffries said, looking in the rearview mirror, "we *are* in Texas."

Polly laughed. But she was not to be deterred.

"You *very* skillfully managed not to stay when you dropped Cleo off the first time. What changed?"

"I guess I'm getting rusty."

"So that's all I'm going to get?"

"That's it," Jeffries said. "Let's talk about you, shall we?"

"Works for me."

Jeffries turned on the windshield wipers as Polly warmed to the topic.

"Do you want to hear about my boyfriend or my plans for the future?" Polly asked.

"Surprise me."

"Well, Poet is leaving soon for Nebraska. I think I told you he's going to work on a wagon train, which is so cool. But I'm not sure he has the personality for that, you know? He's kind of quiet. Sort of like you."

"But I'm not planning on running a wagon train."

Polly giggled. "Anyway, when Erinn interviewed me, she asked about my plans for the future and I said I didn't really have any. But that got me thinking. Maybe I should go with Poet. I could be the friendly one."

"I see," Jeffries said. "What does Poet think of this?"

"He doesn't know yet," Polly said. "But on the other hand, I really like making my hats and other crafts and they're starting to really take off."

"Both directions sound very interesting."

"Can I ask you something? How come you became a chauffeur?"

"I look good in a uniform," Jeffries said. "And it pays better than the military."

"Seriously?"

"No," Jeffries said. "The fact of the matter is, I don't even remember. So, here's my advice—do one or the other. Or do neither and stay in Fat Chance. But own your decision. Don't wake up one day, look at your life, and wonder how you got there."

"OK," Polly said. "Thanks."

They stared out the window, one lost to the future, one to the past.

Erinn and Wesley were falling into a rhythm. Erinn carried the camera and a backpack full of gear while Wesley toted the tripod and light bar. Erinn quickened her pace when she spotted Cleo on the boardwalk.

"Cleo!" Erinn called out, but Cleo walked on. Erinn turned to Wesley. "Can you get her attention?"

"Not in the past twenty-five years," he said, smiling.

Erinn glowered and tried again.

"Cleo," she called. "Ms. Johnson-Primb?"

Cleo turned around and smiled at them. Erinn's antennae went up. Cleo wasn't one to smile. Cleo stood still, waiting for Wesley and Erinn to make their cumbersome way to her.

"She couldn't come to us?" Erinn said under her breath to Wesley.

"Have you met her?" Wesley said, almost looking like a ventriloquist as he spoke through his flashing white teeth while smiling brightly at Cleo.

"Yes?" Cleo asked when Erinn and Wesley finally reached her.

"I was wondering when might be a good time to interview you for the documentary," Erinn said.

"Never," Cleo said, her smile hardening. "Didn't Wesley tell you I never do interviews?"

"You do interviews all the time," Wesley said.

"Not about family, I don't," Cleo said. She turned to Erinn. "When you want to know my opinion on the latest happenings in Beverly Hills, I'll be happy to talk to you."

Cleo turned on the heels of her cowboy boots and started walking toward the inn at the far end of town. Erinn and Wesley watched her go.

"I don't understand," Erinn said. "What's with the reluctant debutante routine? She came here *because* of the documentary, didn't she?"

Wesley didn't say anything.

"Howdy," Powderkeg said, startling Erinn.

"Oh! Hi, Powderkeg," Erinn said.

Powderkeg tipped his hat but kept walking down the boardwalk.

"What am I missing?" she asked, turning to Wesley.

Wesley met her eyes, then looked down the boardwalk toward the end of town. Erinn followed his gaze. Cleo was headed up the stairs of the inn, turning and scanning the boardwalk before heading inside. Powderkeg was taking his time down the final stretch of boardwalk. He stepped into a cloud of dust on Main Street and made a beeline for the inn.

"Oh." Erinn looked up at Wesley.

Wesley barely nodded.

Erinn looked back at the inn and saw Powderkeg disappear inside.

"Oh!" she said.

Erinn mentally crossed Cleo off her to-do list of interviewees. She only had Old Bertha and Titan left, which made her nervous. She should have an angle on the story by now, and she didn't. If anything, the story seemed to be getting away from her. If she were doing a reality show, she thought, she'd have a gold mine. She could almost visualize it: two sisters, estranged, facing old demons for the first time in years. An heiress having a fling with her artisan ex-husband. A disappearing senior citizen leaves behind his heartbroken paramour. And that was just the tip of the iceberg. There was also the boy-crazy but equally talented tough-as-nails hat-maker with a heart of gold, a man the size of a mountain who turned to his craft to distract him from his sorrow over losing a beloved pet (Erinn wasn't sure the MIA buzzard would make the cut, but you never knew), and the thrill and passion of local politics as played out by the café owner and the museum curator.

She stole a glance at Wesley. If only his clients could see him now, sweating and struggling with camera gear as they made their way back down the boardwalk toward the grocery store.

She smiled to herself as she returned to producing the reality show in her mind. Comic relief provided by one of the most respected attorneys in the Golden Triangle of Beverly Hills. Her smile faded when she thought of Jeffries, the man in the background with the biggest secret of them all. He'd confided in her when he found out he'd be driving them all to Fat Chance, on the off chance she could think of a reason for him to stay. She thought of a reason, all right: He could be her production assistant. But Wesley seemed determined to dog her every step. At least Jeffries wasn't banished to Beverly Hills.

So much drama for such a small town.

If only she could capture some of that humanity for her documentary. But she was after more weighty stuff.

"We're here." Wesley's voice brought her back to the present.

Erinn looked up and they were standing in front of the grocery store. She peered in the window and could see Old Bertha stocking the shelves.

"Come on," Erinn said. "Let's see if we can sweet-talk Old Bertha into an interview."

"Maybe you should let me do the talking," Wesley offered as they stumbled into the grocery store. "She can be a little cantankerous."

Erinn gave Wesley a quizzical look.

Wesley shrugged. "I have a way with the ladies. If I do say so myself."

"I hadn't noticed," Erinn said.

She tried not to be a little stung that he hadn't felt an urge to extend that charm to her.

Old Bertha looked up from stocking her three rolls of paper towels. She watched as Erinn and Wesley put their gear down. They stared at one other.

"Got a special going on walnuts," Old Bertha finally said, putting another roll of paper towels on the shelf.

"Bertha, dear," Wesley said. The sappiness in his voice made Erinn cringe. "Could we have a moment of your valuable time?"

"Bertha, *dear*? My *valuable* time?" Old Bertha squinted at him. She turned to Erinn. "Is he trying to sell me snake oil?"

"I need to interview you for my documentary," Erinn said. "If now is a convenient time."

"Good a time as any," Old Bertha said. She turned to Wesley. "Your swanky ways won't get you anywhere with me, young fella."

"Apparently," Wesley said good-naturedly.

Erinn saw that she had perfect natural light streaming through the store windows, so she quickly set two chairs in place. When she turned to set up the camera, she saw that Wesley already had it set on the tripod. He looked at her.

"Lens height OK?" he asked.

Erinn had to admit, the man was a quick study.

Old Bertha sat herself heavily in the chair opposite Erinn.

Bertha Belmont said her name and spelled it, as instructed. At Erinn's prompting, Old Bertha began to reminisce.

"I guess I'm the only one who knew Clarence before he became 'Cutthroat,'" Old Bertha began. "I was barely twenty and he was edging toward thirty. I thought we were so grown-up, but looking back, we were practically kids. I'll never forget the day he hired me to work in his hardware store. I saw him hanging the Help Wanted sign in the window. I wasn't even looking for a job, to tell the truth, but when I saw that sign go up in the window, I didn't think twice. I walked right in and applied for the job. Which turned out to be a cashier. Every girl in town had a crush on Clarence, but he was all business. I didn't really think I had a chance with him, but getting to work in the store was better than nothing. And of course the bragging rights were, as Polly would say, off the hook."

Erinn could see Old Bertha was pleased with her twenty-first-century reference.

"You didn't even know what the job was?" Erinn asked.

Dymphna had been a font of background information, but Erinn hadn't absorbed it all and needed to consult her notes.

"Nope," Old Bertha said, suddenly looking decades younger. "That's one thing Clarence and I always had in common, I guess. We saw an opportunity and we never looked back."

"In your own words, tell me about coming to work one day and finding a Sold sign across the door. How devastated were you?"

"Why?" Old Bertha frowned. "Your words are just fine."

"Because my words don't matter," Erinn said, shaken at the truth of the statement. "Only yours do."

Old Bertha seemed to retreat into herself. Her protective walls seemed to have crashed, leaving her looking smaller and more vulnerable.

"That's all there was to it. I showed up for work one day, the hardware store was closed, and Clarence was gone. It took me nearly fifty years, until I was at Cleo's house for the reading of his will, to know what really happened."

"Which was?" Wesley asked.

Erinn spun around and glowered at him. He put his hands up in surrender.

Old Bertha took a deep breath. "He got a lead on a better investment. I think he said it was a restaurant. Have I got that right, Mr. Tensaw?"

"Yes, I believe that's what he said. Please go on," Wesley said, trying to return the spotlight to Old Bertha.

"In his videotape, he said he used the money he'd saved up for my engagement ring to buy into it," Old Bertha said. "I never knew he was planning on asking me to marry him."

"Would you have said yes?" Erinn asked, realizing she was once again slipping out of the documentarian mode she was trying so hard to maintain.

"What difference does that make?" Old Bertha said forcefully, her protective walls shooting back up.

The interview ended. Erinn noticed that Old Bertha had made some progress on her leather and canvas quilt. It sat lumpily on the checkout counter. Erinn wanted to ask about it, but decided against it. Old Bertha didn't seem to invite conversation about her personal life. Erinn was lucky to get on tape what little information Old Bertha had offered. Erinn thanked her for her time. Old Bertha went about her business and Erinn and Wesley went about theirs.

Rain pounded the limousine as it made its way into Galveston.

"This is some storm," Polly said, squinting through the windshield. "I hope Lucinda's shop is open."

"Lucinda?" Jeffries asked.

"The lady who's buying my hats and stuff," Polly said, looking into the back of the limo to make sure everything was still there. "Can't imagine anybody's out shopping on a day like this."

Polly, luxuriating in cell phone reception, tapped on the weather app.

"Big storm coming through," Polly said.

Jeffries turned on the windshield wipers full blast.

"You really don't need an app to tell you that," he said. Jeffries followed the GPS to a small but elegant store on Moody Street.

He cut the engine and sat, listening to the storm. Hard rain blanketed the entire area from the stretch to the storefront. Suddenly, Polly's passenger door whipped open and a tall woman shielded by an enormous umbrella leaned inside.

"Hey, Polly! Crazy storm, right?" the woman said. She looked at Jeffries. "Nice ride. I'm Lucinda."

"Jeffries," Jeffries said, then glancing at Polly, added, "Donald. Donald Jeffries."

"Well, Jeffries Donald or Donald Jeffries, do you think you can get this boat behind the store so we can unload?" Lucinda asked, pointing up the street. "There's an alley around the corner."

"Sure," Jeffries said.

Lucinda slammed the door and disappeared into the store. Jeffries started the car and headed slowly up the street.

"If only this were a boat," Polly said.

Jeffries noticed Polly was gripping the seat so hard her knuckles were white.

"We'll be fine," Jeffries said. "This car has never let me down."

"There's always a first time," Polly said.

Chapter 27

Fernando watched the clouds grow darker and darker over the grape-vines. The tender stalks trembled on the hills.

He thought back to the days working in Napa alongside his father, shouldering the responsibilities and hard, hot labor of planting and nurturing grapes. He had sworn he would never get lured back into that life, but here he was, staring up at the trellises, willing them to survive whatever monster storm was headed their way.

They get under your skin, he thought. You watch over them like children, watch them grow and do your best to help them be something special. His father always assumed Fernando resented the hard work, but it was the heartbreak when the harvest failed that got to him. If only Professor Johnson could understand that.

As if summoned out of thin air, Professor Johnson suddenly appeared in the archway between the Boozehound and the café. He looked as worried as Fernando.

"Want some peach brandy?" Fernando offered.

Professor Johnson nodded, dropping wearily into a chair at the center table. Fernando watched him. How had this man become his adversary? They'd started out wanting exactly the same thing—a wine in which they could take pride. Their differences of opinion seemed silly now. Worse than silly. A complete waste of resources and energy.

"We're in for it, I think," Professor Johnson said. "I can't get any weather information even on Main Street. But the sky keeps getting darker."

"Green?" Fernando asked as he poured the yellow liquid into two mason jars.

"Pardon?"

"Is the sky green?"

"Now that you mention it, there was a greenish cast."

"That means we're probably going to get a full-blown tornado."

"Can the grapes survive?" Professor Johnson asked, taking a sip of the brandy.

"Maybe yes, maybe no." Fernando shrugged. "Tornados are funny. They can take out one whole side of a street and not even touch the other. They can level a house and the house next to it won't have lost a single shingle."

"I'd hate to see all of this taken away before we even got started."

"I'll drink to that, amigo."

"How do you know so much about tornados?" Professor Johnson asked. "I thought you always lived on the West Coast."

"I did," Fernando said. "But I did a lot of research in my academic career."

"I didn't know you had an academic career."

"See? You've never given me enough credit."

"Where did you go?"

"St. Ellen's," Fernando said. "Did my third grade extra credit report on tornados after seeing *The Wizard of Oz*."

Silence ensued until Professor Johnson said, "Well, I don't think there is anything we can do now to protect the vines from a tornado. Our differences seem ridiculous now. When the storm is over, we might not even have grapes or a road."

"On the other hand, we might have no damage at all," Fernando said. "And we can go right back to fighting."

"To fighting," Professor Johnson said, raising his mason jar.

"*Sí, a peleando*," Fernando said, saluting in return.

Chapter 28

The clouds continued to roll in. An unearthly calm would suddenly give way to howling winds which would in turn subside again into eerie quiet.

Dymphna and Professor Johnson struggled up the hill from town toward the farm. The wind had started to pick up. Dymphna wanted to make sure all the animals were safely inside the barn. Thud's jowls quivered in the breeze.

"If there's a tornado coming, we should get the animals into the cellar," Professor Johnson said.

"I thought we were just supposed to have a storm," Dymphna said.

"Better play it safe," Professor Johnson said, deciding not to repeat all he'd learned from Fernando's third-grade report. "But I'm guessing there is a fine line between storm and tornado around here."

"Do you think we'll survive a tornado?" Dymphna asked. "I know the town has been nearly destroyed twice. Are we in better shape to withstand one?"

"There's no way to calculate that," Professor Johnson said. "It depends on a lot of things. The ferocity of the twister, the improvements to the buildings and road . . ."

"You're not starting on the roads again, are you?" she asked. "We might be headed into a disaster and you're fixating on the road?"

"As a matter of fact, I'm not," Professor Johnson said. They picked up their pace as they got near the gate. "I'm much more worried about the grapes than I am the road."

They ran to the barnyard. Dymphna ran to check on the rabbits while Professor Johnson looked in on the goats. Thud sprinted into the barn, climbed onto a bale of hay, and curled up.

"The chicken coop is empty!" Dymphna raced into the barn, relieved to see her four Angora goats were all right.

She almost ran into Professor Johnson's back. He was staring into a corner of the barn, where the chickens were corralled.

"How did they get in here?" Dymphna asked.

"I brought them inside." Maggie's voice came out of the shadows. "I was thinking I should move the rabbits, too, but their house looks pretty sturdy."

"Actually, if a twister hits, we're going to have to move them all," Professor Johnson said.

"You won't have time to get them into town," Maggie said.

"I was thinking the cellar," Professor Johnson said.

"Is there room?" Maggie asked.

"There has to be," Professor Johnson said.

"Wait a minute! Wait a minute!" Dymphna said. "Excuse me, Maggie, but what made you think we needed your help?"

"Uh, look around you?" Maggie snarled. "A big storm is coming. I'm sorry if I overstepped your precious boundaries."

"I think it was very—" Professor Johnson started.

"Don't help," Dymphna snapped. "You have no idea what's going on here."

"Really?" Maggie arched an eyebrow. "Why don't you tell us then, Dymph. What *is* going on here?"

"I don't know exactly," Dymphna said. "But I know you didn't just come up here to help me save my farm."

"Oh, I forgot," Maggie said. "In the whole world, only *you* love animals."

Maggie stormed out of the barn. The door slammed heavily behind her. Thud looked up, but decided the barn was the place to be. He put his head back down.

"I'm not sure it's safe for her to head back into town," Professor Johnson said.

Dymphna pouted. "Can you believe she said I'm the only person in the world who loves animals?"

"I don't understand what you are so upset about. She was a big help."

"So now you're taking her side," Dymphna said, near tears. "I should have guessed."

She pulled the barn door open. She was hit by a blast of wind. She ran to the gate, her hair whipping around her face. She grabbed onto the gatepost, hoping the wind wouldn't pull her off her feet. When she saw her sister had made it back to town, she turned. Professor Johnson was standing there, looking at her.

"You're not so tough," he said.

Dymphna wrapped her arms round him and they made their way to the house, Thud at their heels.

Titan opened the back door to the forge and pulled Rocket inside. As he tried to settle the longhorn's nerves, Erinn and Wesley hurried in through the front.

"May I help you?" Titan asked.

"I thought we might set up that interview," Erinn said, inspecting her camera for rain damage.

"In this weather?"

"You've been hard to pin down, so I thought now might be as good a time as any," Erinn said.

"I thought I might go see if I can find Fancy, one more time," Titan said. "If she's hurt, she'll never survive this."

"Why don't you sit for my interview and then we'll help you," Erinn said.

She turned to look at Wesley. She hoped he understood the interview was just a ploy. She needed to keep this sweet soul from risking his life for a bird that in all probability was not out there waiting to be rescued. Wesley nodded.

Erinn and Wesley jumped when Rocket lowed. When Erinn turned back she saw Titan already sitting on a stool, looking out at the darkening sky. She and Wesley set up as quickly as they could.

"I know they call you Titan," Erinn said. "But could you tell me your name and spell it, please?"

"My name is Ray . . . well, Raymond Darling," Titan said. "R-A-Y-M-O-N-D D-A-R-L-I-N-G."

"Can you tell me a little about yourself, Titan?"

"There isn't much to tell," Titan said in a voice so soft Erinn had to turn up the audio levels. "I'm the son of Sweet Darling. Did you ever hear of her?"

Erinn nodded. She didn't want to say a word.

"She was a famous singer and dancer. She was the most beautiful person in the world and the best mother," Titan said. "She died one night after a concert went wrong. I was too little to know about it at the time, but they say she got caught lip-syncing and she ran in front of a car. Some of the press said it was suicide, but I don't believe that."

"Why?" Erinn whispered gently.

"Because she loved me," Titan said. "She loved me too much to leave me alone. At the reading of the will, Cutthroat said so. He said my mom would never have left me intentionally. It was almost thirty years later, but I guess he would know."

"What happened to you after that?"

"I grew up." Titan shrugged.

"And you never heard from Cutthroat Clarence in all that time?"

"No," Titan said. "I didn't even know who he was. In his video, he told me that he felt responsible for my mother's death, since he was financing her career. But his lawyer said he couldn't do anything to help me because that would mean he was admitting cul . . . culp . . ."

"Culpability," Wesley said.

"Yeah," Titan said. "That. So, I guess Cutthroat blamed himself, but I don't. Although I do have pretty hard feelings toward that lawyer, that Pennyfeather."

"He was only doing his job," Wesley said.

Erinn glared at him. Wesley knew better than that, both as an attorney *and* a production assistant.

"Sorry if I don't see it that way," Titan said. "I'm very grateful that Cutthroat left me this forge. I've found a real home for myself here. But I can't help but wonder what life would have been like if I'd had my mother all those years. And if I couldn't have my mother, it would have been nice if Pennyfeather had let Cutthroat contact me. I was only *six*. I didn't want his damned money. I wanted someone to care."

Chapter 29

Maggie stalked through the jail and into Pappy's former living quarters. She pulled a small bundle from her waistband, tossing it on the bed. She pulled a faded quilt around her shoulders and tried to still her shivers. She lit the little camping stove. The flame heated the room while Maggie filled a kettle and put it on to boil.

What is wrong with Dymphna? she wondered. *Couldn't she have just thanked me? It's not every day an estranged sister herds your animals out of the way of an approaching storm.*

Of course it's not every day an estranged sister breaks into your farmhouse looking for something, anything, to be used against you. Maggie had found something that she sensed might be of some value because of the way it had been hidden. Someone with less of a history of opportunism might not have noticed the little sliver in the wall that made a secret drawer. It crossed Maggie's mind that Dymphna herself might not even know about it, but she dismissed that. Even her space-cadet sister must know her own house! Maggie had taken a kitchen knife and wiggled the drawer open. Inside was a small pouch. The cloth was old and tied with a stubborn knot. She stuffed it in the waistband of her jeans and headed out the door. As she looked to make sure the coast was clear, she noticed the wind kicking up. The fact that your sister just burglarized your home should *not* negate the fact she took pity on your poor farm animals and got them into the barn.

Maggie made a hot cup of tea. She sat in the rocking chair and thought about how she had found her way to Fat Chance. She remembered telling Polly and Old Bertha how she managed to track Dymphna's knitwear to the store in Dripping Springs and from there to Fat Chance. She'd intentionally left out the middle part of the story. She couldn't find Fat Chance but had stumbled onto Spoonerville, where she'd met Dodge.

"You on your own?" Dodge had said. "Where's your watchdog?"

Maggie looked around the store, wondering if this man was talking to her. In seconds, she realized this man knew her sister.

"I think you have me confused with Dymphna. She's my sister," Maggie said. "I'm Mary Magdalene. Call me Maggie."

"The evil twin?" Dodge said, shaking her hand.

"More like the misjudged younger sister," Maggie said.

"I'm misjudged myself," Dodge said. "Pleased to meet you."

Dodge told her the story of Fat Chance and how Cutthroat Clarence had sent a group of innocent lambs into the Texas Hill Country to salve his own sorry conscience. He painted a picture of how his family had been swindled out of the town not once but twice, and he was always on the lookout for a way to get Fat Chance back. He bought Maggie a Coke and listened sympathetically as she recounted all Dymphna's wrongdoings and desertions. After an hour, Dodge suggested they could be partners and set things right.

"What do you mean by partners?" Maggie asked cautiously.

"I think you and I understand each other," Dodge said. "I'm guessing you're here in the middle of nowhere 'cause you don't have anywhere else to go. Am I right?"

Maggie reddened.

"I thought so," Dodge continued. "Well, you snoop around Fat Chance for a while, get me some dirt. Anything I can use to get my town back. And I'll give you enough money to get settled somewhere else."

"How much is that?" Maggie asked. "What if I want to settle in Manhattan?"

"Bring me something worth Manhattan, and we'll see," Dodge said seriously.

Maggie had not forgotten her deal with Dodge, but as hard as she tried, she had failed to come up with anything—until now. Aside from her sister being there, she found herself really liking the people of Fat Chance, and as time passed, she didn't want to find any dirty laundry. Even so, she kept trying. She had her own sense of honor, no matter how bent. She tried getting to know the men of the town, but that hadn't really worked out as planned. She tried befriending the women, but they didn't have any secrets either. She'd pretty much given up. She avoided Spoonerville so she wouldn't have to explain herself. But Dymphna's refusal to accept her in town was starting to get to her. So she decided to redouble her efforts. She went up to the farm when she knew Dymphna would be on Main Street. She worried that the humongous dog would be lurking or one of the goats would sense her ill will, but she'd walked right on into the farmhouse without a hitch.

The sound of hail on the roof brought Maggie back to the present. Even with the camp stove and the quilt, she couldn't get warm. She noticed the package on the bed. She picked it up and studied it. Whatever it was, it had not been disturbed in a very long time. She delicately pulled at the drawstrings. She stood up and moved under the dim light of the overhead bulb. She pulled something out of the pouch and stared at it. Something about it looked very familiar. Her breath caught when she realized what she was looking at.

"What was this doing at Dymphna's?" she wondered. "It doesn't make any sense."

Then she remembered: Pappy used to live on the farm. This belonged to him!

Jackpot! Dodge will have to finance a trip around the world when I give him this!

Over the wind, she could hear someone entering the jail. She quickly tied the pouch up and stuck it back in her waistband. She tiptoed to the door and peered into the jail.

"Pappy!" she said, trying to keep her voice even. "What are you doing here?"

As she registered the large man in the center of the room coming toward her, the lights went out.

PART THREE

Chapter 30

Dymphna and Professor Johnson moved the rabbits and chickens into the cellar without incident. The rooster and goats were another matter. The young kids scampered around the barn as if playing a game of tag, but the older Angoras knew something was wrong. They refused to deal with either Professor Johnson or Dymphna.

"Is there room in the cellar for all the goats?" Professor Johnson asked.

"There has to be! We can't just leave them!"

"Animals have an instinct when the weather is going to take a turn," Professor Johnson said.

"Really?" Dymphna asked, annoyed that he thought she might not know this. "Is that something you learned at Harvard?"

"No. My degree is in natural sciences. That would be meteorology," Professor Johnson said distractedly, chasing Diego, the Angora buck, into a corner. "Fernando told me."

Dymphna didn't have time to continue the conversation. She leaped at Wobble the rooster as he flapped by her. He managed to get himself onto a perch just above her head. She reached up and he pecked at her reaching fingers.

Thud studied the pandemonium, then blocked the path of the three oldest nanny goats. Professor Johnson managed to get leads on them, but the three nannies and Diego, the buck, wouldn't move. With a twister bearing down on them, Professor Johnson didn't have time for a test of wills.

"Listen, ladies"—Professor Johnson addressed the nanny goats, who huddled together—"I'm at the top of the food chain, and you need to do what I say."

"Don't threaten them! You are not at the top of the food chain,"

Dymphna admonished. "You wouldn't say that if we were in Africa and there were elephants chasing you through the bush."

"One, elephants don't eat meat. Two, we're not in Africa, and three, you are interfering with my intimidation technique," Professor Johnson said.

Dymphna returned her attention to corralling Wobble while Professor Johnson and Thud tried to get the goats to cooperate. Professor Johnson managed to get ahold of Catterlee, and tried to get her into the cellar. He nudged the cellar's heavy wooden door open just an inch with his foot. The storm took note of Professor Johnson's imprudence and roared into the cellar. The nanny goats and kids moved quickly, running out into the barnyard and leaping the fence. Catterlee shook off the professor and followed her sisters. Professor Johnson turned and faced Diego, the buck.

Diego, like all of Dymphna's Angora goats, had a comical fleecy face. The females had short, stubby horns, but Diego sported an impressive spiral set of horns atop his curls. They were impressive at the best of times, but lethal looking as he stared down Professor Johnson. Thud got in front of Professor Johnson and barked at the goat.

"It's okay, Thud," Dymphna said soothingly. "Diego isn't going to hurt anyone."

"Don't lie to my dog," Professor Johnson said quietly, keeping his eyes locked on Diego. "This goat means business."

Diego slipped around Thud and followed the nanny goats into the pasture. Thud brayed. Diego turned and looked at the dog standing at the gate, the goat's mohair blowing majestically in the wind. Diego bowed to his adversary. Dymphna ran to the gate, ready to give chase, but Professor Johnson grabbed her.

"You'll never catch them," Professor Johnson said.

"I know," she said, staring after them.

The nanny goats came to stand with Diego. They stood staring at Dymphna.

"Come on, sweethearts. Come back," she said. "It's not safe out there. Please come back."

It was as if they were deciding what to do. The wind kicked up a notch. Diego turned toward the creek and the nannies followed.

"Let them go," he said. "They know what they're doing."

"They might die," Dymphna said, trying not to cry.

"You've said a hundred times that animals know their own minds and people just don't have enough respect. You need to respect them now. They've made their decision."

She turned and buried her head on Professor Johnson's shoulder. He held her close. He suddenly felt a sharp pain on his foot. He pushed Dymphna back and looked down. Wobble was pecking at his foot. When the rooster sensed he'd gotten the professor's attention, he looked up. Dymphna laughed as she dried her tears.

"It looks like Wobble has made up his mind to join us," she said, gingerly scooping up the rooster. She'd never held him before. He looked even meaner up close.

"Let's get him to the cellar," Professor Johnson said.

Huddled together, they made their way to the cellar. Professor Johnson kept one hand on Dymphna's back, the other holding on to his glasses. Dymphna's hair blew straight back, Wobble's cockscomb fluttered, and Thuds ears flapped.

The farmhouse suddenly seemed very far from town. Then the rain started. Then the hail.

"Looks like the storm is getting closer," Titan said as Erinn and Wesley packed up their gear.

"This doesn't look particularly safe," Wesley said as the wind whistled through the uneven wall boards. "Do you have a place to go? Do you want to come back to the inn with us?"

"I'm not sure any building here is safer than any other," Titan said.

"That's true," Erinn added. "But at least you wouldn't be alone."

"I'm not alone," Titan said, jerking his head toward the longhorn, who still stood in the middle of the forge. "I need to take care of him. He's very upset."

Erinn and Wesley studied the bull, who looked at them with placid eyes.

"He is?" Wesley asked.

"He doesn't show it," Titan said. "But he is aware of everything that's going on. He knows a storm is coming. If he decides the building isn't safe, we'll leave."

"I feel as if we're deserting you," Erinn said. "I know you're an adult and we can't insist, but please come with us."

"We'll be fine," Titan said. "I promise, if it gets really bad, we'll leave."

Erinn and Wesley made their way onto Main Street. The intermittent rain and hail had stopped, but the wind was constant.

"I'm not comfortable leaving him there," Erinn said to Wesley.

"He's a grown man," Wesley said. "And he's right. Who's to say one place is safer than the next? *If* we get a tornado, it could level the whole town or whistle right through without leaving a mark. Titan's guess is as good as ours."

"I feel so sorry for Titan," Erinn yelled over the wind. "If that damn Pennyfeather hadn't been such a . . . a . . ."

"A lawyer?" Wesley ventured.

"Yes," Erinn said. "I mean, that was a brutal call, washing their hands of Titan. Sounds like Pennyfeather was even worse than Cutthroat."

"He was just doing his job."

"I keep forgetting he was a friend of yours," Erinn said.

"Mentor, colleague, whatever. But I wouldn't say we were friends."

"Point taken." Erinn sighed as they climbed the boardwalk stairs. "The lights seem to be off all the way down the boardwalk," she said. She looked into the window of Old Bertha's market, the first store on the boardwalk. "Let's duck into the grocery store. This wind is killing my camera."

"I guess Old Bertha went back to the inn," Erinn said as she peered into the deserted store. "Should we just go in? Do you think she'd mind?"

"Old Bertha? Of course, she'd mind."

They moved on to Powderkeg's place. Wesley opened the door.

"Hello?" he called as they stumbled into the store.

"Doesn't sound like anyone is here," Erinn said. "But I'm sure Powderkeg wouldn't care if we wait here for a reprieve from that wind before we move on."

Wesley fumbled around until his hands found the battery-powered lantern that sat on the counter. The room lit up with a warm glow.

"Well, boss," Wesley said, "you've interviewed everybody. Have you decided on a direction?"

"No," Erinn said, blowing bits of dust off her camera. "There's something bothering me, and I can't put my finger on it."

"Can I help?"

"I don't know. OK, so we've got Cutthroat, who makes it big. He's got natural, ruthless instincts that serve him well in business, but then he gets involved with Pennyfeather, who seems to fuel the fire of his greed."

"That's one way to look at it," Wesley said, an edge to his voice. "Go on."

"So why didn't Pennyfeather come check out Fat Chance with Cutthroat? Why, suddenly, is Pappy the confidant?"

"What do you mean?"

"Think about it! Cutthroat supposedly won't make a move without Pennyfeather's consent, then all of a sudden, the new guy shows up out of the blue, hanging out with Cutthroat and looking at ghost towns in Texas."

"What's so strange about that?" Wesley asked. "We don't know the exact time frame. My best guess is that Cutthroat had gone through a rough time with the Sweet Darling thing, his son and daughter-in-law dying, and Pennyfeather getting killed in that boating accident. But he still had to keep his . . . empire, for lack of a better word . . . going. So he got a new adviser."

"But not an adviser from your firm?"

"Obviously not."

"Even if that's the case, where does Pappy fit in?"

"What does it matter? He's MIA."

"Exactly," Erinn said. "And I think he holds the key."

"I suggest you find another key, 'cause this one doesn't fit."

Erinn blinked as the electric lights flickered back on. She couldn't read the look on Wesley's face.

"You scared me," Maggie said to Pappy. "I didn't know you were back."

"There's a tornado warning," Pappy said. "Figured I better get back here and help out."

"That's very nice of you," Maggie said, making sure her bundle was still secure in her waistband.

"Come with me," Pappy said. "You don't want to take any chances with a tornado coming."

"Where are we going?"

"I'm going to stick you in the bank vault," Pappy said. "Safest place in town."

"That's OK," Maggie said, trying to keep her voice even. "I don't even think we're going to get a tornado."

"It's best to play it safe," Pappy said. "So let's go."

"No. Thanks, really, but I'm staying here."

"I'm sorry you feel that way," Pappy said, advancing on her.

She turned to run, but Pappy caught her. He hoisted her over his shoulder like a sack of potatoes and headed to the door.

"It's only one building over," Pappy said, and he walked out the door into the driving rain, holding Maggie as she flailed in his arms. "This won't hurt a bit."

Old Bertha was in the back room when she heard the knock on the grocery store door. She refused to answer it. What damn fool would come looking for groceries in the middle of a storm? It must be some crazy cowboys looking for munchies. She listened to make sure they went away. One of these days, the people of Fat Chance would have to get locks, damn it! She peered into the store. Except for the screaming wind and rain dripping through the holes in the roof, everything was quiet. She walked to the front window and looked out. As a flash of lightning flashed across the sky, she saw a large man carrying someone over his shoulder and walking down the boardwalk.

Crazy cowboys! Just like I thought.

She went back to the back room, lit a candle, and returned to her accounting.

Cleo and Powderkeg were asleep in Cleo's room at the Creakside Inn. Cleo awoke when an ice-cold droplet of water fell from the ceiling onto her nose. She sat up in bed with a jolt. She pulled the covers around her naked body and looked at the sleeping man beside her. She rubbed tentatively at the raw spot that heated her jawline. How long had it been since she'd had a bad case of whisker-burn, she wondered. Another droplet hit her, this time on top of her head. She shivered and pulled the covers tighter. She reached for the bedside lamp and tried to click it on.

Nothing.

Listening to the rain, she realized a storm was raging outside. Was the electricity out? It wouldn't surprise her. This town was held together with spit and chewing gum as far as she could tell. She looked at Powderkeg again. She had no regrets that they'd slept together. They were good together in bed. If only they were as good together out of bed.

The inn creaked and moaned in the storm. Cleo sat up and listened. She heard someone walking downstairs. The footsteps were heavy, so they couldn't belong to Polly. Cleo remembered that Polly was in Galveston. Cleo knew that if they were being hit with a storm of this magnitude in Hays County, chances were good it was worse down by the Gulf. She prayed Polly had enough sense to get out of the storm if it came down to it. Then she remembered that Polly was with Jeffries. She breathed a sigh of relief.

Good old reliable Jeffries. Solid as a piece of snakewood.

She lightly touched Powderkeg's shoulder and smiled. She remembered when he'd had her memorize the top ten hardest woods in the world when she was still pretending she was interested in carpentry. Snakewood was the only one she remembered because it was so unusual looking, its grain mimicking the look of a snake's skin. At the time, she was just grateful he had another interest besides making leather belts.

Jeffries would be lucky to be remotely as interesting as snakewood.

The footsteps must belong to Old Bertha. Cleo settled back down, but the raindrops had soaked her pillow. She let out a little shriek. Powderkeg woke up.

"Sorry I woke you," Cleo whispered.

"I'm not," Powderkeg said. He reached for her, but she pulled away.

"Is there a problem?" he asked.

Cleo sighed. "Not a new problem. We always seem to take one step forward and two steps back."

"Correction," he said. "*You* always take one step forward and two steps back. I'm pretty much standing still, waiting for you to stop moving."

"Except for the pilot."

"And where is she now? Cleo, we're getting older. We need to stop fooling around."

"I thought you liked fooling around?"

"You know damn well what I mean. You keep coming back here for a reason."

"And you think that reason is you?" Cleo sat up, a steely tone creeping into her voice. Powderkeg was about to answer, but Cleo stopped him. "Shhhh," she said. "Do you hear that?"

Creaking on the stairs started softly, but grew louder as it got closer.

"It's just Old Bertha," Powderkeg said. "Nothing to worry about."

"No, it's not! Those steps are too heavy."

Suddenly the door crashed open. Cleo screamed and pulled the blankets around her. Powderkeg jumped out of bed, buck naked.

Lightning lit up the room.

"Pappy?" Cleo asked in astonishment.

"What the hell are you doing here?" Powderkeg groused as he pulled on his underwear.

"Come to rescue you fools," Pappy said. "Get dressed. And quick."

Chapter 31

Pappy led Cleo, Powderkeg, and the mules, Jerry Lee and Patsy, up the boardwalk.

"You drove through this?" Cleo yelled over the wind.

"Yeah, and it wasn't easy," Pappy said. "The wind tore the canvas top off the Covered Volkswagen. Probably gonna turn the thing into a swimming pool by the time this is over."

It wasn't easy getting Jerry Lee up the stairs. The animal was frightened of the storm and always hated the boardwalk. Patsy daintily climbed the stairs and watched as Pappy swore and pulled Jerry Lee's bridle while Powderkeg and Cleo pushed from behind. A crack of thunder from the sky finally convinced Jerry Lee to get a move on, and he trotted to the top of the stairs.

"Go into the bank," Pappy yelled over the rain.

"The bank?" Powderkeg roared back. Their voices were being lost on the wind.

"We need to get to the vault," Pappy said. "Already got Maggie locked up in there."

They entered the bank, pulling the mules behind them. Jerry Lee knew instinctually he was not supposed to be inside a bank and protested loudly with bared teeth and a honk. Patsy was better behaved. She was used to being inside. She was so small that Old Bertha couldn't resist bringing her inside the inn. Pappy, Powderkeg, and Cleo shook rain from their clothes. Pappy had explained that they needed to wait out the tornado in the vault, and since the townspeople almost always did what Pappy said when it came to survival, they followed him.

"What do you mean, you've got Maggie locked in the vault?" Cleo said. "Can she breathe?"

"She wouldn't be able to in an air-tight vault," Pappy said. "But there's plenty of air in ours. It got broken into around 1900. The thieves used gunpowder and the door has never been the same. Fat Chance's vault isn't much better than the rest of the town."

"Then why are we going there?" Cleo asked, backing toward the door.

"I said the vault wasn't *much* better than the rest of the town," Pappy said. "But it's still our best bet."

Pappy spun the lock and pulled open the massive vault door. Maggie sprung out, but he was waiting for her. He held on to her as if he were struggling with a puppy.

"You crazy old man," Maggie screeched. "I could have died in there."

"I'm trying to *keep* you from dying," Pappy said, handing her over to Powderkeg. "Get everybody in there and don't come out. Even if the building gets ripped to shreds, this is your best bet. You hear me?"

"Is the building going to be ripped to shreds?" Maggie was suddenly contrite.

"Do I look like God?" Pappy asked as he ushered the group into the vault.

With his long white beard, wild hair, and commanding way, Maggie thought he did look a little like God.

But she knew better—and she just needed to get out of this disaster alive to prove it.

The mules went silently into the tiny room, taking up more than their fair share of space.

"We're not going to fit in there with those animals," Cleo said.

"Suit yourself," Pappy said. "Feel free to take your chances out here."

Cleo started to argue, but just then the door to the bank swung open and Fernando walked in, drenched to the skin.

"I saw you heading over here from the hill," Fernando said. "The grapevines are taking a beating."

"You were out gardening?" Pappy said in disgust. He threw Fernando a blanket that covered one of the bank chairs. "Get in here."

"Where are you going?" Powderkeg said.

"We're still missing some folks," Pappy said. "It looks like Professor Johnson and Dymphna knew enough to go to their cellar, but I still need to make the rounds in town. The vault has as many people as it can handle, so I'll figure something else out."

"I'm going to close you in," he said as he gave Fernando the code to the lock. "I tested the inside lock. You'll be able to get yourselves out if something happens to . . . if something happens. There's some lanterns. Use 'em. It gets mighty dark in there."

"You didn't tell me we had lanterns," Maggie said indignantly. "I was sitting here in the dark!"

"Just stay until you know the tornado has passed," Pappy said, ignoring her.

"How will we know that?" Maggie said in a quaking voice. The vault was so crowded, she was pressed against Jerry Lee.

Pappy stared at their terrified, ashen faces.

"You'll know," he said as he started to swing the door into place.

"Pappy?" Powderkeg's voice echoed in the steel room.

Pappy stopped and looked in.

Powderkeg saluted. Pappy returned his salute and closed the vault door.

Old Bertha's candle blew out as the wind rustled through the cracks in the back office of her store. She let out a big sigh. She was never going to get any work done. She might as well pack it in and head back to the inn.

She lit the candle again and made her way to the front of the store. She looked out and was shocked how hostile the weather had turned in the few hours she'd been in the back. It was even worse than when those drunken cowboys had come by. She looked down the boardwalk and saw that boards were splintering from the hail and wind. It was too dark to try to walk all the way to the inn. Main Street was a muddy river, so that was out. She saw a flicker of light coming from the forge. She admonished herself. She was a big girl. She would just stay by herself here in the grocery store. How much worse could it get?

A bolt of lightning crashed down onto Main Street, lighting up the town for a brief second. Old Bertha grabbed her shawl and put it over her head. She opened the door and realized the shawl would be sodden in an instant. She rushed back into the store and felt around behind the counter. Her fingers grasped the rough canvas and leather quilt she was working on. She swapped it out for her shawl, taking only a second to think about her encounter with that awful Maggie. Accusing her of stealing! She took a deep breath and waded toward the forge.

* * *

Erinn paced Powderkeg's shop. The answers to her questions about Pappy were just out of reach. Suddenly, she stopped and turned to Wesley. The two of them were so absorbed in their battle of wits they barely noticed the squall.

"I think you're focused on the wrong people," Wesley said. "You don't have Cutthroat, you don't have Pennyfeather, and you don't have Pappy. Why not concentrate on what you do have?"

"Which is what?"

"The story of the human spirit."

"You must be joking."

"No, I'm not. Cutthroat set up this town and gave a bunch of misdirected people a chance at the American Dream. They took it and ran with it. It's very uplifting, you have to admit."

"Of course it's uplifting," Erinn said, trying to keep the "who gives a shit" out of her voice. "But anyone could tell that story."

"I think you're wrong."

"That's why I'm the director and you're the production assistant."

"Then we're back to square one."

"Maybe," Erinn said. "Maybe not."

"What do you mean?"

Erinn noticed a hint of panic in Wesley's voice. She thought back to the last few days as he'd followed her around. She'd heard that tone before.

There is something he doesn't want me to find out.

Her guard was suddenly up.

"Let's say—for the sake of argument—that I change directions. Who is the weak link in the plot? Cutthroat?" she said.

"No. You can't tell the story without Cutthroat."

"So . . . Pennyfeather? Pappy?"

"I don't think you'll find an angle there with either one of them. I really don't."

Bingo.

Erinn and Wesley continued to stare at one another, unaware that a twister was going to strike at any moment.

"So . . . even though Pappy and Pennyfeather are of no interest, let me ask you this," Erinn said. "Why one and then the other? Why did Pappy just suddenly show up out of thin air? Why wasn't your law firm on top of this guy? I mean, do you even know who Pappy is? We don't have a real name. That should have been easy to find out, shouldn't it?"

"You act as if Cutthroat were obliged to give us information," Wesley said. "He wasn't. We weren't managing his life, just his legal work, and gave counsel and recommendations on financial matters that might—"

"That might get him in trouble with inconvenient laws?"

"Now, you aren't really expecting an answer on that, are you?" Wesley's smooth side reasserted itself.

"Did it ever occur to you that Cutthroat asked that a junior partner, still wet behind the ears—"

"Meaning me?"

"No offense."

"Some taken, but go on."

"Wasn't it possible that Cutthroat wanted a less . . . experienced attorney at the helm, so he could have a little more freedom? So he wouldn't be watched as closely?"

"You're desperate to get an interesting story going. Why can't you just admit you don't have one?"

"I'll admit it when you convince me. You haven't."

"Why would Cutthroat do that? You think he'd put all his business and personal wealth at stake so he could have a little fun?"

"Not exactly."

"What then?"

"Maybe he was hiding something."

"Oh! Now he's hiding something. I'll bite. What was he hiding?"

"I don't know. But I just have a feeling it has something to do with this Pennyfeather and Pappy."

Erinn started pacing. "No, wait! I think if we could establish a timeline, we could see where all this intersects. We need to know why and when Cutthroat turned from Pennyfeather to Pappy. Why did he just give Pappy the OK to stay in Fat Chance? On whose dime? Just out of friendship? There are too many unanswered questions."

"You're forcing the issue, you know that," Wesley said.

"Look, I don't have all the answers, but I'm thinking something like this—Cutthroat is completely reliant on Pennyfeather. Maybe the next beat is . . . I mean, maybe the next thing that happens is Pennyfeather dies. For some reason, Cutthroat turns the law firm over to a kid and takes up with an eccentric nobody had ever heard of and leaves him in a ghost town. Does that sound about right?"

"It's a possibility, yes. So what?"

"You don't think it's an odd coincidence that Pennyfeather suddenly disappears and Pappy moves into his spot? Cutthroat, who trusted only one man and then so easily replaces him?"

"So now what? You think Pappy killed Pennyfeather? That would be an interesting twist."

Erinn stopped pacing and looked at Wesley. How could she have missed it? Wesley was dogging her every step because he already knew the truth and wanted to make sure she didn't stumble on it.

"I agree," Erinn said. "It would be very interesting. But that's not the truth, is it?"

Pappy tilted into the lashing rain. His heart beat faster. If Old Bertha wasn't in the grocery store, he didn't know where else to look. He'd expected to find her at the inn and was surprised when she wasn't there. He didn't have time to think about how surprised he was to find Cleo and Powderkeg in bed together and he was already trying to forget the image of Powderkeg standing naked in front of him.

He was so focused on making his way down the disintegrating boardwalk, he luckily didn't see a tiny light shine from Powderkeg's store, where Erinn and Wesley continued their sparring. Unluckily, he didn't see Old Bertha trudging through the mud on her way to the forge.

Pappy went into the grocery store. He knew immediately it was empty. Should he go back to the inn? Maybe Old Bertha passed him when he was in the bank.

Where is that damned woman?

When Pappy had seen the sky turn green, he knew he had to return to Fat Chance. It was a risk, but one he knew he had to take. He had grown to love not only Old Bertha but the entire band of misfits with their passion for life and their squabbles over asphalt and grapes. He loved them but knew they didn't have two brain cells among them when it came to anything practical—like weather.

Pappy stood in the middle of Main Street, barely breathing. He listened. The wind had died down. There wasn't a sound. The tornado was upon Fat Chance. After making sure everyone he could find was as safe as they could be in an old ghost town caught in a tornado, he found himself the most vulnerable of all.

He braced for the fight.

Let's do this.

Chapter 32

Titan opened the door of the forge and Old Bertha rushed in. She busied herself shaking off the quilt and brushing mud from her skirt. When she looked up, she let out a curse. She found herself staring into Rocket's eyes.

"What's that damned bull doing in here?" she asked.

"Same as us," Titan said. "Waiting out the storm."

"I didn't think I could make it back to the inn," Old Bertha said.

"Not a problem," Titan said. "We're happy to have the company."

Titan walked over to the small window that faced Main Street. Old Bertha knew what he was thinking. She opened her mouth to tell him he just needed to let go of the idea that Fancy would ever be coming back. She stared at his broad back and found she didn't have the heart to set him straight.

"You know, that buzzard of yours is one smart bird," she said. "I don't think she's going to try to make it back to Fat Chance in this weather."

"You're probably right," Titan said. "She'll wait out the storm."

His posture straightened. Old Bertha was pleased with herself. Maybe she should try to be nice more often. Old Bertha heard a sound like rain drumming on a tin roof. She looked up, knowing full well that the forge had a patched roof.

"What's that sound?" she asked.

"Just the rain beating on the Cinderella carriage out back," Titan said. "I tried to move it inside, but Rocket is pretty much taking up every square inch."

Old Bertha was about to say the longhorn was taking up too much room. He was not exactly domesticated. But then it flashed through Old Bertha's mind that Jerry Lee and Patsy were at the inn.

"Your mules are as smart as Fancy," Titan said, as if reading her mind. "They'll know how to take care of themselves."

She nodded, but since she herself was lying about Fancy being smart, she took no solace from his comment. She looked at Rocket. She'd heard that animals had an innate sense about where to go and what to do when something like a tornado or earthquake was imminent, but this huge beast looked dumb as a stump. She exhaled, realizing she was holding her breath. She prayed that there was someone at the inn who was taking care of her precious animals.

She looked back at Rocket. He was moving his horns from side to side.

"What's the matter with your cow?" Old Bertha said.

"He's a bull," Titan said, walking quickly to Rocket, who let out a loud bellow. "What's up, big guy?"

Suddenly the bull reared back. Titan pulled Old Bertha out of Rocket's way as the bull charged the back door. The door splintered into three large pieces. The bull ran past the Cinderella carriage with incredible speed. It was easy to see why he'd been named Rocket.

"That bull ruined—" Old Bertha started to say.

"Shh," Titan said. "Listen."

Old Bertha could hear it. It sounded like a train coming through. *Clickity-clack, clickity-clack*, first faint, but getting stronger.

"What is that?" Old Bertha asked.

"It's the twister," Titan said.

"Oh my God."

Titan picked her up and started running toward the front of the building. He stopped just in time, as an enormous beam blocked his path. Pivoting on his heels, he faced the back door—or where the back door used to be before Rocket crashed through it.

There was no choice. He'd have to make a run for it.

Dymphna put her head in Professor Johnson's lap, hands over her ears to block out the sound of the twister. Professor Johnson patted her hair with one hand and held on to Thud's collar with the other. Thud was barking at the cellar door.

"It's taking the house," Dymphna whimpered.

"Yes," Professor Johnson said.

Dymphna sat up. Wobble glared at her from a top shelf. The chickens huddled together as did the rabbits.

"Nobody's freaking out," Dymphna said as she studied them.

"They know you're taking care of them," Professor Johnson said.

Dymphna started to cry. Professor Johnson sat next to her silently. Her tears could be about so many different things. The animals that were here with them? The goats who bolted and were out there in the storm somewhere? The fact that the farm was coming down around their heads? The fact that she now had a perfect out to leave Fat Chance, and felt guilty?

That, of course, was all contingent on their making it out alive.

Even in the cellar, they could tell that the sky had lightened. It was late afternoon, but the sky had been as black as Polly's Goth makeup. Birds had started to sing again. Thud stopped barking.

"Do you think we should try going up?" Dymphna asked.

Professor Johnson wasn't sure. It was fairly obvious from the sound of things that the house was gone. Had the shredded lumber fallen on the cellar door? The door opened out, which meant they'd be trapped. Before he could make a decision, there was a banging at the door. Dymphna started. It was not the sound of a friend knocking on the door. It was fierce and aggressive.

"What is that?" Dymphna asked, shaking.

Professor Johnson looked at her, then at Thud. Thud gave him a slobbery kiss.

"Thud's not barking," he said. "I think we're safe to take a look."

Professor Johnson stood up. Thud was already at the door, wagging his tail. Dymphna tried to slow her heartbeat, but the crazy banging continued. While Dymphna calmed herself by attending to the animals, Professor Johnson unhooked the latch and pushed on one side of the door. It didn't give an inch.

"Hello?" he called as casually as he could. He tried to take Thud's goodwill as a sign that they weren't in any danger, although he couldn't for the life of him figure out who or what was making that ungodly racket. He tried to push again, with as much force as he could muster.

Nothing.

He wondered how long it would take for someone in town to come up to the farmhouse . . . well, what was left of the farmhouse. Professor Johnson felt his breath grow ragged. In his entire life, he never had anyone he could truly call a friend, and now he had a whole town full of people he could count on. The thought of fighting with Fernando about the grapes and Dymphna about the road now seemed so inconsequential. He'd make it up to them when they got out of this.

The banging started again.

If *we get out of this.*

He knew the farmhouse was gone, but it hit him—and hit him hard—that the grapes might be gone as well, that the entire town might be gone, his friends might be gone. Twisters chose loopy and random paths, but it was foolhardy to think Fat Chance had survived unscathed. He had heard the damage, if not yet seen it. *History repeats itself,* he thought. Twisters had nearly destroyed the town twice in the past; maybe three times was the charm. The erratic banging continued. He tried pushing the other door.

It opened easily.

He looked back at Dymphna, who was studying one of the rabbits, singing softly to it and stroking its long, soft hair. He was happy she was distracted. He wanted a chance to assess the damage. As he tried to make his way quietly up the stairs, Thud shot past him. Professor Johnson tried to catch him, fearful that whatever was making the racket outside the cellar was foe, not friend. But he only managed to grab hold of the dog's tail, which whipped through his fingers without Thud even noticing. Professor Johnson climbed out of the cellar. He reeled back instantly. At first he had no idea what he was seeing, he was so close to it. But then he knew.

He was staring into Rocket's eyes.

The longhorn's right hoof was stuck in some timber. He was standing on one side of the cellar door, trying to dislodge it.

"You were making a lot of noise there, Rocket," Professor Johnson said, grabbing the wood that trapped the longhorn. "Gave us quite a scare."

Once freed, the longhorn scampered off and Professor Johnson made his way the rest of the way out of the cellar. He steeled himself, then turned around. He staggered backwards as he surveyed the devastated farmhouse. It had been reduced to rubble. Rocket and Thud nosed curiously around the devastation. Professor Johnson realized he was holding the piece of wood that had entrapped the longhorn. He looked at it. It was one of the lovingly painted floorboards from Polly's welcome mat.

Dymphna's voice echoed up the stairs. "Watch out, Wobble's on his way."

Professor Johnson had to duck as the rooster shot out of the cellar. The rooster flapped his way to his customary fence post, but the fence post wasn't there. He turned and glowered at Professor Johnson accusingly.

"Can we come out?" Dymphna called from inside the cellar.

"Not yet," Professor Johnson said. "Let me make sure it's safe."

He was lying. He didn't want her to see what had become of her home.

It was gone.

Erinn and Wesley clung to each other. The sky had returned to its usual benign self, but neither would let go of the other. They'd been arguing about Pappy, Erinn joyfully cornering Wesley and Wesley deftly avoiding the most damning accusations. They were each so intent on their arguments and counter-arguments that they'd forgotten about the giant stomping through the town. They heard the deafening roar at the same time. Wesley had his finger raised, mid-point. Erinn had her arms folded and her eyes blazed. They looked at each other. As the sound got closer and closer, they'd rushed into each other's arms.

"You have been the worst PA in the history of the world," Erinn had said. "And I've loved spending every minute with you."

"You're the most fascinating woman I've ever met," Wesley said.

"I agree," Erinn said. "Not that I'm the most fascinating woman you've ever met! But I think you're a remarkable man. A *most* remarkable man."

"You know you might not get to make that documentary after all," he said. "I think that ticking sound is wood splintering."

"We who are about to die, salute you," Erinn had said to the wind as she stared at the window.

She'd buried her head in Wesley's chest. She had always thought she was too politically correct to take solace in a man's arms.

Forgive me, Gloria Steinem.

She had been scared to death and he felt like safety. They held on tight.

Erinn was the first to let go. When she was a young playwright on Broadway, she'd had her share of too-casual encounters that left her feeling embarrassed in the morning. She'd found a way to at least *pretend* the morning after wasn't awkward. But that was a lifetime ago and she was out of practice.

"Looks like we made it," Wesley said, letting his arms drop to his sides.

"Yes," Erinn said, walking to the window and looking out. "The boardwalk looks like hell."

"What else is new?" Wesley said.

Erinn was looking out the window rather than at Wesley. She could tell by his voice that they were going to play this as if those last words had never been uttered. That was fine with her; she wasn't exactly proud of her role as damsel in distress. She looked up and down the splintered boardwalk.

"I see Jerry Lee and Patsy," she said.

They stepped out onto what was left of the boardwalk. The animals leapt off the planks onto Main Street—and into the sticky mud. Fernando, Maggie, Cleo, and Powderkeg were running out of the bank toward them, their faces grim. The buildings were a mess; there was mud everywhere. But Fat Chance appeared to be standing.

"We're OK," Erinn said as the group advanced, but everyone ran right by her. Erinn's smile faded. She turned to see what had them in such a panic and then she saw it as well. She gasped and grabbed Wesley's hand.

The forge had collapsed. The walls and shingles were strewn everywhere, splintered wood piled high over the Cinderella coach.

Pappy was standing in the rubble.

Where did he come from?

Erinn felt Wesley release her hand when he saw the old man. Erinn and Wesley exchanged a look. They both knew it meant that they were calling a truce until the damage was assessed. Then they followed the rest of the townspeople toward what was once the proud forge of Fat Chance, Texas.

Chapter 33

Pappy was grimly moving wood, kicking at mangled tools and swearing.

"Titan?" he called. "Come on, buddy, where are you?"

Pappy stopped his macabre hunt and staggered, but he regained his footing. He looked at the paralyzed group.

"Some help here?" he asked gruffly.

As if coming out of a dream, the group snapped out of their disbelief. As they helped each other move heavy pieces of wood and machinery amid jangled nerves and tears, a new sound diverted their attention. An engine whined from the road above Fat Chance. The group turned to look as the limousine, now almost brown with mud, came soaring down the road, metal scraping and shooting sparks when it hit the asphalt.

"My God," Powderkeg said. "Jeffries *drove* through this?"

The limousine screeched to a halt. Polly and Jeffries flew out of the front doors.

"Titan!" Jeffries cried. "Titan!"

His surprising outburst momentarily stopped everyone in their tracks. But they mobilized as Jeffries threw off his jacket and started running into the dangerous mass of wood and metal.

"Hey," Pappy said. "Be careful there."

But Jeffries wouldn't listen. He seemed possessed.

"Slow down, partner," Powderkeg said to Jeffries as he grabbed him. "We don't want any more . . ."

A huge piece of lumber from the middle of the rubble suddenly crashed to the ground, shaking the ground and frightening everyone. Was another twister on the way? Another piece of wood moved as a strong, mocha-colored hand pushed it aside.

"It's Titan," Fernando called out. "Sweet Lady of Guadalupe! It's Titan!"

The inhabitants of Fat Chance fought through the mountain of debris, trying to reach him.

"There is no way he could have lived through that!" Powderkeg said.

"It's a miracle," Fernando said. "I wish my mother was here to see this. She was a big believer in miracles."

As Titan pushed and the people of Fat Chance pulled, the impossibly sturdy and heavy Cinderella carriage slowly revealed itself.

Polly turned to look down the street to the other end of Fat Chance. Jerry Lee and Patsy stood in front of the inn as if nothing unusual was going on.

"The inn made it," Polly said to Cleo, as Polly wiped a tear from her eye. "As soon as we get Titan out of there, I'll go check on Old Bertha. She must be freaked."

Cleo exchanged a look with Powderkeg.

"Old Bertha's not at the inn," Maggie said absently. "Everybody who was there went to wait out the tornado in the bank vault. It was nuts . . ."

Polly wasn't listening. She let out a howl.

"Bertha!" She started down the street. "Bertha! Oh please! Answer me! Bertha?"

Powderkeg overtook her, grabbing her around the waist. She was hysterical.

"She's all right," Powderkeg said. "She's all right! Look!"

He pointed back to the Cinderella carriage. The rubble had been pulled away and Titan was standing on the ground, his hand extended into the carriage. Old Bertha's hand was reaching for his. Powderkeg held the sobbing girl as they watched the surreal fairy tale play out. It was as if Cinderella had fallen asleep inside her coach and emerged a grouchy and ample-bottomed eighty-year-old.

Polly ran to Old Bertha and threw herself into the old woman's arms.

"Calm down, now," Old Bertha said, patting the girl. "It's fine. Titan got us into the carriage just in time."

Old Bertha looked at Pappy.

"So you decided to come back, did you?" she said.

"I did," Pappy said.

"You're a mess," she said, looking him up and down. "Don't expect dinner until you clean up."

Cleo was watching Jeffries. He was still moving boards off the coach.

"You don't have to do that," Titan said. "I can clean it up later."

Jeffries threw down a piece of wood angrily.

"Fine," he said. "Handle it yourself. See if I care." He started to storm away, but Titan grabbed his arm.

"I'm sorry," Titan said. "I'm sorry I've been ignoring you. I just . . . I just thought it was for the best."

"You remember?" Jeffries said.

"Of course I do. How could I forget?"

The two men embraced. As they kissed, Cleo turned to Powderkeg.

"Jeffries is *gay?*" she asked.

"Woman, he's worked for you for twenty-five years," Powderkeg said. "How is it you didn't know he was gay?"

"I really need to start paying more attention," Cleo mused, returning her gaze to the two men leaning against the dented Cinderella carriage.

"Now I understand," Wesley said to Erinn. "Jeffries confided in you that he wanted to see Titan. That's why you offered to take him on as a PA."

"That's right," Erinn said.

"That was very kind of you," Wesley said. "I mean, he has no PA experience."

"Unlike you?"

The flirtatious banter didn't fool either one of them. This was merely a brief détente. The secrets of Fat Chance were going to continue to come out. Jeffries and Titan were just the tip of the iceberg.

Dymphna refused to look at the space where her farmhouse used to be. She got the chickens and rabbits resettled. The barn and rabbits' habitat were unscathed, but the fence was mangled. The goats were heading back to them, looking like aliens with their sodden, matted hair. For now, the barn seemed to be where the goats wanted to be. They went into the barn single file, ignoring Professor Johnson and Thud along the way.

Professor Johnson went to Dymphna, who was studiously concentrating on the rabbits.

"The animals seem all right," he said. "The goats got home OK." Dymphna nodded.

"I'll accept any decision you make," Professor Johnson said.

Dymphna looked up, startled. "I'm sorry—" She shook her hair as if trying to clear a fog in her head. "What decision?"

"Even though I thought I knew you, I didn't," Professor Johnson said. "When I had to go back to Los Angeles for six months, it never occurred to me we wouldn't make it. It wasn't until *you* left that I started to worry. When Maggie showed up—"

"Maggie doesn't—" Dymphna interrupted hotly, but Professor Johnson held up his hand. She backed down.

"When Maggie showed up and mentioned that you took to the hills whenever things got tough, I didn't really believe it."

"But now you do?" Dymphna said in a small voice.

"Well, I'm not going to lie to you," he said. "It did get me thinking. I didn't know you had a sister. I didn't know anything about your life before you lost your land in Malibu, and I only knew that because Cutthroat told us when Wesley played the DVD."

"I just don't like to talk about the past." Dymphna looked out over the land rather than at Professor Johnson.

"I'm not asking you to. What I'm saying is, if this is too much for you and you decide to take your rabbits back to Los Angeles, I'll understand."

"Is that what you want?" she asked.

"Is that what *you* want?" he asked right back.

"There's Rocket," Maggie shouted, pointing to the longhorn rambling over the rise from Dymphna's farm.

"I can't believe how lucky we've been," Titan said, as he and Jeffries walked quickly toward the bull.

As Titan reached the section of Main Street where Dymphna's farm started to become visible, he realized something was very wrong. He turned back to the townspeople, who were starting to disburse.

"I can see the barn, but I can't see the house," Titan shouted.

"Oh no!" Maggie cried, as she broke into a run. "Dymphna!"

She shot passed the rest of the townspeople as she raced up the hill. It was slippery from the rain and there were chunks of missing earth, which caused all of them to fall on their way toward the top of the hill.

Maggie was the first to see her sister and Professor Johnson standing in the barnyard. Before, the space had been anchored by the house on one side and the barn on the other. Now there was only the barn, standing like a confused and lonely bookend.

Maggie stopped running and took a deep breath. She tried to quiet her heart. It would not do for Dymphna to see her panic, or even show sadness, at the prospect of her older sister coming to harm. After all, she knew both of them had fantasized about the other's unfortunate demise since they were children, sent to their separate rooms for fighting. Seeing her sister standing in the ruin of her life made Maggie's heart ache, but she had to be tough. She might meet Dymphna halfway, but she wasn't going to be the first to offer an olive branch. She might get a poke in the eye.

She dug deep inside for all the evidence of Dymphna's failings as an older sister. The fact that both her parents had admired Dymphna was something she'd lived with until her parents died. The sound of her father's pride when he announced "Dymphna won the spelling bee" to her mother's cheerful chirp of "Dymphna is selling her own line of knitwear to boutiques" grated on her even now. Tired of recounting the injustices, she moved on to the slings and arrows of following Dymphna through school. Dymphna with her art awards, Dymphna with her 4-H awards, Dymphna with her posse of cute boyfriends. As they got older, the playing field leveled. Maggie might not have been able to get her parents' attention, but she could make Dymphna's boyfriends sit up and take notice.

She smiled grimly at the memory of seducing Dymphna's sophomore-year boyfriend. The exhilaration of the conquest had been short-lived. Dymphna's brokenhearted wails rang through the house for a week. Her parents had endless discussions about Maggie for once. It wasn't exactly winning first place in something, but it was much more fun, more empowering and easier. Taking things from Dymphna became an addiction. She'd swear to herself she was going to stop, but the temptation would get too great and she would think "OK, only one more time."

And then Dymphna just left. Dymphna took off as soon as she turned eighteen, leaving Maggie to deal with brokenhearted parents, who blamed *her*! It was the final drop in a heart full of resentment. Her cup runneth over.

As she got closer to the farm, it occurred to her that Dymphna and Professor Johnson were working at cleaning up, but seemed to be working separately, not together. Her view was obscured from time to time, because everyone but Pappy, who was helping Old Bertha up the hill, had passed her by.

Now that she was calm again, she reached in her waistband to make sure her treasure was safe. There might have been one minute when she was locked in the vault and feared for her life that she was tempted to give up her treasure, but the urge passed as quickly as the tornado. She stood still as Pappy and Old Bertha huffed by. She smiled grimly to herself. The only thing more fun than ruining something special for Dymphna was ruining something special for the people whom Dymphna loved.

Taking down Fat Chance was going to be epic!

"It looks like your sister is safe at least," Pappy said to Maggie. When she didn't respond, he added, "You OK?"

"Yes," Maggie said.

But she wasn't.

Chapter 34

Titan was the first to reach Dymphna. He swooped her up in a bone-crunching hug.

"Titan," she said softly, "my house is gone."

"I know, sugar," he said. "Mine too. The forge got hit. But Rocket is OK. We're all OK. That's all that really matters." He put Dymphna back on the ground. Jeffries came up and put his arm around Titan.

"You can come back to Los Angeles. I'll take care of you," Jeffries said.

"I just might," Titan said. "There isn't anything left for me here."

Dymphna's heart started to pound.

She was angry when Professor Johnson gave her the out of leaving. She wanted to prove she had what it took to finally stay in one place and to make things work. But maybe it wasn't going to be her choice this time.

Was this the end of Fat Chance?

She tried to smile at the two men.

"I see this disaster had one good outcome," she said. "You two got over yourselves!"

Dymphna knew that after the reading of the will, Titan had been so upset he'd bolted from the living room as soon as they were dismissed. When Dymphna was leaving, she went to find him. Even though they had just met, she knew he was going to be the one she leaned on in the months ahead. She'd found him in a darkened hallway, locked in an embrace with Jeffries. The men broke apart immediately and Jeffries put his butler-mask back on and excused himself.

Dymphna wasn't sure if Titan had wanted to talk about it, so she walked with him down the long driveway in silence. He was the one who spoke.

"I guess that looked a little weird," he said.

"Do you even know that man?" Dymphna had asked, then decided to be quiet rather than sound the tiniest bit judgmental.

"No," Titan said. "I was just trying to find a corner in that humongous house where I could be alone. I hate crying in public. I thought that hallway was safe, but the butler saw me and came to see if I was OK. Next thing I knew, we were kissing!"

"Wow."

"I know."

When Jeffries had first shown up in Fat Chance, Texas, having driven Cleo to the turnout above the town, Dymphna had taken her cue from the two men; they'd acted as if they'd never laid eyes on each other. After Jeffries drove away, Dymphna asked Titan why he hadn't run up to Jeffries.

"You must have been surprised to see him," Dymphna said. "You could have at least given him a hug."

"Jeffries isn't out of the closet," Titan said. "In case you haven't noticed."

"But he drove all this way!" Dymphna said. "He might have come all this way to see you."

"Maybe," Titan said, "but maybe not."

"You didn't give him a chance," Dymphna said.

"He didn't give me a chance to give him a chance!" Titan said huffily.

Dymphna had let it go.

"That's all behind us now," Titan said, bringing Dymphna back to the present. "It was a misunderstanding. I thought he didn't want to acknowledge me and he thought I didn't want to acknowledge him."

"Nothing like a near-death experience to clear the head," Jeffries said.

"Nooooooooooo," came a wail from the rubble.

Dymphna, Titan, and Jeffries turned to see Erinn standing ankle deep in mud, holding the remains of her computer. Polly strode over to her and examined the mangled piece of technology.

"Yeah," Polly said. "This is toast."

"I don't have a backup!" Erinn said.

"Shit," Powderkeg said.

"Watch your language," Cleo said. "That doesn't help."

"I knew it," Erinn said. "I knew I was risking everything shooting here without access to the cloud!"

"Is she delirious?" Old Bertha whispered to Fernando.

"The cloud is . . ." Fernando started, but looked at Old Bertha's puzzled face and realized it was futile. "The cloud is a thing. An important computer thing."

Old Bertha nodded.

"So," Pappy asked Fernando, "everything she shot is gone?"

"Most everything," Fernando said. "She might have an interview or two still on her camera, but from the look on her face, she's in big trouble."

Pappy tried not to show the relief he felt.

"Well, that just sucks," Maggie said. "Do you think she'll start over?"

"Can't say," Pappy said.

Maggie noticed that Pappy was eyeing the debris carefully but surreptitiously.

You'll never find what you're looking for, she thought.

As if agreeing with Maggie's unspoken thoughts, Pappy let out a heavy sigh. He finally grabbed Old Bertha's elbow to help her down the hill. Bertha turned back to the group.

"It's gonna be dark soon," she said. "Best you all get back to town as soon as you can."

Dymphna said that she and Professor Johnson would come down as soon as they made sure the animals were safe for the night.

"We can make room for you at the inn," Old Bertha said.

"We can stay behind the Boozehound," Professor Johnson said.

"That's right," Polly said. "I forgot you had a little place back there."

"We'll need a place," Titan said, taking Jeffries's hand.

Old Bertha paled. "I don't have any more rooms," she said quickly.

"But you just said you could always make more room," Maggie said.

"Well, that was before I realized all the rooms were taken."

"I see," Jeffries said. "Well, we can always sleep in the limousine."

"Like hell!" Cleo burst out.

Everyone turned to stare at her.

"What I mean is," Cleo said, regaining her composure, "I can move over to Powderkeg's and you two can have my room."

Once the group internalized the old-new development between Powderkeg and Cleo, all eyes turned back to Old Bertha.

"Oh, what the hell," she finally said. "Fernando, I think you need to feed all of us. That is, if the food didn't all blow away. I'll fix up a room for these boys."

"You got it," Fernando said.

Pappy, Old Bertha, Powderkeg, Cleo, Maggie, Polly, Titan, and Jeffries headed down the soggy hillside. Erinn stood cemented to the earth where her computer had met its end.

"Let's go back to town," Wesley said.

"It's all gone," Erinn said.

"Those interviews aren't the story anyway," Wesley said gently. "You said so yourself."

"Aha!" Erinn said. "I knew I was on the right track, Mr. Wesley Tensaw."

"You're impossible," he said.

"Really?" Erinn stomped through the mud as they headed into town. "I thought I was remarkable."

"No," Wesley said. "You said *I* was remarkable."

After the other townspeople left, it was very quiet on the farm. Dymphna and Professor Johnson looked down over Fat Chance.

"We should get down there pretty soon," Professor Johnson said. "That hillside will be tough to navigate in the dark."

"Do you think it makes sense to rebuild?" Dymphna asked.

"That depends on whether you want to stay," Professor Johnson said.

"Maybe I'd stay if it made sense to rebuild."

"That's not much of a reason."

"If I didn't rebuild, you could use this land for grapes."

"Yes, I could."

Dymphna shivered in the rapidly cooling breeze.

"We better get down to town," she said.

Chapter 35

Night was merciful. As the inhabitants of Fat Chance sat around the big center table at the café, it was easy to ignore the ruin they would face in the morning. While the Creekside Inn and the stores on the boardwalk had been spared destruction, the giant had not left the place unscathed. Mud covered all the buildings, Main Street was a river of sludge, and the boardwalk had gaping holes.

Erinn retrieved her camera from Powderkeg's store. She knew she had the interviews with Old Bertha and Titan, which were both compelling pieces. If her hunch was right, and she could get around Wesley, the interview with Titan would be gold.

She looked around the table, trying to gauge the group dynamic. Fernando and Polly just seemed absorbed in getting the food on the table. Polly enlisted Maggie's help. Professor Johnson and Dymphna appeared to be barely speaking. Erinn was glad to see Jeffries and Titan staring moonily into each other's eyes. If Titan was going to leave Fat Chance, now that the forge was gone, he'd need all the support he could get. Cleo and Powderkeg were also playing the role of lovebirds, but that seemed to be a familiar story to the townspeople. Old Bertha and Pappy seemed drained by the events of the day, but Pappy seemed alert. Erinn noticed that Wesley kept trying to catch Pappy's eye, but Pappy studiously avoided eye contact with the big-city attorney.

Erinn was itching to get to Pappy. If her suspicions were right, she'd have the story of the century. The fact that he seemed wary of Wesley checked yet another box on her list of theories. She needed to keep an eye on him. He'd bolted once; she wanted to make sure he wouldn't get a chance to do it again.

Pappy suddenly stood up and tapped his mason jar with a spoon.

Unlike the *ping ping* of fine crystal, the mason jar sounded a flat *ponk ponk ponk.* But it got everyone's attention.

"I know this has been a rough day for everybody," Pappy said. Turning to Titan and then to Dymphna, he added, "Some more than others. But as mayor of Fat Chance . . ."

He glared at Professor Johnson, daring him to wage a war of words over Pappy's self-appointed office. None came. Pappy resumed his speech.

"I am calling a town meeting in a half hour."

This is it, thought Erinn.

This is it, thought Maggie.

They each had their suspicions, but none of them knew for certain what Pappy was going to say. If Erinn was right, she'd make a name for herself in the respected world of documentarians. If Maggie was right, she'd blow the town apart.

"Why not just have the meeting right now?" Powderkeg asked. "We're all pretty beat."

"This is official business—sorta," Pappy said. "Plus, I want to talk privately to Bertha. She deserves to hear this first. So I'll see you all in City Hall in one half hour. Do. Not. Be. Late." Pappy turned and escorted Old Bertha out the door to the boardwalk.

Erinn stood in the back of City Hall, camera perched on the tripod, ready to record and make history. Wesley stood beside her.

"I guess there is no sense in trying to get you to hear him out before you shoot this," he said.

"I don't think I need to answer that, do I?"

"No," he said. "I just thought I'd give it a shot."

"I'm just doing my job."

"Spare me," Wesley said. "Nobody has hidden behind that line more than I."

Pappy and Old Bertha walked in, hand and hand. Bertha's eyes were swollen. She looked grim but resigned. The din of conversation came to a halt as they made their way to the front of the room. Old Bertha sat in the front row, next to Polly, Cleo, and Powderkeg.

"This isn't going to be easy," Pappy said.

Erinn quickly pushed "play." She looked in the viewfinder. It was a little dark, but she irised down and got a little more light on Pappy. She put in her earbuds. If she was right, the audio was going to be even more important than the video. She waited, along with the rest of the room, for Pappy to speak.

"I know y'all are used to me taking off now and then," Pappy said. "It's not easy being mayor and sometimes I just get sick of you guys and need a break."

"This isn't news, Pappy," Powderkeg said and yawned.

"Keep your pants on," Pappy snarled. "This time was a little different. Not the part about needing a break. I was pretty fed up with all the fighting about the road and the grapes. I see the young lady in the back is taping this, so for the record, I'm on Professor Johnson's side about the road and Fernando's side about the grapes, should that be of any interest."

"It isn't," Powderkeg said. "Could you get to the point?"

"May we have a private conversation before you proceed?" Wesley blurted out.

"Request denied, Counsel," Pappy said.

Everyone in the room stiffened. What was happening?

"I'll start with what you know. Going way back, Clarence 'Cutthroat' Johnson learned how to make money. He earned his nickname. He never broke the law, but he'd mow an opponent down as easy as look at him. He was a powerful man, more powerful than any of you could imagine. Except maybe Mr. Tensaw over there. He could probably imagine."

Everyone turned to stare at Wesley, who sat stone-faced.

"Anyway, as he got more and more powerful, he couldn't manage his empire by himself. He would have if he could, but just keeping the jackals at bay takes backup. So he hired Sebastian Pennyfeather. Sebastian Pennyfeather was equally ruthless. Maybe more so, because he didn't have Cutthroat's instincts. So he had to be twice as cold-blooded. The media never knew this, but once Cutthroat Clarence had kids, and then a grandkid, for cryin' out loud, he'd every once in a while exhibit a few moments of compassion. But Sebastian Pennyfeather would get him right back on track. Until the Sweet Darling tragedy."

Pappy stopped and wiped his glasses. He looked frightened, something the people of Fat Chance had never seen before. He put his glasses back on. He avoided looking at Titan as he continued.

"When Sweet ran into that car, everything changed. For months, the press hounded Cutthroat, and Pennyfeather was so busy with damage control that he didn't realize . . . he didn't want to realize . . . that maybe there was more to life than making money. He was so busy arguing with Cutthroat, insisting that he couldn't take any responsibility for Sweet's death or help her little boy, that he forgot his . . . his humanity."

"I think you're being very unfair to Uncle Sebastian," Cleo said. "He was a good man."

"No, he wasn't," Pappy said. "No. He wasn't."

"Well, you're entitled to your opinion," Cleo said frostily. "I guess you can say anything you want, since he's not here."

"He is here," Pappy said. "I'm Sebastian Pennyfeather."

Silence enveloped the room. Nobody moved. Suddenly, Titan sprang up with such force that his chair tipped over. Every muscle in his immense body was tensed. Pappy didn't say a word, but he didn't shrink back.

"You . . ." Titan said, pointing at Pappy.

Titan ran from the room. Jeffries leapt up to chase after him, but Professor Johnson stopped him.

"Titan wants to be alone," Professor Johnson said.

"It's pitch-black," Jeffries argued.

"Titan knows this country like the back of his hand. If anything happens to you, this situation will only get worse."

"I can't just sit here," Jeffries said, pushing past the professor and running outside.

Chapter 36

Tremors of disbelief filled the hall.

"I think that's enough for tonight," the man they once knew as Pappy said. "We can take this up in the morning. I got to go after that damn fool."

"I don't think Titan wants to talk to you right now," Fernando said, not unkindly.

"I know that," Pappy snapped. "I'm talking about Jeffries. He'll get himself killed out there."

With that, Pappy was gone. The rest of the group filed out slowly, too stunned to speak.

Erinn shut off her camera. She could feel Wesley's accusing stare boring into her back. She straightened her spine and met his glare.

"Did you get everything you wanted to ruin a man's life?" Wesley said.

"I'd say Papp ... Pennyfeather did a fine job of that, himself," Erinn said. "I don't understand why *I'm* the bad guy here."

"Because Mr. Pennyfeather must have suspected you were getting close," Wesley said. "That's why he ran in the first place."

"I don't think so," Erinn said. "He was gone long before I started to get the pieces to fit. I think he ran because he recognized *you*."

"That's ... that's possible."

"In which case," Erinn said, snapping her camera off the tripod, "*you're* to blame for ruining his life. You knew all along?"

"I suspected all along. As you said, it didn't make sense that this Pappy character just showed up out of nowhere. Plus, when he 'died,' Pennyfeather had no insurance policies, no next-of-kin, no will leaving his money to charity. If my assumptions were correct, Pennyfeather hadn't broken any laws. For years, I was too busy trying to stay afloat as the new head of a very important law firm to give it much thought. After this 'Pappy' surfaced, it all started to make sense."

"Why didn't you do anything about it?"

"On the one hand, the man hadn't broken any laws, so what did it matter to me?"

"And on the other hand?"

"He left me a law firm. With one faked accident, he'd made my career. Why would I ever want to find him?"

"What changed?"

"I didn't want *you* to find him."

"So you've basically just been trying to thwart me?" Erinn asked.

"Pretty much," Wesley said. "It's nothing personal. I'm just a huge fan of letting sleeping dogs lie."

"This sleeping dog couldn't tell more lies if you paid him."

She started to pack up her camera, then she stopped abruptly. "I just realized something."

"What's that?"

"I have no place to sleep tonight. I was up at the farm."

"You can stay with me."

Professor Johnson and Dymphna retreated to the little living space Professor Johnson had created in the back of the Boozehound before he abandoned it to live up at the farm. Professor Johnson stoked the fire while Dymphna looked for blankets. The two of them made the bed without speaking. When the room was warm enough, they crawled into bed. Dymphna could feel Professor Johnson shaking. She snuggled against him.

"Are you cold?" she asked.

"No," he said. "I'm just overwhelmed by Pappy's confession. I mean, I *knew* Sebastian Pennyfeather. How could I not have known in these last few years?"

"First of all, you were gone for six months, so it's really been only two-and-a-half years," Dymphna said. "And you were just a little boy when Pennyfeather died. Didn't die. When Pennyfeather left. I'm sure he wasn't a gray-haired, gun-toting cowboy when he was running around Beverly Hills."

"No, he wasn't," Professor Johnson said.

Dymphna could feel him relax into sleep. She realized how exhausted she was. She tried not to think about what they would all face in the morning. Everything she had was gone. It would only make sense to leave. She kissed Professor Johnson's shoulder. She felt something cold and wet on her arm. More rain? She saw Thud's large head propped up on the edge of the mattress. She looked at him. His tail started wagging furiously. She knew he was waiting on an invitation to join them in the small bed. Dymphna scooted over.

"You can come up," she said. "But if you wake your dad, you're in big trouble."

Maggie moved back to the jail cell. She figured Pappy probably wasn't coming back tonight, but she didn't want to be anywhere near his place if he did. He was, after all, a lawyer. He might sue her or something.

Maggie put the pouch under the mattress. She lay on the cot in the cell, hands clasped over her head. She wondered if she had lost all her leverage with Dodge, now that Pappy had confessed. She sighed. Maybe she could fake Dodge out and get the pouch to him before Erinn broke her story. He didn't actually *need* to have something to hold over Fat Chance; he only had to *think* he did until Maggie got her traveling money.

She'd contact Dodge tomorrow.

I'll miss this place, she thought, then fell fast asleep.

"How could you not recognize him?" Cleo asked Powderkeg as she smoothed another quilt over them.

"He was your fake uncle," Powderkeg said. "Not mine."

"But you knew him, too," Cleo insisted. "And you were in the military."

"What has that got to do with anything?"

"Weren't you trained to notice things like that?"

"I was in the army," he said. "I wasn't James Bond."

"What happens now? Am I supposed to go back to calling him Uncle Sebastian?"

"I don't think so. I think he became Pappy and now that's who he is."

"Until that horrible woman breaks the story," Cleo said. "I never liked her."

"Sweetheart," Powderkeg said sleepily, "you never like anyone."

* * *

Pappy found Jeffries some time later. He was scratched and bleeding, sitting on a log about a mile down the creek from Fat Chance. The sun was just coming up.

"Mind if I join you?" Pappy asked.

"If you can keep from saying 'I told you so,'" Jeffries said.

"Deal."

"Actually, I can't stop you." Jeffries winced. "I think I sprained my ankle."

"In that case," Pappy said, sitting heavily on the log, "I told you so." The two men sat silently, listening to the hills come to life.

"Can I ask you something?" Jeffries said.

"Go ahead," Pappy said. "It'll be good practice."

"Why'd you do it?"

"What?" Pappy said. "Disappear thirty years ago or confess just now?"

"Take your pick."

"I strong-armed Cutthroat into staying as far away from the Sweet Darling fiasco as he could. One chink in the armor and the press would have taken him down. It was my job to protect him. But I just couldn't get Sweet out of my mind," Pappy said. "I was kind of in love with her. We all were. She never knew it, of course, but I was really crazy about that girl. That's what made it all so terrible. I loved her and I turned my back on her little boy."

"Why couldn't you just come clean and admit you pushed the girl into doing something she didn't want to do?"

"It was my job to keep Cutthroat out of hot water. He was a friend as well as a client, you know. I tried everything I could to find a way to live with the pain and the guilt. Cutthroat and I traveled a lot. When we got to Fat Chance, I knew I wanted to disappear here. It was perfect. Nobody saw us. By the time we'd put the plan in place, Sebastian Pennyfeather was out on an extended fishing vacation on his yacht and I'd grown enough hair to play the hermit of Fat Chance."

"You must have panicked when Cutthroat said he was sending people to Fat Chance after all those years."

"I couldn't believe it!" Pappy said, the surprise still in his voice. "I figured I could get away with it when it was a bunch of strangers, but then he started with the family members—Cleo, Elwood, and Marshall . . . I mean Cleo, Professor Johnson, and Powderkeg."

"I know who Elwood and Marshall are," Jeffries said. "I work at the mansion, remember? Well, 'worked,' I suspect. Were you worried they'd recognize you?"

"Not really." Pappy shrugged. "Cleo never really noticed anybody, Elwood was just a little kid, and Powderkeg wasn't around much. They were already having problems. Besides, by that time, I barely recognized myself.

"And then he hit me with the hardest part of all. He said he was sending Titan. I blew a fuse. I told him I wouldn't stand for it. I couldn't bear to see that boy. I begged him to reconsider. But he said if he owed anybody, it was Titan. He knew I'd have no comeback to that."

"You left when we came in that night in the limousine. Was it because of Erinn?"

"I didn't know Erinn from a hole in the head," Pappy said dismissively. "It was when I saw Wesley that I panicked. I had no idea why he'd come, but I figured he either knew the truth or would figure it out pretty quick. So I ran."

"But you came back."

"I couldn't leave these lambs to the slaughter of a twister," Pappy said. "I had to come back."

"But why confess?"

"When Cutthroat finally reached me to tell me he was dying, he said, 'You know, Penny, you can't hide forever.' I didn't believe him, but he was right. I want to marry Old Bertha, but how do you ask someone to trust you with her life when your own life is a lie?"

"I hear you," Jeffries said softly.

"Plus, when I left, I didn't know this, but that Erinn is one sharp gal. I could tell by the way she looked at me that she had my number. Wesley too. I'd rather bust this story open than have it busted open for me."

"One more question," Jeffries said. "Why are you telling me all this?"

"Because I'm going to go find Titan. And he might not listen to me. So I want you to know the facts. I hope you two have a long, happy life together and maybe one day he'll want to hear this," Pappy said, looking down at Jeffries's ankle. "How bad is that ankle?"

"It hurts," Jeffries said, rotating it gingerly. "But I can get myself back to town."

"You sure?"

"Go find Titan."

Without another word, Pappy stood up and walked down along the creek.

Chapter 37

Titan came across a tree that had fallen over the once-peaceful creek in the storm. He strode across a makeshift bridge over the swollen, raging water below. He'd walked all night and wasn't sure exactly where he was. Exhausted, he stretched out on a large, flat rock that jutted over the fast-moving water and closed his eyes. The boulder was still cold, but the morning sun felt comforting on his face.

Like a mother's touch.

He wasn't sure if he'd fallen asleep, but he felt a shadow come between him and the sun. He opened his eyes.

"I don't think it's a good idea for you to be here," he said, sitting up and glaring at Pappy. "I'm not feeling very friendly right now."

"I understand," Pappy said. "And I wouldn't blame you if you threw me off this rock and into the river. I'd rather you didn't, but that's up to you."

Pappy sat down on the rock. He waited for Titan to speak.

"I'm really mad at you," Titan said.

"I know."

"I trusted you."

"I know."

"I feel betrayed."

"I know."

"Don't you have anything else to say?" Titan asked.

"I have a million things to say," Pappy said. "But I really don't want you to throw me in the river."

"The worst part," Titan said, "is that I felt like you were the father I never had, like the parent I never had. And now I find out that's all a lie."

"Hold on," Pappy said, turning to face Titan squarely. "My whole life here had been a lie. Until you came. Because the feeling is mutual, Titan. You're the son I never had. And if I had a son, I wish he could have been just like you."

Titan started to tear up. "You're just saying that so I don't throw you in the river."

"That's my boy," Pappy said as he put a meaty paw on Titan's shoulder. "Why'd you pick this spot to stop?"

"I don't know," Titan said. "I just got tired. Why?"

"Because this is the exact spot I first saw Fancy years ago. I was fishing and saw this poor old bird hopping around the creek. I could tell her wing was broke."

"Mr. Pennyfeather, I think the bad grammar sounds a little fake at this point," Titan said.

"I'll make a deal with you," Pappy said. "You never, ever refer to me as Mr. Pennyfeather and I'll give up the coy grammar."

"Sounds fair."

"At first, I just shooed her away. Buzzards throw up on you as a defense, so I wasn't exactly going to ask her to dance. But I knew she wouldn't live long out here with that wing. I tried to catch her. But even on the ground, she was too fast for me."

"So what happened?"

"One day, I was sitting on a bench on the boardwalk, and she just showed up. Used to hang around Fat Chance, which was fine with me. If anybody happened by, they'd hightail it out of there when they got a look at her. Of course, by that time, I could see that besides the broken wing, she was missing an eye."

"Was she your pet, then?"

"No," Pappy said. "She never came near me. She never came near anybody till you showed up. She might be ugly, but she's a good judge of character."

"Where'd you say you first saw her?"

"Right over there in that rotten log," Pappy said, pointing uphill. "Of course, it wasn't quite that rotted back then, but I'll never forget it."

Titan stood up and started walking toward the log. Pappy watched him, grateful that for now, at least, they had moved on. As Titan scrambled up the slope, two young birds flew into the sky in front of him. Titan turned back to Pappy with a smile.

"Looks like the buzzards are still using this place as a breeding ground," Titan said.

"Buzzards are weird birds," Pappy said. "They make their nests on the ground instead of in trees. The parents stay with their offspring for two or three months and then the babies just . . . fly away. Like those two!"

Pappy and Titan watched the baby birds fly toward the trees.

"I hope mama bird was ready to have them fly the coop," Titan said. "I'd hate for her to be mad at me. Not in the mood to be thrown up on by a buzzard."

"Those birds were strong and ready to take off," Pappy said, squinting into the sun as the birds disappeared. "I think you're safe."

"Maybe that's a sign," Titan said. "Of a new beginning."

Chapter 38

Breakfast got started early. Fernando knew that even though everyone was exhausted from the giant's visit, no one would get much sleep waiting on Pappy, Titan, and Jeffries. His heart ached when he realized he'd never have to sound the dinner triangle again to call Dymphna, Professor Johnson, and Thud from up on the hill or Titan from the forge.

Never say never.

Jeffries was the first into the café, limping and leaning on a piece of wood he was using as a walking stick. Fernando helped him off with his shoe and was examining his ankle when Polly came bounding in.

"I saw Jeffries from my window," Polly said to Fernando.

She was breathless, having obviously run from the inn.

"Want me to take a look at that foot?" she asked Jeffries, nudging Fernando aside.

"Do you have any medical training?" Jeffries asked, after getting a look of alarm from Fernando.

"No," Polly said. "But I might be working on a wagon train soon and I need the practice."

She realized this was the first time she'd said those words and meant it. She glanced quickly at Fernando, who looked pensive.

"It might not make sense for *any* of us to stay here," she said quietly.

"I'm not ready to face that," Fernando said. "But you might be right."

Professor Johnson and Dymphna walked through the archway that connected the café to the Boozehound.

"I forgot you were staying in town," Fernando said. "I guess I'll have to get used to that."

Professor Johnson and Dymphna both realized this was a perfect opening to mention their future plans, but neither did. Instead, Professor Johnson said, "How are the grapes doing?"

Dymphna's mouth tightened.

"As far as I can tell, we lost about a third," Fernando said. "We'll have to get a more accurate count, of course, but I think that's going to be what we find. We'll have to scale back, but we can still move forward, if that's what you're asking."

"It is," Professor Johnson said.

"I'm surprised you didn't already check," Fernando said.

"I've had my hands full trying to figure out what to do about Dymphna's farmhouse," he said.

As soon as they smelled biscuits being baked and coffee being brewed, most of the townspeople straggled to the center table. Maggie was pacing Main Street, trying to find a cell phone signal.

It was still two hours before the café actually opened, but they knew they were welcome and they needed to be together. It had been a long night.

Jeffries told and retold how he twisted his ankle and how Pappy had set out to find Titan. A sigh of relief went up. Pappy might be a deceitful charlatan, but he was still Pappy, and the best scout in the area.

Pappy and Titan walked through the door, ridiculous grins on their faces. Cleo, being younger, beat Old Bertha to the punch of being the first to hug Pappy, and Dymphna was the first to hug Titan. No one was pretending that life was going to be the same, but at least everyone made it through the night.

"Quiet! Quiet!" Pappy bawled.

The group went silent.

"Titan found something he'd like y'all to see," Pappy said.

Titan, still grinning, opened the door as wide as he could.

Fancy limped in, giving them all her one-eyed squint. Amid cries of surprise, Thud was on his feet in a heartbeat. He charged. Fancy let out a loud squawk and scurried out as Titan caught Thud by the collar. The joy everyone was feeling disintegrated as they realized Fancy was heading for the forge.

"I'll be right back," Titan said to the group.

Titan gave Thud a hard stare as he let go of his collar and the dog sat down.

As he took off after Fancy, the group crowded around the window. Titan and Fancy walked slowly down still-sodden Main Street to the flattened forge, passing Maggie on the way. Maggie jumped out of the way when she saw Fancy, but still punched at her cell phone screen.

Rocket was standing sentry by the Cinderella coach.

"The coach," Erinn breathed. "Titan built the coach for Fancy."

Titan swept a few pieces of wood out of Fancy's path. He bowed as the bird crab-walked up the three shallow steps and disappeared inside.

"Hope she likes it," Powderkeg said.

"It's actually very comfortable." Old Bertha sniffed, glad to be an authority on something.

Once Fancy was installed in her coach, the inhabitants of Fat Chance watched as Titan picked his way back to Main Street. He stopped and studied the ground for a minute. He heaved a chunk of metal out of the way and pulled out a large, wet mass of brown and tan fabric.

"My quilt!" Old Bertha cried. "He found my quilt!"

As Titan approached, the group hurried back to their seats but kept their eyes on the window, watching as Titan snapped the leather and canvas quilt in the breeze, sending even more mud flying.

"I just washed those windows," Fernando complained. At Bertha's look, he went silent.

Titan returned to the café. The townspeople made a fuss over Old Bertha's quilt, praising her for her insight of using leather and canvas. No ordinary cotton quilt would ever have survived.

"What *is* this?" Pappy said, studying the lump.

"It was going to be a quilt for you." Old Bertha blushed. "I know it's kind of crazy."

"Actually," Pappy said, standing up and letting the quilt roll out to its full length, "if you could make it a little longer, this would be an impressive new top for the Covered Volkswagen."

Old Bertha beamed. The hard questions no one knew how to ask about Pappy or about the future of the town were set aside while Titan recounted finding Fancy. He told them about stumbling upon the nest just as the baby birds were taking flight.

"All of a sudden, I heard Pappy give a low whistle and say 'holy f—'" He turned to Pappy, in apology for busting him. "Pappy said the f-word."

The group looked reproachfully at Pappy. Everyone knew Titan didn't like swearing.

"Go on," Pappy said in his authoritative, gravelly voice.

"I looked down at the log and there she was," Titan said, a quaver in his voice. "She only left to have some babies!"

"That daddy buzzard must have been drunk," Powderkeg said, shaking his head. "I forgot how nasty-looking that old girl is."

As the coffeepot was emptied, the fate of the town hung in the air.

"I have some clothes you can borrow," Polly whispered to Dymphna. "Everything will be too long, but I can hem stuff."

Dymphna nodded, afraid of grateful tears if she tried to speak. She looked out the café window at her sister, still marching up and down Main Street. Maggie's clothes would fit her perfectly, but it seemed obvious to everyone that Maggie was not going to lend a helping hand.

Professor Johnson stood up. Everyone quieted down.

"We have so much to be grateful for," Professor Johnson said. "But we have to make some decisions. Some can wait, but some have to be addressed immediately."

"Like what?"

"Well, Main Street, for one."

A unified moan escaped the group. Professor Johnson rapped his knuckles on the table.

"We need to rebuild," Professor Johnson said, carefully avoiding Dymphna's eyes. "I mean, if enough of us decide to stay, we're going to have to have supplies delivered and Main Street is almost gone. In case you haven't noticed, there's an inch-thick covering of mud on everything—and most of that mud came from Main Street."

"He has a point," Fernando said, surprising everyone with his about-face. Fernando had been the strongest opponent to paving the street.

"Hey," Fernando said, indignantly, "I can admit when I'm wrong."

"He has a point, if enough of us stay here," Old Bertha said. She turned with huge, scared eyes to Pappy. "We are staying, aren't we?"

"That's up to this young lady," Pappy said, indicating Erinn.

Erinn realized the masterful move on Pappy's part. She looked at

Wesley, who looked as expectant as the rest of the table. She was saved from having to answer as Maggie barged in.

"I have some good news," Maggie chirped. "Dodge says to tell you the paint came in right before the storm hit. Spoonerville is fine and there's minimal damage to the ranch. He'll bring the paint over as soon as he can. I told him Main Street was a mess, but he says his truck can handle it."

"Why were you talking to Dodge?" Cleo asked.

No one in Fat Chance liked Dodge Durham, but for Cleo, he was Public Enemy #1—at least in Texas.

Maggie ignored the question as she plopped down in a chair. In contrast to everyone else, who looked haggard and pale, Maggie was practically glowing.

"I guess I'll ask the question everyone is thinking," Professor Johnson said. "What paint?"

Maggie just shrugged as she reached for a biscuit.

"I can explain," Dymphna said. She looked imploringly at Professor Johnson. "I thought the grapes and Main Street had become hot-button issues and I just . . . well . . . Titan and I just thought a group project might unify us."

"So you bought *paint*?" Cleo asked incredulously.

"Whitewash," Dymphna said, hanging her head. "It seemed a good idea at the time."

"It's brilliant!" Powderkeg bellowed. "Let's face it, once we scrape the mud off these buildings, they're going to need a coat of paint."

"And who's going to paint them?" Cleo asked.

"My point exactly," Professor Johnson said. "But that's the question: Who's staying?"

There was a painful silence at the table.

"All right," Professor Johnson said. "We'll take this one at a time. Fernando?"

"I'm staying," he said simply.

"Titan?" Professor Johnson asked.

Titan and Jeffries were looking at each other. Jeffries gave a nod so brief, Professor Johnson wasn't sure he'd seen it.

But Titan had. He took Jeffries's hand.

"We're staying."

"Powderkeg? Auntie?" Professor Johnson turned toward them.

"We're staying," Powderkeg said at the same time Cleo said, "We're not staying."

"You can't be serious," Cleo said to Powderkeg. "The town has always been a wreck and now it's a disaster! Why would you want to stay here?"

"I belong here," Powderkeg said simply. "My shop is still here and I have orders to fill that will take me through next year."

"But this place is regularly hit by tornadoes," Cleo said.

"Says the woman who lives in a desert prone to earthquakes," Powderkeg said. "And, until now, there hasn't been a tornado here in eighty years."

"So, you're planning on staying here and rebuilding, is that what you're saying?"

"That's about right," Powderkeg said.

"You'd be crazy to start all this again," she said.

"Tell that to the people of New Orleans," Powderkeg said.

"Don't get me started on New Orleans," Cleo said.

"Cleo, honey, every time you go back to Los Angeles, you find a reason to come back here," he said. "Doesn't that tell you something?"

"Yes," Cleo said, forgetting that she was sitting with a group of people. She put her hand over his weathered one and continued. "I keep coming back for *you*."

"And I'm always right here."

Polly let out a small sniffle and wiped at a tear running down her cheek. Fernando glared at her. This was good stuff, but the group had silently determined to pretend they weren't privy to the intimacy of the moment.

"What would I do here?" Cleo asked dramatically, sweeping her arms wide. "Fernando has made more of a success with his dismal cowboy food than I ever did with my French cooking." She blinked at the group, as if surprised to find them all there, and added, "No insult intended, Fernando."

"None taken," Fernando said, heaving a sigh of relief that she wasn't going to demand the café back.

"Auntie," Professor Johnson said. "If I may be so bold, you've got more money than God, and we could use an investment in the vineyard. You know wine and you must know people in the wine business."

"Don't be obtuse, Elwood," Cleo said. "Of course I know people in the wine business."

"You could be the face of Fat Chance wines and get it into prestigious wine competitions that we'd never get into otherwise. We need to win some medals."

"Wait a minute," Fernando said, trying to keep the excitement out of his voice. "You mean . . ."

"The logical thing would still be to go about this my way and create a reliable wine that would have a steady client base," Professor Johnson said. "But when that tornado was tearing our lives to shreds, it made me think. Did I really want my epitaph to be 'Here lies a man who made dependable wine'? That's not who I want to be."

Cheers erupted from the table.

"I can't promise I'll stay," Cleo said to Powderkeg. "But I'll take on the winery."

"We'll take it one day at time," Powderkeg said.

Professor Johnson moved on with his questioning. "Polly?"

"I don't know," Polly said. "I love everyone here, but I'm only twenty-four. Part of me wants to stay, part of me wants to go. Poet wants me to go to Nebraska with him and Lucinda in Galveston wants me to move there and take over her shop."

"OK," Professor Johnson said. "So . . . we'll put you down as a 'maybe'?"

Polly nodded as she and Old Bertha both started crying.

"Pappy?" Professor Johnson said. "That brings us back to you."

"Same answer as before," Pappy said. "It's up to Erinn . . . and Wesley."

"It has nothing to do with me," Wesley said. "You haven't broken any laws and nobody is looking for you. I'm happy to go back to Los Angeles and pretend this never happened."

All eyes turned to Erinn. She gripped her camera to her chest, as if protecting her baby from a pack of wolves.

"You must understand this is a big story," Erinn said. "One of the biggest."

No one spoke.

"Even with all the footage I lost . . ." Erinn began.

Old Bertha leaned in to explain to Titan, "Because there were no clouds."

"I could make my reputation with this," Erinn said, looking around imploringly. "But," she said as she put her camera on the table, "Professor Johnson is right. Do I want my legacy to be the woman who ruined the lives of the most interesting, courageous group of people she ever met?"

"I'm hoping the answer to that is no," Pappy said quietly.

"The answer *is* no." Erinn sighed, opening her camera and pulling out the tiny memory chip. She put it on the table. "I'm going to close my eyes, and maybe the rest of my footage will disappear. I don't have the fortitude to destroy it myself, but if it should happen to disappear in the next few seconds, I won't have a story."

She closed her eyes. When she opened them, the chip was gone.

"Thank you," Old Bertha whispered without looking at Erinn.

"We're staying," Pappy said, his verve returning. "Bertha and I are staying. I'm getting old and might retire as mayor, but we're staying."

"You can't retire," Professor Johnson said.

"Why, Professor Johnson, I didn't know you cared," Pappy said.

"You can't retire because you are not the mayor!" Professor Johnson said.

"You're a consistent fellow, I'll give you that," Pappy said with a smirk.

"You haven't asked me if I'm staying," Dymphna said so quietly no one but Professor Johnson heard her.

"Because I'm afraid to ask you," he said.

"Why? Why would you be afraid to ask me?"

"Because you have no reason to stay," Professor Johnson said. "You can take your animals and go anywhere. Your home is gone."

"No, it isn't," Dymphna said. "As long as you're living and breathing, I have a home."

Professor Johnson pulled her out of her chair, swept back her hair and kissed her. Both of them had tears in their eyes.

"I didn't dare hope . . ." Professor Johnson said. "I've been focused on all the wrong things, and I—"

"Shhh," Dymphna said. "No, you weren't. When you told Fernando that you were more worried about my house than the grapes, I realized I was the one focusing on the wrong things, adding up all the stupid little slings and arrows."

Thud scrambled to his feet and tried to join their embrace. When the dog stood on his hind legs, he was taller than Dymphna. Professor Johnson had become adept at holding them both up. It was second nature to all three of them to stand that way.

"Does anybody care if I'm staying?" Maggie blurted resentfully.

There was a stunned silence. No one spoke.

"Well, I'm not," Maggie said.

"Where are you going?" Polly said, genuinely interested.

The telltale vibration of trucks coming down the road from the highway interrupted her reply. Maggie knew it was Dodge, although it sounded as if he had several men with him as well.

"I don't know exactly where I'm going," Maggie said, "but I think I'm about to get a whole bunch of options."

As the trucks hit the sludge of Main Street, the whine of gears shifting into low ran through the café.

"Better put more coffee on," Fernando said. "Sounds like it's going to be business as usual."

No, Maggie thought as Fernando and Polly headed to the kitchen. *It's not.*

Chapter 39

Dodge was putting down his tailgate as Maggie fought her way through the steady stream of cowboys heading into the café. Ranch hands and Fat Chance locals exchanged horror stories of the day before, a new Texas tall tale being born every minute.

"You got something for me?" Dodge growled at Maggie.

"I do," Maggie said. But before she could reach for the pouch, the residents of Fat Chance came out on the boardwalk.

"You have our paint?" Dymphna asked excitedly. "This is perfect timing! If we'd painted the buildings two days ago, it would have been a waste."

"That really would have been a damn shame," Dodge said, a huge smile on his face. "Here you go."

He gestured toward the back of his truck. Dymphna and Titan looked in. Excited anticipation dropping from their faces.

"What is this?" Dymphna asked.

"The paint you ordered," Dodge said, barely containing his glee.

"But we ordered whitewash," Dymphna said.

"I don't understand," Titan said, taking in the truck-bed full of paint cans. "What are all these colors? Do any of them even match?"

"Sure," Dodge said genially. "There are four cans of Ruddy Rose, four cans of Sunburst, four cans of Lemon Maze, four cans of Green Apple, four cans of Sky, four cans of In-Ya-Go Blue and my favorite, Old Bruise . . . it's a kind of purple."

Titan tried again. "We ordered white."

"If you remember, I said I could get you a deal. This is what I got a deal on." Dodge sneered. "You should like it, Titan. It's the rainbow."

Jeffries and Fernando took a step forward, but Powderkeg stopped them.

"Let Titan handle it," he said.

"But we gave you a thousand dollars," Titan said in disbelief.

All the townspeople and cowboys were now on the porch, witnessing Dodge's victory.

"Wow, Dodge, you can be a real asshole," came a voice no one knew.

It was Poet.

"Watch your mouth, Poet, or you're fired," Dodge said.

"I don't work for you," Poet said, jumping off the boardwalk and standing under Dodge's nose. He was half Dodge's size. He looked into the truck, then back at Polly.

"What do you say, Polly, you think your hat store would look better in Old Bruise or Green Apple?" asked Poet.

"Well," Polly said, considering, "if we've got red, orange, yellow, green, blue, indigo, and violet, maybe we should paint the town in order of the rainbow?"

"Nah," Poet said. "This is Texas. Let's make our own rainbow."

"My God," Old Bertha said. "He is a poet."

Dodge stood, in all his pettiness, yelling at the Rolling Fork Ranch cowboys as they helped unload the paint. Some had already started to clear the mud from the buildings. Old Bertha insisted the inn, as the biggest building in town, needed two colors.

Maggie watched as her sister and Professor Johnson seriously discussed which horrible color to paint the Boozehound. Fernando was laughing with two huge ranch hands who were scraping big chunks of mud off the Cowboy Food Café. Erinn and Wesley helped Jeffries clean the limousine.

"All right," Dodge said, "let's get down to business. What have you got for me?"

Maggie stared at him. She was alone. The outsider. Again. The difference this time was that she didn't blame her sister. These people had been ready to accept her when she arrived in Fat Chance. Her sister had not run Maggie out of town when Dymphna walked in on Maggie hitting on Professor Johnson. Old Bertha had taken Maggie in until Maggie accused Old Bertha of stealing. Powderkeg had given her a job. Cleo had found her a place to stay—even if it was just to keep Maggie away from Cleo's ex. And Cleo had reason to worry. Maggie knew she had made herself the outsider. But it didn't have to be that way. And maybe it wasn't too late to change.

"For you?" Maggie asked. "I've got nothing for you."

She walked away down the boardwalk until she reached Powderkeg and Cleo. Cleo showed Maggie the can of In-Ya-Go Blue.

"For Powderkeg's shop," Cleo said. "What do you think?"

"I like it," Maggie said.

She watched Dodge's truck screech up the road. She knew he was fuming, thwarted by his own pettiness.

That's the epitaph I don't *want*, Maggie thought. *"Here lies a woman thwarted by her own pettiness."*

She made her way to Pappy's side.

"I have something for you," she said.

She walked behind the building and Pappy followed. She handed him the pouch. His hands shook as he held it.

"I found it up at the farm one day," she said.

"It was hidden," Pappy said. "It's been hidden for years."

"I know."

"What were you looking for?"

"Trouble," Maggie said. "I was looking for trouble. But now I'm not, so I thought you might like to have it, you know, as a souvenir of other days."

"A souvenir of another life," Pappy said, almost to himself.

"I'll leave you to it," Maggie said. "I'm going to see if I can help my sister." She left Pappy standing alone. She didn't look back.

With shaking fingers, Pappy undid the strings.

He lifted out an old belt.

The buckle was copper, almost green now. He rubbed his thumb over the etched feather.

He thought he'd dodged a bullet with Erinn, but all the time there was this other time bomb waiting to go off. Maggie could have taken his life away from him and she chose not to. He knew better than to think he was safe forever. But he had to admit he'd been pretty lucky so far. He might still be exposed one day. But now that Titan and Old Bertha knew his terrible secret, he was free to build a life with Bertha— and to be a real father figure to Titan.

If Titan wanted him. But that was for Titan to decide.

Pappy found Old Bertha sitting on the swing on her front porch. She was looking down Main Street, watching Polly and Poet fall further in love. Pappy sat down and put his arm around her.

"I don't want her to go," Old Bertha said. "She's become like a daughter to me."

"I know she has," Pappy said. "But that happens with daughters—and sons. They go their own way if and when the time is right."

"Maybe if I told her . . ."

"Now, Bertha, damn it, you can't go guilting the girl," Pappy said. "If she's gonna go, she's gonna go, and it would be wrong to stop her."

"You're right," Old Bertha said, looking toward Polly. "But when she does, I'm sure gonna miss her."

Jeffries looked up at Erinn and Wesley as they brought buckets of clean water to wash off the limousine.

"Excuse me, sir," Jeffries said, reverting to his formal speech pattern. "If I'm staying here, what are you going to do about getting home?"

Erinn stopped in her tracks. She hadn't thought about that!

"I told you before," Wesley said. "I know how to drive one of these. I was a chauffeur in college."

"You were?" Erinn asked.

"I was," Wesley said. "I haven't always been the world's worst production assistant. I paid my dues."

Erinn went to collect more water and saw Dymphna sitting by herself on the edge of the boardwalk. Erinn sat down next to her.

"Wesley and I are going to head out in the morning," she said. "But maybe I'll come back when the town is strutting its stripes. Maybe I can get a story out of it."

"I'm sorry this has been a waste of time," Dymphna said.

"It wasn't a waste of time," Erinn said. "Not at all. I've learned a lot of valuable lessons here."

"Like what?"

"Well, for one thing, it looks like I can date a Republican."

Dymphna smiled the confused smile she found herself using around Erinn.

"Anything else?"

"Yes," Erinn said, looking around at the marvel that was this little town and the people who loved and protected it so fiercely.

"What happens in Fat Chance, Texas, stays in Fat Chance, Texas."

See how it all began in Celia Bonaduce's

WELCOME TO FAT CHANCE, TEXAS

For champion professional knitter Dymphna Pearl, inheriting part of a sun-blasted ghost town in the Texas hill country isn't just unexpected, it's a little daunting. To earn a cash bequest that could change her life, she'll have to leave California to live in tiny, run-down Fat Chance for six months—with seven strangers. Impossible! Or is it?

Trading her sandals for cowboy boots, Dymphna dives into her new life with equal parts anxiety and excitement. After all, she's never felt quite at home in Santa Monica anyway. Maybe Fat Chance will be her second chance. But making it habitable is going take more than a lasso and Wild West spirit. With an opinionated buzzard overlooking the proceedings and mismatched strangers learning to become friends, Dymphna wonders if unlocking the secrets of her own heart is the way to strike real gold . . .

A Lyrical e-book on sale now!

CHAPTER 1

"Please don't talk to anyone at the yoga stand," Erinn Wolf said. "Those people are dead to us."

"That's a bit harsh," Dymphna Pearl said.

"They threw down the gauntlet," Erinn replied. "Not us."

"I just don't want there to be any hurt feelings," Dymphna said, as she loaded two of her Angora rabbits into the hatchback of the car. Erinn, who was her best friend, landlady, and business partner, filled the backseat with knitwear—hats, scarves, bags, and gloves. When Erinn was upset, it was as if she lived in some medieval melodrama—or at least with the New York Mafia.

"Yes," Dymphna said, as she buckled herself into the passenger side of the car. "But we won. We have to see those people every Sunday. Don't you think it would be nicer to offer an olive branch?"

"By 'olive branch' I take it you mean 'carrot cake'?" Erinn asked as she pulled out of the driveway.

Dymphna winced. "How did you know?" she asked, eyes downcast.

"I could smell it as soon as I woke up!" Erinn said. "I could smell it *before* I woke up. I dreamt the gingerbread man was chasing me—until I realized it was the cinnamon and cloves coming from the guesthouse. I knew to what you were up."

Even when Erinn was in scolding mode, her grammar was perfect.

"I just think we could take the high road," Dymphna said. "I don't want to have enemies at the farmers' market."

"As Franklin Roosevelt once said, 'I ask you to judge me by the enemies I have made,'" Erinn said.

Dymphna thought that Erinn might want to rethink that particular philosophy. Did she really want to be judged by *these* enemies—people offering peace and spinal alignment?

Erinn drove down a deserted Ocean Avenue toward the Santa Monica Farmers' Market on Main Street, where Dymphna had a booth called Knit and Pearl. Dymphna was a bit of a celebrity, since she was the host of a video podcast—produced by Erinn—also called *Knit and Pearl*. The show fueled sales at the farmers' market and the clientele at the farmers' market created new viewers. Erinn, who knew what it took to get attention, insisted that a giant Angora rabbit would trump any display of yoga pants on the aisle, so Dymphna always brought at least two of her six angora yarn–producing rabbits. It seemed like a straightforward business plan, until the owners of the Midnight at the Mirage yoga stand complained the animals were disrupting the quiet zone that was imperative to the success of their business. Dymphna could see their point—people often came to her booth just to pet the fluffy fur of the animals that looked like an explosion in a cotton factory. It was anything but calm.

But Erinn would have none of it. She told the farmers' market board that Dymphna was using the rabbits as educational tools—teaching the public about the proper care of Angora rabbits and their fur. Knit and Pearl was every bit as *enlightening* as a chakra massage. Erinn won, but Dymphna got a stomachache every time the owners of Midnight at the Mirage looked over at a family squealing with delight over one of her rabbits. Dymphna didn't want to stir up Erinn's wrath, which was formidable no matter what the issue, but she thought maybe she'd sneak the carrot cake over to the yoga instructors when Erinn wasn't looking.

Dymphna understood all too well that sinking feeling when you thought your business was threatened. One of her greatest regrets was that she had never made a go of her shepherding business. She had tried to raise a small herd of sheep in Malibu, but when the land she was renting got sold out from under her it just proved to be too expensive. So she traded in her sheep for six Angora rabbits and moved out of the hills. Sometimes she felt guilty about trying to raise rabbits in Santa Monica. Dymphna wasn't sure city life was healthy for rabbits.

Erinn stopped the car near their allotted space and started to unload the collapsible tables and the knitted accessories, while Dymphna tended to Snow D'Winter and Spot, the two giant Angoras chosen to represent the show at the stall.

By midmorning, the farmers' market was humming. Once the booth was set up and everything was running smoothly, Erinn usually headed off to shop for produce. She offered to go shopping for Dymphna, who was stuck at the booth all day, but Dymphna could never gather up all her various scraps of paper on which she'd written reminders of what she needed. At one point, Erinn tried to relieve Dymphna at the booth so she could do her own shopping, but the customers all wanted to talk to Dymphna Pearl, designer of the knit creations, or they wanted to ask questions about the rabbits—questions to which only Dymphna had answers. Dymphna was perfectly content buying her groceries at an actual grocery store, but she knew better than to share that with Erinn.

Erinn started to gather her shopping bags and her detailed list. She turned to Dymphna and held out her palm. "Let me have it."

"Have what?" Dymphna asked.

"The carrot cake. I don't want you to have a weak moment."

Dymphna handed over the carrot cake and watched Erinn stride purposefully into the crowd. On one hand, Erinn could be exasperating, but on the other you had to hand it to her—she had amazing instincts.

Dymphna gave Spot and Snow D'Winter some fresh water. When she turned back toward the front of the booth, a tense-looking woman was standing in front of a display of knitted scarves. She didn't appear to be all that interested in them, though. Instead she was staring intently at Dymphna.

"May I help you?" Dymphna inquired.

The woman seemed startled that Dymphna was talking to her. Nothing about this woman suggested she resided in a casual beach neighborhood. Dymphna guessed the woman to be in her midfifties, her salon-highlighted hair glinting expensively in the sun. She extended a long French-manicured talon and snatched up a cream- and rust-colored scarf.

"Yes," the woman said. "I want to buy this." She thrust the scarf at Dymphna.

"Great!" Dymphna said, taking a charge card from the woman and sliding it through a contraption on her smartphone. She held her breath. She couldn't believe her phone could actually ring up sales. Dymphna handed the card back to the shopper. The name on the credit card was C. J. Primb.

"Thank you, Ms. Primb," Dymphna said. "Would you like me to e-mail you a receipt?"

Ms. Primb looked startled. "No," she said. "Absolutely not!"

"All right," Dymphna said, handing over the knitwear. "I hope you'll enjoy the scarf."

As the woman took the scarf, Dymphna noticed a small gold band on C. J. Primb's left hand. It was sitting on the index finger, between the first and second knuckle joints. *Such odd placement*, Dymphna thought. She herself would never be able to get any real work done without losing a ring so precariously placed.

Perhaps that's the point.

Dymphna was happy to turn her attention to another shopper, who was scanning the hats. Ms. Primb was making her nervous. She couldn't put her finger on it, but there was just something about the woman that made her very uncomfortable.

The shopper wandered over to the booth and caressed a green-and-blue beret. She saluted Dymphna with her biodegradable cup of chai tea, purchased from a stall across the asphalt. "I love your TV show," she said.

"Podcast," Dymphna said in a breathy whisper. "It's just on the web. It isn't a real TV show."

The shopper held the hat up to the Southern California sky. The yarns sparkled, changing colors like a prism. She then expertly popped it on her head at a jaunty angle, studying herself in the mirror.

"Video, podcast, TV show, I don't care, I just love it all," the woman said, handing the hat to Dymphna with a smile. "This beret is just fabulous."

Dymphna stared down at the beret. Did the woman want to purchase it? Or was she just handing it back? There were more compliments than sales at the Santa Monica Farmers' Market. It was times like these when she wished she were a little more like Erinn—assertive and self-assured. Erinn would just come right out and ask the customer if she wanted to buy the hat. But Dymphna could never bring herself to be so blunt. She would just wait it out, until the woman made whatever decision she was going to make.

"Excuse me, ma'am, but are you going to buy that hat or not?"

Dymphna looked up. Sometimes people could get pushy and she was not one for conflict. It was Ms. Primb. Why was she still here? What did she want?

"So," Ms. Primb said again to the shopper and pointed an accusing finger at the hat in Dymphna's hand. "Are you buying that or not? We don't have all day."

We?

"Yes," said the woman, handing over her charge card to Dymphna and blinking aggressively at C. J. Primb. "I am."

Dymphna hurriedly rang up the sale and started to put the hat in a paper bag. Whatever weirdness was going on with Ms. Primb, Dymphna didn't want to distress one of her customers.

The woman took her charge card back and put her fingertips on Dymphna's arm. "That's OK, sweetie," she said. "I don't need a bag. No need to kill a forest on my behalf."

"I wouldn't," Dymphna said.

"Pardon me?" the woman said as she adjusted her new hat in the mirror. "You wouldn't what?"

"I wouldn't kill a forest on your behalf."

The woman nodded quickly, first to Dymphna and then to C. J. Primb. Dymphna watched her as she drifted down the aisle to the vintage jewelry. Dymphna suddenly realized C. J. Primb was still studying the merchandise—or was she studying Dymphna? Their eyes met. Ms. Primb made no attempt to leave.

"May I show you anything else?" Dymphna asked.

"Not really. I just wanted to get a good look at you."

Dymphna tried not to show her surprise. Many people watched the show and felt as if they knew her—and could say anything they wanted.

"Well, feel free to look around," Dymphna said cautiously while looking around herself—mostly for something to do. She wished Erinn would come back. She started arranging embellished half gloves on a smooth manzanita branch that she used as a display rack. She tried to ignore the woman, who just stood, rooted, in front of her booth.

"Let me ask you something," Ms. Primb said.

"Yes?"

"If you had all the money in the world, what would you do with yourself?"

"I . . . I really don't know," Dymphna said. "I've never thought about having all the money in the world."

"Oh, really?" Ms. Primb practically snorted in disdain.

"What about you?" Dymphna asked. She had read somewhere that people loved to talk about themselves, and you could get out of practically any uncomfortable situation by asking your tormenters to talk about themselves. "What would *you* do if you had all the money in the world?"

"I *do* have all the money in the world," Ms. Primb said as she walked away.

Photo Credit: © William Christoff Photography

Celia Bonaduce is the author of six novels and is currently a Field Producer on HGTV's *House Hunters*. She has covered a lot of ground in TV programming, including field-producing ABC's *Extreme Makeover: Home Edition* and writing for many of Nickelodeon's animated series, including *Hey, Arnold* and *Chalkzone*. Her successful Tea-Shoppe Stops, lectures and readings of *The Venice Beach Romance Series*; *Merchant of Venice Beach*, *A Comedy of Erinn* and *Much Ado About Mother* will continue across the country with the *Welcome to Fat Chance* series, although a better venue might be local rodeos. Celia lives in Santa Monica, California with palm trees, the Pacific Ocean and her husband, Bill.

Website: http://www.celiabonaduce.com/
Facebook: https://www.facebook.com/pages/Celia-Bonaduce/
352890508156101
Twitter: @celiabonaduce
Instagram: Yocelia
Media: http://www.celiab.name/

CELIA BONADUCE

Slim Pickins' In FAT CHANCE, TEXAS

It's been a year since an eccentric billionaire summoned seven strangers to the dilapidated, postage stamp-sized town of Fat Chance, Texas. To win a cash bequest, each was required to spend six months in the ghost town to see if they could transform it—and themselves—into something extraordinary. But by the time pastry chef Fernando Cruz arrives, several members of the original gang have already skedaddled . . .

Fernando's hopes of starting a new life in Fat Chance are dashed when the town's handful of ragtag residents—and a mysterious low-flying plane—show him just how weird the place actually is. His hopes of making over the town's sole café into a BBQ restaurant for nearby ranchers threaten to turn to dust as a string of bizarre secrets are revealed. But just when the pickins' couldn't get any slimmer, the citizens of Fat Chance realize they might be able to build exactly the kind of hometown they all need—but never knew they wanted . . .

the
Merchant of
venice beach

Take the first step
on the way to
happiness...

CELIA
BONADUCE

The Rollicking Bun—Home of the Epic Scone—is the center of
Suzanna Wolf's life. Part tea shop, part bookstore, part home,
it's everything she's ever wanted right on the Venice Beach
boardwalk, including partnership with her two best friends from
high school, Eric and Fernando. But with thirty-three just around
the corner, suddenly Suzanna wants something more—
something strictly her own. Salsa lessons, especially with a
gorgeous instructor, seem like a good start—a harmless secret,
and just maybe the start of a fling. But before she knows it,
Suzanna is learning steps she never imagined—and dancing
her way into confusion.

"*The Merchant of Venice Beach* has a fresh, heartwarming voice
that will keep readers smiling as they dance through this
charming story by Celia Bonaduce."
—Jodi Thomas, *New York Times* bestselling author

Your best shot at love...

A *Comedy* OF *Erinn*

CELIA
BONADUCE

Erinn Wolf needs to reinvent herself. A once celebrated playwright turned photographer, she's almost broke, a little lonely, and tired of her sister's constant worry. When a job on a reality TV show falls into her lap, she's thrilled to be making a paycheck—and when a hot Italian actor named Massimo rents her guesthouse, she's certain her life is getting a romantic subplot. But with the director, brash, gorgeous young Jude, dogging her every step, she can't help but look at herself through his lens—and wonder if she's been reading the wrong script all along . . .

A VENICE BEACH ROMANCE

MUCH *Ado* ABOUT

Mother

When it comes to life's
big questions, who knows best?

CELIA
BONADUCE

Look out, Venice Beach—the Wolf women are all together again. But when 70-year-old Virginia arrives with her teacup Chihuahua and unshakeable confidence, she senses trouble. Erinn is keeping secrets—like being broke and out of work—and Suzanna is paying too much attention to the wrong man—a Latino dance instructor who nearly broke her heart once before. Virginia's ready for the third act of her life, and she intends to make it rousing and romantic. Now she just has to convince her daughters to throw out their old scripts. If life has taught Virginia anything, it's this: there's more than one way to a "happily ever after" . . .